Every Sweet Regret

Every Sweet Regret

New York Times Bestselling Author

LEXI RYAN

Cover design © 2020 by Hang Le

Cover photo © 2020 by Sara Eirew

Ebook ISBN: 978-1-940832-17-3

Print ISBN: 978-1-940832-18-0

❀ Created with Vellum

For Tina,
who's read them all and cheered me
on every step of the way

ABOUT EVERY SWEET REGRET

New York Times **bestselling author Lexi Ryan brings you Every Sweet Regret, a sexy standalone romance about a single dad and the reformed party girl who's loved him all her life.**

Her brother's best friend. Her lifelong crush. Her sweetest regret.

For as long as I can remember, Kace Matthews has been my brother's best friend and my not-so-secret crush. But I knew nothing would ever happen between us. The successful single dad doesn't fall for the hot mess party girl. Kace + Stella exists in the doodles in my high school notebooks and in my dreams. Never in real life.

Until he finds me on a hookup app and starts flirting shamelessly.

It turns out high school Stella was not prepared for Kace Matthews. Adult Stella isn't much better, but I manage to break down the walls to show Kace the real me--not just the life-of-the-party exterior, but the vulnerable pieces I hide from the world. Combine that with the combustible chemistry we have in real life, and I'm a goner.

Too bad it takes me so long to realize Kace doesn't know

I'm the girl he's been falling for online. Telling him the truth now that he knows my secrets could mean losing everything, and that's one regret that could break me.

CHAPTER ONE

STELLA

$\mathcal{T}$he woman seated at the bar next to Kace Matthews has been flirting with him for thirty minutes straight. Not that I'm surprised. Kace's rough exterior, matched with his gooey insides, make him a bit of a unicorn. I've known single women who've scoured the dating desert for years searching for a guy like him. With jaw-length brown hair, a neatly trimmed beard, and those piercing whiskey eyes, he looks like he belongs on an episode of *Sons of Anarchy*. But see his dimples appear when he talks about his four-year-old daughter, and . . . *ovary explosion.*

The woman tilts forward. Now, if Kace just happens to glance down, he'll get an eyeful of her cleavage. But the man's absolutely clueless, bless his sexy li'l heart.

The woman's pretty—if you're into that skinny, blond, flawless-beauty kind of look, and, well, Kace is. But only if his ex-wife is the flawless beauty in question. The man has eyes for no one else. If I know Kace—and after years as his best friend's little sister, I do—this chick will be going home alone.

"This place is kind of lame, babe. Let's bounce."

I jerk my attention back to the guy sitting across from me—Jared, who arrived fifteen minutes late and has been trying to fast-forward to the sexy-times part of the evening since he sat down. Not that I should be shocked. I met the guy on Random, and that's kind of the point of the app. Not small talk. Not sharing drinks at my favorite bar. Not love matches. *Hookups.*

Unfortunately, any chemistry I felt with Jared during our brief exchanges on the app fizzled out the second he turned his nose up at my favorite watering hole. He sneered when he walked in the door. Then again, maybe Jared's snobbery isn't the real culprit here. Maybe my sudden lack of enthusiasm for ending this dry spell has everything to do with Mr. Unattainable at the bar.

Jared grins and licks his lips. "So . . . yeah?"

"How old are you?" His profile said twenty-six, but he's got such a frat-boy vibe (emphasis on *boy*) that I'm suddenly not so sure.

"Why?" Leaning across the table, he snatches my martini from in front of me and takes a big drink. He could be drinking his own shit if he'd bothered to order anything, but no. When I suggested he get a drink, he laughed, as if it was ridiculous to get too comfortable when he was only here to get off. Now, he's slurping up *my* expensive vodka like a cow at the trough. "Age is a state of mind."

I won't roll my eyes. I won't. But I do turn away to hide my annoyance—which means I put Kace in my line of vision just in time to see him make a beeline to the entrance, where his ex-wife now stands.

Amy's too busy messing with her phone to notice him. Then she's too busy noticing the athletic stranger who's pulling her into his arms. Kace stops dead in his tracks.

"Who are you staring at?" Jared asks, glancing over his shoulder toward the depressing tableau at the door.

Sighing, I nod to Kace. "That's a friend of mine."

"That lumberjack-looking guy?" Jared spreads his legs and glares. "You know him?"

I won't *roll my eyes.* "Easier to be friends that way, yeah."

"You *fucking* him?" His gaze whips back to me. "Is that why you're suddenly acting like such a frigid bitch?"

Once again, this less-than man manages to drag my attention away from the best guy in the room. "Excuse me?"

"Come on, you were ready to ride my dick when we made these plans. Something's changed." He lowers his voice and leans closer. "You don't have to pretend with me. I know Reggie's brother, and so I know you."

What. The. Actual. Fuck? There's nothing that makes me go cold faster than the name of my asshole college boyfriend. I lean back in my chair and shake my head. "Yeah, it's time to go."

He exhales, and his shoulders sag. "Thank Christ. Let's get out of here."

"You go. Alone. Without me."

He throws up his hands. "Why? What did I say? You can't deny we had *plans* when we decided to meet here. But I'm onto girls like you—throwing out suggestive messages to get guys to buy you a few drinks and then never following through with what was promised. But joke's on you." He wags a finger at me. "That's why I never order anything."

Is this guy for real? "Hey, sweetie." I paste on my most saccharine smile then scoot my chair around the table so I'm next to him. The sneer falls off his face. "Can I tell you a secret?"

He swallows, his gaze dipping to my cleavage. I wore my hottest red dress for him, and the reminder just pisses me off more. My breasts look fucking fantastic, and he does not deserve their company. "Sure." He doesn't bother to lift his gaze.

"Those *girls like me*? You're right to believe they aren't being honest with you, but you're wrong about them wanting free drinks. You see, they're trying to figure out if their date is a potential creeper before they go home with him, and since you can't hide that shit in person, I bet you have a lot of experience with women backing out once they meet you face to face."

He pulls back. "What the fuck do you know, cheap porno bitch?"

"I know they call *girls like me* bitches when we decide *guys like you* aren't entitled to our bodies. The only difference between them and me is that I don't care if you call me a bitch, and I wouldn't let you buy me a drink even if being roofied sounded like a good time. You give all the bad vibes, Jared—starting with lying about your age. Do yourself a favor before you use any hookup or dating app again: learn how to treat a woman. Until then, leave."

His chair screeches as he pushes it away from the table and jumps out of it. "I wouldn't stick my dick in your diseased cunt if you paid me."

"What'd you say to her?"

Jared spins around and finds his face inches from Kace Matthews' broad chest.

I shrink into my chair and scan the room for a rock to crawl under. I didn't mean for Kace to run over here and play hero. For once, I wish he were still focused on his undeserving ex just so that judgmental gaze wasn't cast in my direction.

Hello there, disapproving Adonis. Yes, I'm still the hot-mess Stella you know and love, and here's the proof, since you think you need to rescue me from this hellish non-date.

Jared stumbles back a step, and Kace moves closer.

"If I ever hear you talk to Stella or *any* woman like that ever again—"

"Whatever, man. I'm outta here." Jared scrambles away and out the door, and I'm sure he can feel the burn of Kace's angry gaze with every step.

Only when Jared disappears from view does Kace turn back to me, eyes worried and jaw tense beneath his beard. "You okay?"

"I'm fine." I'm not fine. I'm exhausted. I'm sick of attracting all the creeps and falling for all the assholes. Because I do. Every time, with the lone exception of Kace, who I've wanted for as long as I can remember and who's never been even the slightest bit interested in me in return. I'm lonely, and I miss sex.

"Where do you find these assholes?"

"There's a secret catalogue," I say, flipping my hair over one shoulder. "I usually pick the ones with the biggest muscles and hope they won't ruin my fun by talking."

Kace ignores my sass and glares at the window, as if daring Jared to reappear. "It's like you want to be treated badly or something."

"Whoa. Way to victim-blame, Kace."

His gaze snaps back to mine. "I'm not blaming you. I'm pointing out a pattern of behavior."

"I'm sorry. I didn't realize you were my therapist. Sit down so I can tell you all about my sex addiction and the trouble it gets me into."

His jaw unhinges, and he draws in a sharp breath before snapping it shut again. "I . . . Shit, I didn't realize you had a . . ." He clears his throat.

"It was a *joke*." But a badly chosen one, because "sex addict" probably fits right into the little box Kace has me in. I'm pretty sure said box is labeled *Irresponsible Party Girl.* That's me.

He draws his mouth into a thin line of disapproval. "Well, I wasn't joking about your patterns." He shoves his hands into his pockets. "What would've happened if he'd taken you home?"

As *if.* I might date jerks, but Jared never stood a chance. My *pattern* shows I prefer the guys who reel you in and get you attached before they let their jerk flag fly. Jared never stood a chance. I sigh. "I had it under control."

I think he's about to give me a lecture, so I'm relieved when my friend Abbi appears at my table and waves at her brother. "Hey, Kace."

"Hey, Abs." He returns her smile, but it's tight, and when his gaze drifts back to me, disapproval is written all over his face. He shakes his head, already retreating. "Just . . . be careful. Okay?"

I want to reach for him. *Don't go. Stay. Sit down and remind me there are good guys in this world.*

But I don't say a word. I sink back in my chair and let him walk back to the bar. For a beat, I let myself imagine what it'd be like to be the recipient of one of his broad grins. What would it be like to be the object of Kace Matthews' affection? What would it be like to have him flirt with me? There's a very small club of women who've experienced those things, and I'll never be part of it. I've made my peace with that. *Mostly.*

I reach for my drink, then remember Jared the Asshole put his mouth on my glass, and I yank my hand away like I just touched a hot stove. I shift my attention to Abbi. "How are you, pretty?"

She pulls out the chair opposite me and lowers herself into it. "I'm . . . meh. Just had the longest day ever and decided to treat myself." She takes the small menu out from under the napkin holder and studies it. "Have you eaten yet?"

My stomach growls. "No, but I want something salty and greasy."

She narrows her eyes, studying me over the top of the laminated menu. "Is this that thing where you talk about the junk food so much you give *me* a craving, and then you decide to get a grilled chicken salad while I cave and get the nacho-cheese-smothered tater tots?"

"That!" I grin and point at her. "That's what I want."

"Wait—seriously? I thought you and Savvy were doing that cleanse shit. Your body's a temple, and no grease allowed past those lips, et cetera, et cetera?"

I narrow my eyes. "Shut up. I'm PMSing." I wave at Smithy, the bar's owner. I could wait for my waitress, but Smithy will treat me if I ask nicely.

His eyes light up when he spots me, and he rushes over. "Stella, Abbi, what can I do for you two beautiful women tonight?"

"Nacho tots," Abbi says.

"The big one," I add. "I'm bitchy and bloated, and I want to eat my feelings."

"Hormonal cravings." Smithy bobs his head as if he too is afflicted by a monthly cycle. "Maybe some fried pickles too, then?"

I moan. "God, yes."

Abbi grins in triumph. "I like you tonight."

"And booze." I point to my glass. "The dickwad who just left soiled mine by putting his nasty-ass mouth on it."

"Whatcha drinking?" Smithy asks.

I should choose something with fewer calories to balance out the junk food, but . . . "Another lemon drop martini?" There's nothing like a fancy drink with greasy bar food, and Smithy makes the best lemon drops.

Abbi bounces in her seat. "Oh! Me too!"

"As you wish." He sweeps the glass off the table. "And Stella, I happen to know a guy who'd treat you right if you're ever interested." He winks then walks away.

"Think he meant himself?" Abbi asks.

"Or the monk he roomed with that time in Rome." I shrug. "You never know with Smithy."

Abbi laughs. "So tell me how you ended up in *that dress* while PMSing. Because when I'm bloated, I want PJs and oversized hoodies."

I arch a brow. "Hoodies in June?"

She shrugs. "That's what AC is for. Stop avoiding the question."

"I had a date. Well, sort of." I yank at the neckline of my dress ineffectually, wishing it covered a smidge more skin. I felt sexy when I left home, but sitting across from Abbi in her jeans and T-shirt has me feeling ridiculous in my "look at me" red dress. "It wasn't a date exactly." When she raises a brow in question, I add, "Random."

Abbi snorts. "You're still using that app? I swear it's the same ten guys, and they're all . . . Well, my standards might not be the highest, but they're higher than *that*."

I shrug, understanding what she means. Orchid Valley isn't *quite* big enough for an app like Random. Unless you're cool with hooking up with your high school geometry teacher—and let me tell you from experience, that's a *bad* idea. "I usually choose the bigger radius to grab some of the north Atlanta suburbs guys."

"Ooh." She folds her arms on the table and leans forward. "Teach me your ways, wise one."

I don't know if she's serious or mocking me, so I just shake my head. "Seriously, don't get advice from me. No one's caught my interest for weeks, then I finally agree to meet this guy and . . ." I give an exaggerated shudder. "I should've run the moment he walked in the door. Creeper city."

"Really?"

"It was a vibe, know what I mean? Anyway, he left—but not before your brother threatened to beat the shit out of him."

"Is that why Kace was looking at you like he just bailed you out of jail?" Abbi frowns as her gaze tracks across the bar to find her brother sitting on a stool, nursing his beer and surreptitiously keeping an eye on his ex-wife. "How'd he even know the guy was a creep?"

"My guess? Kace decided to intervene when he heard Jared use the words *diseased cunt*."

Abbi flinches. "Yikes. I'm surprised Kace didn't make good on his threat."

"Nah, Jared scampered off pretty quick after that." I shrug. "Anyway, my dry spell continues."

"You were in Jamaica with your ex two months ago. That's hardly a dry spell."

"Well, we're not talking about Bobby."

"Hmm. I think you should, though."

I don't get embarrassed easily, so I'm not sure what my issue is with telling my friends about what happened in Jamaica. I just don't want to admit that I fell for the wrong guy. *Again.* "You know how when you go online shopping, you can filter out certain brands or items above a certain price? I wish I could do that with dating—or, hell, even with hookups. No more assholes. No more users. No more cheaters."

"I'm not sure Random is the best place to be if those are your criteria."

"Is Random really the problem? Because I feel like I might have *I love jerks* tattooed to my forehead. Or maybe I screwed up somewhere, and that's my profile pic."

"What pic are you using now?" She points at my phone. "Let me see."

I unlock it and open the app, sighing when I remember I have to go into Settings and then Profile to see my picture or profile details. This app is so rudimentary that its success might just prove above all else what incredible horndogs people are. "There," I say when I get to it. I turn the phone so she can see the image of me in a yellow dress. I always liked this picture. Brinley took it when we were at the park last year. I'm leaning against a gnarled oak tree and grinning at the camera. I look *happy.*

Abbi lets out a long, low whistle. "Girl, they're totally clicking on you for your hot bod."

I'm *not* all that, but I'm experienced enough to know that a lot of guys have a weakness for my curves and think my red hair is a sign of my sexual proclivities. Then again, maybe that's the problem. I put myself out there with my looks, and then I'm heartbroken when guys never see past them. I tried so hard to make things different with Bobby.

I laugh. "I keep threatening to change my profile pic to a cartoon avatar. Maybe I'll do it."

She snorts. "If I looked like that, I wouldn't hide behind a cartoon."

I shrug, lock the screen on my phone, and slide it back into my purse. "I'd rather find a guy who wants me for my personality than one who wants me for my appearance."

"Must be a nice problem to have." She sighs. "Not that I'd know."

I ball up my napkin and throw it at her. "You're fucking *gorgeous.* Just because you can't see that doesn't mean it's not true."

She shrugs and throws the napkin back at me. "No, *you're* gorgeous. I'm . . ." She shakes her head.

"What?"

"Nope. Nothing. We're not doing that."

"Doing what?"

"That thing where I express my insecurities and you spend the rest of the night trying to reassure me, and then I just feel doubly awkward. Not in the mood."

"Abs," I say.

"Nope." She points at me. "Back to you and your reasons for needing a cartoon avatar."

I feel like we should talk about *her* for once, but once Abbi shuts that down, it's over, so I let it go. "I don't know." I shrug. "Maybe if guys actually talked to me for a bit rather than jumping right into 'Can I fuck your titties?' I'd find someone who wants to know what's going on in my head."

She snorts. "Again, maybe try an app other than *Random*."

I sigh. After what Bobby put me through, I'm not ready for another relationship, but hookups are rarely worthwhile. I just need a reliable fuck buddy. Still, Abbi has a point.

"Drinks, ladies!" Smithy slides two martinis onto the table, then the waitress behind him settles two plates between us. One's piled with cheesy tater tots, and the other what must be a triple order of fried pickles. Smithy spoils us. "Enjoy."

"Thank you," we chorus.

Abbi and I go quiet as we fill our plates with salty, fried goodness. Abbi digs in, and I let my gaze drift back to Kace. Bless his broken heart. He's trying to ignore Amy, but he keeps looking in her direction as she threads her fingers in her date's hair and laughs at his jokes.

Abbi follows my gaze. "I wish he wouldn't torture himself."

I shake my head. "Dean says he's over her, but I don't think so."

Abbi scoffs. "He's definitely not. He admitted to me just last weekend that he doesn't want to start dating in case she decides to come home."

Those words are a punch in the solar plexus.

Nodding, Abbi licks the sugared rim of her glass. "He wants what they had. I can't blame him."

"He wants what he *thinks* they had," I mutter.

Abbi shrugs. "I know what you mean, but we all get like that about past relationships, don't we?"

I give a noncommittal hum. Frankly, Abbi doesn't know

what I mean, because she doesn't know Amy's secrets. I, however, know more than I'd like to.

Abbi nudges my plate toward me. "Eat. Not only will it cheer you up, I'll curse you tomorrow if I tear through all this by myself."

"Wouldn't want to let you down." I laugh and pop a nacho-cheese-coated tot into my mouth. As good as a greasy meal sounded, my heart's just not in it tonight.

"Are you coming tomorrow?"

"Tomorrow?"

"Kace's party?" she says. "Friends, beer, barbecue, and pool time?"

I sigh, remembering. Kace is having a pool party at his new house, and my best friends will be there. "I'm at The Orchid until five, but I'll come over after." I hesitate, swirling a tater tot in cheese, but I have to ask. "Will Amy be there?"

"I think so." Abbi gives me a sympathetic smile. "They have a child together. Even if Kace doesn't get the reunion he wants, she's not going anywhere."

"He deserves someone good."

Abbi glances at Kace again and shakes her head. "Stella, baby, you know I love you, but you two are all wrong for each other."

I scoff. "That's not what I meant. I know Kace and I are never happening. But he needs someone . . . someone *good*," I repeat. Because that's seriously what I want for him. "And don't look at me like that. Kace might star in my go-to fantasies, but I know better than to think I'm the girl for him."

She frowns. "You really do just want him to be happy. That's sweet."

I shrug. It doesn't matter what I want. As long as he's hung up on his ex, his soul mate could be standing right in front of him, and he'd never notice her—especially if she's the redheaded wild child who's been in love with him since seventh grade.

CHAPTER TWO

KACE

My wife is on a date. This is nothing new, but tonight she brought her date to Smithy's bar, which means all I have to do is turn around, and I get to witness every flirtatious touch, every lust-filled stare. Obviously, I'm keeping my eyes on my beer, because who needs that kind of misery in their life?

"Smell that?" Smithy asks, sniffing the air. He pulls the tap and pours a beer, bopping along to that special drumbeat only he can hear.

"What?"

"Smoke, man."

Frowning, I sniff the air then look around. I smell burgers, beer, and the light pine scent of Smithy's mop bucket. He might be a goof, and a bit too fond of the ganja, but he keeps his place clean. "I don't smell anything."

He sniffs again. "You sure you don't smell smoke? Because Stella looks *fire* tonight."

I glance over my shoulder, playing it cool. As if I didn't notice my best friend's little sister the second she walked in. As if I haven't been noticing her way too much for months now.

Not checking out Stella takes physical effort, and the minute my gaze lands on her, relief washes over me. It's the feeling of putting down a weight you've been holding for too long. The feeling of drawing in a breath when you break the surface of the water. It feels good to look at her, and I wish I could get away with doing it a whole lot more.

Sometime during the past ten years, Stella became a bombshell. There's no other word for it, and right now she reminds me of a centerfold more than the pest who'd follow Dean and me around all summer. She's sass and smiles. Her curves make it really fucking hard not to stare under normal circumstances. In a skimpy red dress, she's the focal point my gaze has returned to again and again since she arrived an hour ago. *That's* the fastest way to get my mind off my ex-wife. I can hardly remember other women exist when Stella's in front of me. She's bad fucking news—as evidenced by her dickhead date—and I know this, at least rationally. She's a mess, the all-drama, too-much-trouble party girl I've been programmed to protect, and the polar opposite of what I'd want if I was interested in bringing another woman into my life. But my dick doesn't care about reason, apparently.

Bad for me or not, I do worry about her, especially when I see her with guys who treat women like they exist purely for their pleasure. But at least Abbi showed up and saved me from my instinctive need to hover over her table and stand guard when that douchebag left.

Stella notices me staring and smirks. *Busted.*

My phone buzzes in my back pocket, and I retrieve it to see she's sent me a text.

> Stella: Would you stop checking me out? I'm THIRSTY, and it's not nice to tease.
> Me: Need me to bring you another drink?

Her laughter rings across the bar—bold, loud, sexy, and shameless, just like everything else about her. My gaze drifts her way again, and she shakes her head before her fingers fly across the screen and my phone dings again.

> Stella: Is that what you think THIRSTY means?
> Me: Honestly? I have no fucking idea.

I've turned on my barstool to face her side of the room, and I don't bother taking my eyes off her as she grins down at her phone and taps out a reply.

"Smithy, what are Stella and Abbi drinking tonight?" I ask without taking my eyes off her.

"The usual."

I turn and stare at him, because I have no idea what that is.

He gives me a disappointed shake of his head. "Lemon drop martinis. You buying the next round?"

"Sure. Why not?" Hope is with my mom tonight, and Amy gets her tomorrow, so it's either hang at Smithy's and buy some drinks or go home to an empty house. If buying drinks means I get to give Stella my attention a little longer, it's a damn easy decision.

My phone buzzes, and I practically feel the endorphins hitting my system when I see Stella's name on the screen. This girl is addictive.

> Stella: Okay, old man. I'll give you this nugget
> of wisdom for free. When a girl catches
> you gawking at her tits and tells you she's
> THIRSTY, she means she's hard up.

I freeze and reread the text three times. *Well, fuck me.* This information won't help me get my mind out of the gutter. I bite back a smile as I reply.

> Me: Hard up? Like, for money?

I'm totally fucking with her now, but it's worth it.

> Stella: Like for DICK, Kace. Oh my God. Do
> you need a tutor? Here's another piece of
> knowledge that might come in handy . . .
> the eggplant emoji has nothing to do with
> a balanced diet.

I grunt out a laugh and wait for Smithy to finish with the girls' martinis. "I'll take them," I tell him as he pours the pale yellow drink into frosted glasses.

"It's not busy," he says. "I can do it."

"Let me." I take the drinks before he can object again. Honestly, I need to prove to Stella and to myself that I'm not going to get all weird now that I know she's "thirsty." That's all this is about. Nothing else.

Stella's eyes go wide when I slide the cold martini glasses onto the table. "Seriously?"

"Thanks, Kace," Abbi says. "You're the best."

"Right?" Stella says. "Is it any wonder I want to have his babies?"

I grunt. "No one can claim you're hard to please."

She looks at the ceiling and screws her mouth up in a thoughtful grimace. "I mean, I guess that depends on the context."

"Eww," Abbi says. "Stop."

I bark out a laugh. "I walked right into that one."

Abbi mimes puking.

"You're too easy, Mr. Matthews," Stella says. She lifts the martini to her lips and flicks her tongue across the sugared rim.

I swallow. Hard. *Don't be a creep, Kace.* "No more trouble from that asshole from earlier, I hope?"

"Nah, he's history." She sips her martini, sighs, and mutters, "The dry spell continues."

Abbi scoffs. "She thinks she knows what a dry spell is. Meanwhile, I'm living in the Sahara over here."

I clear my throat and step back, grappling for a subject change. I do *not* want to talk sex with my baby sister. But *fuck*, maybe I should blame that red dress, because tonight I *really* want to talk about it with Stella. Well, maybe not *talk*. . .

"Thanks for this," Stella says, wiggling her glass.

"You're welcome. Wouldn't want you to get *thirsty*."

Her eyes go wide and her lips part. For the first time in my life, I think I've thrown Stella Jacob off guard and not the other way around. I like it *way* more than I should, so I make myself head back to my seat. I feel her eyes on me every step of the way.

My smile falls from my face when I see Amy leaning her elbows on the bar right by my beer. *Fuck.*

"What was that about?" Amy asks, turning to me as I sit.

Grabbing my beer, I punch down the feeling that I was doing something wrong by flirting with another woman in my wife's presence. *Not your wife. Your* ex. "What?"

"Is Stella playing her usual games? Trying to get your attention by any means necessary?"

I sigh. "No games. She's just hanging with Abbi."

"Then why are you being so defensive?"

"I'm not." But the words come out sharp, undercutting my claim. I *hate* how Amy talks about Stella. Maybe Stella deserves it after the stunts she pulled when she and Amy worked together, but I have no interest being in the middle. "Stop looking for drama, Ames."

Amy arches a brow and looks me over. "Jesus, you need to get laid."

Beer in the windpipe. I sputter and choke. From anyone else, these words might not faze me. But from the woman I planned to grow old with? The mother of my child? Yeah. There's a damn reason Amy's declaration sends me into a coughing fit.

"What? I speak the truth," she says, throwing up her hands. "How long's it been?"

"We're not having this conversation," I wheeze between coughs. I'd rather play hacky sack with my nuts than talk about my sex life with her. Especially since she's the one on a date right now, and from the way she's been hanging on to him, I'd bet they're going home together.

She tucks a platinum curl behind her ear in a futile attempt to get the new short layers out of her face. It'll come loose before I can count to ten, like it does every time. She's never had it this short in all the years I've known her, and I miss the way she used to wear it—just past her shoulders and naturally curly. I miss a lot of things. Including, yes, sex, though I'm not going to rewrite history and pretend I wasn't missing that long before she moved out. "Come on, Kace. We're friends, right?"

"Friends who don't talk about sex."

She frowns. "Are you okay?"

It's her new favorite question for me. *Are you okay?* For a long time, I wasn't. She was the one who wanted the divorce. I was the one who thought we had something worth fighting for. It hasn't been easy to bury my resentment, but I did. For my daughter *and* for Amy. I did the impossible for the two women I love most in this world. "I'm okay. I'm *happy*."

Her frown deepens as she studies me. "Have you tried dating yet?"

The answer to that question is *hell no*, but considering she had her first date the night she moved out, I know how she'd feel about that, so I shrug. "I'm busy." I take a long pull off my beer. I'm in a good mood and don't want to ruin it.

"Kace." Her eyes widen in horror as she studies me. "I moved out a year ago. Please tell me you've screwed *someone* since then."

I cough. *Again.* She's going to kill me before this conversation's over. "Excuse me?"

"Sex is *healthy*." She nudges me with her elbow. "And your hand doesn't count."

"I'm not looking to hook up."

"Why not? You're kid-free every other weekend."

I roll my eyes. "Kind of busy."

She scoffs. "Yet here you sit at a bar on a Friday night. You could be on a date. You know, you're allowed to see people casually. Not everyone is looking for happily-ever-after. Some people just want to get off." Her expression softens, and she clenches her eyes shut for a beat. "Just because our marriage lacked passion doesn't mean—"

"Don't. Please? Just don't." Rather than meet her knowing gaze, I watch a couple of guys in Lamda Chi T-shirts pretend to play pool while they check out Stella for the hundredth time tonight. Fuckers had better keep to their side of the bar.

"I just want you to be happy," Amy says. "There are hundreds of women out there who'd die to be with you, but you'll never know, because you won't even go on a stupid date."

"I don't need the complication in my life."

Amy reaches around me and grabs my phone out of my back pocket. She enters in my passcode—I should probably change that—and starts tapping on the screen. "Other divorced women complain about all the ass their exes are chasing, and here I am, your only hope of getting laid."

I wince. "That's fucked up, Ames. Give it back."

She spins away before I can grab it from her hands. "What do you want your username to be?"

"My username for what?"

"Random."

"Random what? Wait—the hookup app? You can't be serious."

"GoodHands69," she says, winking.

"Oh, yeah. That's a great username," I deadpan, "for a fifteen-year-old boy."

She ignores this, thumbs tapping on the screen. "Recently divorced. Looking for *companionship*, not love. Good with my hands." She flashes me a wink.

I'm gonna be sick. "You've gotta be fucking kidding me right now."

Her blue eyes widen, pure innocence. "Am I lying?"

I drain my beer, but it doesn't do anything to diminish this twilight zone feeling. My ex-wife is setting up my account on a hookup app.

"When I made you promise we'd still be friends, this is *not* what I meant." I sigh.

She waggles her brows then drops her attention back to the app. "Let's see who's online now and is within . . ." She taps her chin thoughtfully. "Let's go with thirty miles. Don't want your booty call to be on the other side of Atlanta traffic."

I wave to Smithy and point to my empty glass to let him know I need another beer, though if she keeps this up, I should probably switch to something stronger. "You're mental."

"Oh!" She studies the screen, her smile growing. "This could be fun."

Really, once Amy sets her mind to something, there's no point in interfering, so all I can do is wait until she's done and then try to minimize the damage.

"I'm going to tap 'interested' on this one." She turns the screen to me for a beat, and I see a flash of cleavage. "Nice rack, huh?"

There isn't enough alcohol in the world. "Is that her *profile* pic?"

She shrugs. "Yeah. That's the way Random works. This isn't about finding a pretty *face*."

"Whatever," I mutter. I take the fresh glass from Smithy and force myself to sip when I want to chug.

"And . . . that was fast. She's interested back." The woman I vowed to love till death is not only trying to get me laid, she's downright giddy about it. "What should I type?"

"How about, *This is Kace's ex-wife, and I'm acting like a creep right now. He'll apologize as soon as I give him his phone back.*"

She lifts her gaze to mine, as if considering this. "Nah." She returns the phone. "My work here's done."

"Save me," I mutter. "What did you do? You know what?" I slide my phone into my back pocket. "Never mind. I don't want to know."

"Hey, baby, you ready?" The guy Amy was hanging on earlier stands a few feet away and nods toward the door.

"Gotta go," she says. She wriggles her fingers in a little wave. "Enjoy yourself tonight."

I shift on my stool to check on Stella, but she's gone. So much for enjoying myself.

CHAPTER THREE

KACE

*T*he sun is shining, the smell of barbecue is in the air, the beer is cold, and my favorite people are scattered in groups around the pool and in the yard beyond. *This* is why I wanted to buy this house—not because of how it could look once restored to its former glory, not because of the backyard privacy fence so tall I forget I even have neighbors, but because of whom it could hold. This'll be the place where Hope has her birthday parties. It'll be the place where I invite my friends for pool parties in the summer and gluttonous feasts at Thanksgiving. If I couldn't keep the family I planned, I'll celebrate the one I have in my friends.

It's far from perfect, and the few months of work I've put in have barely scratched the surface, but today I'm reminded of why I took the plunge and bought the old plantation-style home in Orchid Valley's historic district. I needed to get out of the house where I thought I'd grow old with my wife.

When I got home last night, the quiet was so deafening that I almost considered opening up that app Amy installed for me. *Almost.* Instead, I focused on last-minute prep work for today's cookout and then crashed, trying not to think about Amy going home with that guy. Finally, my mind settled on thoughts of Stella . . . and stayed there until I forgot about Amy completely.

Now Stella's stretched out by my pool in an itsy-bitsy, pink-striped bikini I've been trying like hell not to appreciate since the moment she peeled off her sundress. Her red hair is piled in a messy bun on top of her head, and one long leg is stretched out in front of her, the other bent at the knee. Her sunglasses are perched on the tip of her nose, and she's biting her tongue between her teeth while she messes around on her phone.

Is she messaging someone? Some guy who might be willing to do something about the thirst she mentioned last night?

I'd bet she has a list of guys who'd run right over if she asked. And from the way she talks, I'm pretty sure she *asks* as often as she pleases, which—good for her. She's young and single. She can do whatever and whomever the fuck she pleases. And if the idea bugs me more than it should? Well, that's something I'll be taking to my grave.

I stoop to the cooler and pull out a White Claw—Stella hates beer—and take it to her. "For you," I say, offering the can.

She drops her phone between her legs and props her sunglasses on the top of her head before taking it from me.

"Thank you." She grins. "Is serving me, like, your thing now?"

She said *serving me*, but my brain heard *servicing me*, and my imagination grabs on to that with both hands. *Fuck.* "You're welcome." My gaze dips to her cleavage and the sheen of sweat that's gathered in the afternoon sun. I'm pretty sure this is the part where I walk away, but I don't want to. I don't want to say anything to encourage her, either, so I go all boring-dad mode on her instead. "I hope you have sunblock on."

"If I said no, would you help me get my back?"

I cough. *Don't make it weird.* "Sure. Whatever."

She chuckles, a low, husky sound that seems to reroute all my blood to south of my waistband. There's nothing that amuses Stella more than watching me get awkward when she pretends to throw herself at me. The thing is, it wouldn't be awkward at all if I weren't so determined to resist. If she were serious and I decided to indulge in that little fantasy . . . Fuck. I already know it'd be damn good.

"Good to know." She cracks open the can and brings it to her lips. I'm mesmerized by the single drop of sweat that rolls down her neck as she tilts her head back and drinks. When she pulls the can away, she grins, like she knows just what I was thinking.

Friend zone. Keep it in the friend zone. "Thanks for coming today, Freckles."

She smiles at her old nickname and stretches her legs in front of her, pointing her toes. "I'll hang out at your pool any time you want for as long as you want."

I arch a brow and let my gaze slide over her. "And will you wear *that*?" Apparently the beer and the warm sun have made me forget all my better judgment.

She glances down, and her tongue swipes a bead of moisture from her bottom lip. "Just say the word."

"Tempting."

"Kace!" Amy calls from the porch. "Come here for a minute?"

When I look back to Stella, her smile's fallen away. "Go ahead," she says. "I won't keep you."

"I want to talk more about this later," I say, and honestly, I have no idea why I'm making a promise like that, but I know I intend to keep it.

I head to the shade of the porch, where Amy's waiting.

"It's a great party," she says as I climb the steps. She scans the yard and the guests scattered about. "Even Hopey's having fun."

Across the yard, my four-year-old's white-blond hair flies out of her tiny pigtails as she races her friend Cami across the yard. I love seeing Hope this happy. When Amy told me she was moving out, I was convinced our divorce would mean years of heartache for our daughter. In reality, she adjusted quickly. The first night Amy wasn't home, Hope asked if Mommy was going to tuck her in, and I felt like I was behind the wheel of a car flying off a cliff. I swallowed and reminded her that Mommy was staying in her new house. I thought my daughter would cry and ask me why I couldn't keep her mommy happy (*hello, projecting*). Instead, she smiled and said, "Oh yeah! I get to go there tomorrow. Mommy's making my room a princess palace." And that was that.

"You always knew how to throw the best parties," Amy says, pulling my attention back to her.

My chest warms at the fondness in her tone. Amy and I met at one of my parties. The chemistry was instant, and our lives clicked together so seamlessly that I believed we were just meant to be. "Some of my best memories are of throwing them with you," I confess, but then discomfort warps her features, and I regret the words. "Sorry."

"Have you used the app yet?" she asks, and I grimace. "How did I guess? Come on, Kace. You need some sexy fun in your life."

I shrug. "I'm not sure it's my thing." I haven't even looked to see who she connected me with. I'll probably delete it before I'm desperate enough to find out.

"How will you know if you don't try?" Sighing, she shakes her head. "Anyway, I just wanted to thank you for inviting me over."

Sorrow tugs through my chest at the sight of her smile. It reminds me of the girl I fell in love with. The one I proposed to in New York and made love to on the beach in Mexico. Sometimes I can't decide what's worse—how much I miss Amy, or my grief over the life I thought we'd have. But honestly? We lost that life long before she moved out. "Thanks for coming. It means a lot to me."

"Of course. I *want* us to be friends, Kace." She wriggles her brows. "But now I'll get out of here so you can enjoy the rest of your party kid-free. Cut loose. Have *fun*. *Use the app*."

I laugh. What does she want me to do? Leave my own party to hook up with some stranger? Honestly, these friends are like family, and I could leave if I needed to. But this is where I want to be. "We'll see."

"Hope," Amy calls across the yard. "We need to go, baby. We have to get ready for Tyson's birthday party."

Hope wraps her little arms around Cami's waist, squeezing the ten-year-old tight before charging toward the deck. She barrels into me and hugs my legs. "Gotta go. Love you, Daddy."

"Love you too, Snickerdoodle. I'll see you Monday after school."

Amy ruffles Hope's hair. "Grab your bag and meet me at the car." She waits until Hope's inside before turning back to me. "See you later, Kace."

"Later." I return her smile, then watch her walk away. After a year, it's getting easier, that sight, the reminder that I'll be sleeping alone, that there will be no one there for me to bring coffee to in the morning or to share a drink with after we put Hope to bed.

When the gate swings closed behind her, I turn back to the party. Amy thinks I need to get laid, and she might be onto something.

It takes my eyes less than five seconds to lock on Stella again. Stella, who catches me staring, pulls her sunglasses down to the tip of her nose and *winks*. Stella, who's the embodiment of *sexy fun*.

Her attention shifts back to her phone, and then mine buzzes in my back pocket. My blood hums with anticipation as I pull it out to see what she's texted.

> Stella: You gonna put that lotion on me or let
> me burn?

Rub lotion on Stella? *So. Fucking. Tempting.* But I already know how this conversation will go. We'll do that thing we do where she tells me how hot she thinks I am and assumes I don't feel the same about her, and I'll be the nice guy who won't take advantage of a woman he cares about. Attraction has never been my issue with Stella. Not even when I was in college and she was the high school senior who decided to crawl into my bed. I told myself that touching my buddy's younger sister was screwed up and put the brakes on that moment, but I'd be lying if I said it was easy. Or that it's easy to pretend her nonstop innuendos do nothing for me.

I'll be damned if I'm going to go over there and have her tease me more while I rub sunblock on her back. I'm a little buzzed and don't trust my hands.

> Me: I'm sure Dean would do that for you. I'm
> busy.
> Stella: Um, my brother could not, would not
> do the kind of lotion application I have in
> mind. And you're drinking a beer by your
> pool. How busy can you be?
> Me: I've found myself with a Random profile.
> I guess I need to decide if I'm going to
> delete it or check it out.
> Stella: Random, huh? Bold move.

No shit. Going from no love life at all to using a hookup app kind of feels like jumping into the deep end. Assuming the deep end is ice-cold and shark-infested.

Since my divorce, I haven't been interested in dating. I'm not even sure how dating works when it's just casual, when you're not looking for a *partner*. But Stella would know. She's all fun and wild impulse. Honestly, if I'm going to do this, she might be the best person to get advice from. The problem is, I don't want *advice* from Stella. I want something altogether riskier. And I've wanted it for a long while now.

I've been attracted to Stella since long before I was

married. It never meant anything, and I never planned to act on it. I brushed it off as a physiological response to a hot woman. Then, sometime in the past couple of months, something clicked in my brain. We could stop dancing around each other and enjoy ourselves. If she wants me and I want her, we could do this. That doesn't mean it's not a bad idea, but ever since I allowed myself to really consider it, I can't *stop* considering.

> Stella: I'm personally on hiatus, but I might open the app again if you'll be on there. ;)
> Me: I could use some casual fun—not exactly ready for the real thing. That said . . . I'm still not sure the app's for me.
> Stella: You're recently divorced and don't want to find Hope her stepmom just yet. I feel ya.

I shouldn't be surprised she understands how I feel about getting involved with someone. Stella and I might not be close, but we have the same circle of friends. She knows me and my situation. Maybe I haven't given her enough credit.

> Me: I'm new to this . . . Is casual possible? As in, sex with no expectations?

Am I a manipulative ass to put it out there like that? Jesus. I pride myself in being honest and straightforward. In my work. In my relationships. Can I really tell Stella I want to do dirty, dirty things to her with the caveat that she has to promise not to catch feelings?

Stella: It's possible. Are you telling me you've
     NEVER hooked up with someone? As in
     no-strings-attached hooked up?

Me: It's never been my style.

Stella: What's nice about Random is you
     don't have to have the awkward
     conversation. If you meet on there, what
     you're looking for is understood. Just be
     safe, okay?

Me: You say that like you're sending me off
     into battle.

Stella: I kind of feel like I am.

I look up from my phone, and she's holding up three fingers in the *Hunger Games* salute. I laugh and watch as she taps out another message.

Stella: The girls on there are going to gobble
     you up. And fuuuuuck . . .

How can one intentionally misspelled curse have me half hard? Probably because I can practically hear her saying it, and the sound is accompanied by a vivid image. I'd peel off those bikini bottoms, then slide my mouth over her belly—lower—and she'd close her eyes and her lips would part on the word and . . . *Fuuuuuck*.

Me: What???

Stella: I'm just jealous. You put ideas in my
     head, looking at me the way you did last
     night. . . I'll get over it. I always do.

I blame the potent combo of good beer, too much sun, and that hot-as-fuck bikini for the reply I type out next.

> Me: Don't do that. You want something from me, come and get it.

I'm not drunk by any means, but I'm just relaxed enough that my guard is down. What would happen if we were the only ones here right now? I'd drag her inside and show her just what I wanted to do that night she crawled into my bed. I can't imagine how we could do that without changing . . . everything, but lately I've been less and less worried about the consequences of acting on this attraction. We're adults. We can figure it out.

> Stella: You're killing me. I need it straight up —is this heading toward you fucking me against the wall in the pool house, or should I brace myself for the lonely company of my hand tonight?

Suddenly, the crowd of friends I was so happy to see in my backyard is a frustrating obstacle between me and the thing I want most—to have Stella alone.

"Great party, Kace," Dean says behind me.

I look away from my phone so quickly that a muscle in my neck throbs. "Hey," I say, but I'm fixated on Stella's last text. My dick is half hard and I can barely think straight and . . . there's her brother. I feel like I should apologize or something. Dean's not some overprotective asshole who thinks no guy should touch his sister. He respects Stella enough to let her make her own choices, and he generally stays out of her love life—with one or two notable exceptions where *someone* needed to school Stella on a guy's true colors. I wouldn't feel so damn guilty if I were interested in a relationship with her, but I'm not. I'm just another asshole who dreams about those tits and that mouth of hers way too often.

"Having a good time?" I ask, and I've never been so glad for my poker face.

Dean reaches into the cooler for a beer, hands it to me, then grabs another. "Yeah. It's a gorgeous day. I'm glad I came." He takes a pull of his beer and settles back into his chair. "Amy left early. Did you two argue or something?"

I shake my head. "Nah, we're good. Hope had a friend's birthday party she needed to get to."

He lifts his chin. "Got it. It's good to see you and Amy getting along."

"It's easier than I thought it'd be," I admit. When Amy told me she was moving out and filing for divorce but wanted us to *stay friends*, I thought she was crazy. I shrug. "It's all for Hope."

"I love that," he says. "You two are awesome parents."

"Thanks."

Dean glances around the party, and even though it's totally reasonable for him to come over here to hang by me, I wish he hadn't. I want to get back to my conversation with Stella.

I want to kick everyone out and finally turn the corner on this endless flirtation.

My phone dings with another notification. I don't look. I'm ready to tell Stella exactly what I want to do to her, but not while her brother's sitting across from me.

I twist the top off my beer, focusing on my friend, and

catch movement out of the corner of my eye. Stella's heading toward the pool house.

The pool house.

I lean back in my chair and look right at Dean, clearing my throat to get his attention. I don't want him to see where Stella's going, just in case he notices me slipping in there as soon as I can excuse myself from this conversation. "You need anything? Did you get enough to eat?"

"Nah, I'm good." He stares at the table between us and wipes away the condensation from his beer. He's acting weird as fuck. Or maybe I'm feeling awkward and projecting? Either way, Stella's waiting for me, and I need to pick up my phone and get a rain check or follow her.

I know what I *want* to do.

I stand and stretch. "Well, I need to hit the head."

"Sure." He takes a sip of his beer and nods. "Catch you after."

I've known this guy all my life, and I know when something's bugging him. Normally, I'd pry the truth out of him, but right now I have other priorities.

I try to be inconspicuous as I make my way across the patio, but I feel like my secret is written all over my face. The problem with me and Stella is it wouldn't just affect us. Her brother's my best friend, and she's good friends with my sister, Abbi. Then there's Stella's best friend, Brinley, who's like a sister to me, and Brinley's daughter, Cami, who's like a niece to me and also close to Stella. And I don't even want to think about how Amy would react. They worked together a few years ago and Stella made some immature choices, leaving a terrible impression on Amy.

If we screw this up, everyone I care about will be affected as well.

By the time I'm sliding the glass door closed behind me, I'm wondering if this is a terrible idea altogether.

Despite the wall of windows that overlook the pool, the pool house is dark in the afternoons and evenings, and it takes a minute for my eyes to adjust. I don't turn on a light or call out her name.

I scan the living area of the small structure and the kitchenette against the far wall. After a quick look around, I realize Stella's not waiting for me in the open. The sleeping loft is currently being used as storage, and I can't imagine she would've sneaked behind the path I roped off—not with all those chipped tiles—so I assume she's not up there, either. Which leaves the bathroom. The door's cracked, and after I take two steps in that direction, Stella pokes her head out and grins.

"Come here," she whispers.

All my uncertainty disappears behind a haze of lust. I push into the bathroom and kick the door closed behind me. I wouldn't think there'd be anything sexier than that bikini, but Stella's confident grin definitely tops it. And her freckles—she has new ones dusting the bridge of her nose.

"This is crazy," I whisper, but my hands are already on her sweat-slicked skin—palms on her stomach and sliding around to her back, pulling her against my bare chest. Holy hell, she feels good. Soft and warm. Perfect and . . . dangerous. "What are we doing?"

"I think I'm teaching you how casual works," she whispers. "I'm a good friend like that."

There it is—the permission I need, the acknowledgment that she understands the limits of what I'm offering. I hold her gaze, then search her face for any sign of hesitation. "Are you sure?"

CHAPTER FOUR

STELLA

*a*m I *sure?* Kace has his hands on me and is looking at me like a starved man and dropping not-so-subtle hints that he's craving *me,* and he thinks I'm going to back out now? I'm sure I like Coke more than Pepsi. I'm sure I'm cranky if I don't get at least six hours of sleep. Him asking if I'm sure I want him to touch me is akin to asking if I'm sure I need oxygen.

"So sure."

His lips part, and his gaze skims over every inch of my face before dropping to my throat, my collarbone, and finally to the swell of my breasts.

I bite my thumb *hard*, but nope. I don't wake up. Maybe I'm crazy and this is going to make shit real awkward, but I can't back off. Kace is . . . everything. And he's right in front of me.

"I couldn't take my eyes off you today," he says.

"I noticed."

"Or last night," he says, his voice rough.

Not just today. And not just last night. I've given Kace shit for years, but the past month or so, I've noticed the way he looks at me when we end up in the same room together. I've recognized the interest in his eyes, and yet until his last text, I thought he was either in denial about the chemistry between us or determined to never act on it.

His hands skim up my sides, thumbs stopping just shy of the underside of my breasts, before heading back down. "I keep waiting for Dean to catch me ogling his sister and give me a lecture."

"Would that have kept you from joining me?"

He shakes his head then shrugs before his gaze settles on my mouth again. "I don't know."

"Kace." Reaching up, I tangle my fingers into his hair and tug gently. "Are you going to kiss my mouth or just keep looking at it?"

His lips quirk into a crooked grin. "Both?" Then slowly, so slowly I want to whimper in frustration, he dips his head. When those lips finally brush mine, a hot shiver rolls down my spine.

I want to climb him, wrap myself around him and hold on tight. Or kiss my way down his body and fulfill another fantasy. But I ignore the thoughts that beg me to rush to the next part and focus on how surprisingly soft his lips are, how the air around us seems to crackle with the chemistry of our bodies finally touching.

"Is this what you wanted?" His lips brush mine with each word.

"It's on the road to what I want," I admit. "But only if you want it too."

He grunts. "You have no idea."

I slide my hands around his hips, over his waistband, up and over the powerful muscles of his back. Kace might spend the better part of his workday behind a desk now, but he's built like he's still hauling wood and hanging drywall and whatever the hell else those guys do.

"Do you have any idea how hot you look in this bikini?" He drags his mouth across my jaw and to my ear, where he pulls the lobe between his teeth and sucks. His hands are everywhere—rough fingertips skimming the skin just above the top of my bikini bottoms then trailing up, thumbs ghosting over my nipples before they descend. He's touching me all over, and it's not enough. "I've spent the whole day wanting to peel it off you with my teeth. Or maybe just tease you through the fabric until you're begging to feel my tongue on your bare skin."

I draw in a little shocked gasp. Holy hell, who knew Kace could bring the dirty talk? I like it. Way too much. "Either works for me."

He chuckles in my ear. "Patience, Freckles."

"Time for a lesson about hookups," I say between heavy breaths—because the sucking, licking, kissing thing he's doing to my ear right now is making it hard to focus on anything else. "Hookups aren't about patience. Quite the opposite, in fact. It's about getting the job done."

"Fuck that. Maybe *I'm* the one who needs to be teaching *you*." His mouth trails lower, and my laughter turns to a moan as his teeth nip at the swell of my breasts.

Holy shit, this man's mouth is going to be the death of me in more ways than one. "Sorry if this disappoints you, but I don't need a tutor. I consider myself an expert."

"Really?" He straightens, and those liquid honey eyes

burn into mine. "Have you ever even been with a good man? One who knows that treating a woman like a queen doesn't stop at the bedroom door?" He cups my breast, and when his thumb circles my nipple through my suit, I arch into him. "One who worships you the way you were built to be worshipped?"

"I'm not a virgin." I release a ragged exhale as I thread my fingers through his hair. I tug gently and guide his mouth back to mine, kissing him with all the hunger I've felt for years. "I know what it's like to be fucked."

"Such a dirty mouth," he murmurs, but there's only approval in his tone. When he kisses me again, his tongue is velvety soft against mine, and his guttural groan makes my thighs clench. He tastes like his favorite IPA—slightly citrusy and a lot hoppy. I hate beer, but it's good on him. I want to drink him in until I can't taste anything else.

He tears his mouth away, and I whimper, but my sounds of protest turn to moans of pleasure as he kisses his way down my throat and nuzzles his face between my breasts, gently nipping at the swell of each before soothing away the sting with his tongue. My nipples tighten painfully. God, I need that mouth lower. Need to feel his teeth against that sensitive peak.

He works his way back up to my ear with his mouth and back down to my thighs with his hands. "You know what it's like to be fucked, but do you have any idea what it's like to be *savored?* To have a man who wants to earn every moan, every sweet gasp from those lips?" He nudges my legs apart, and his fingertips brush faintly against the fabric between my thighs. It's hardly a touch. It's a whisper. A promise of what's to come. And when I jerk my hips toward him in a raw, physical plea for his touch, he pulls away enough for me to see his smile.

"Tease," I say.

Just as Kace parts his lips to reply, there's a knock on the door. "Kace? You okay in there?"

He drops his hands, his eyes wide. Now I really do whimper. Leave it to Smithy to have the worst timing.

"Uh . . . Kace?" Smithy sounds equal parts worried and curious.

"What the fuck, man? I'm in the bathroom." He throws his head back in frustration and closes his eyes. I'm feeling pretty frustrated too, considering those big fingers that were dancing between my legs a minute ago are now hanging at his side.

"Shit. Right." Smithy chuckles. "Sorry to catch you with your pants down."

Smithy's laughter is contagious, and I have to bite my bottom lip so my own doesn't give us away.

"Dean was looking for you, and I thought . . ." Smithy clears his throat. "I thought it might be better if I was the one who found you, if you know what I mean? I told him you were in the kitchen to throw him off your trail."

Kace scrubs a hand over his beard. "Tell him I'll be out in a minute."

"I'll stall so you can . . . you know." He clears his throat. "Finish and whatnot."

I wait until I hear the sliding doors open and close again before I speak. "Smithy must've seen us both come in here." I swallow. "I'll talk to him. Tell him I needed your help with something."

"Thanks," Kace says. His light brown eyes meet mine,

and he looks . . . remorseful. "Sorry, Freckles. This was a bad idea."

My stomach sinks. Of course. I'm Stella. *Party girl. Dean's little sister. Walking disaster.* He's Kace. *Businessman. Responsible father. All things good and noble.* Of course I knew he'd decide this was a bad idea. I just didn't know he'd decide that *after* I found out about his dirty, dirty mouth.

I try to retreat, but the vanity hits the small of my back, and I can't. I'm trapped in a bathroom between a sink and a man who doesn't want to want me. I lift my chin. I promised myself long ago that I wouldn't cry any more tears over Kace Matthews. "If you say so."

He cuts his gaze to the door and shakes his head. "I think everyone's planning on hanging around, so I can't promise it'll be as soon as I want, but if you don't mind being the last to leave . . ." He smiles at me again. And his dimples melt all my walls. "You deserve better than a quickie in a bathroom, anyway."

I blink at him, and he must take my confusion for irritation, because he says, "It's fine either way. I totally get it if you have plans or—"

"I don't have plans." The mistake was the *bathroom* and the *timing*, not the hookup? Holy. Fucking. Shit.

He traces my bottom lip with his thumb. "Good." He drags his bottom lip between his teeth. "Because I'm really looking forward to teaching you what it's like to be worshipped."

Dead. I'm dead.

RIP, Stella Jacob. She died of thirst.

He looks me over one last time and winks before straightening and backing toward the door.

"Want me to come with you?" I ask. "To talk to Dean? I

LEXI RYAN

won't let him be all overprotective. He knows I'm a big girl and make my own decisions." Panic flashes in his eyes, and I realize that before I opened my mouth, it hadn't occurred to Kace that Dean might want to talk because he knows we're in here together.

He swallows and shakes his head. "Nah. I've got this."

KACE

I'm a grown-ass man, but as I wander around the backyard looking for Dean, I feel a little bit like a kid on his way to the principal's office. *Dean wants to talk to you.*

Those words might not have bothered me much if we hadn't been talking right before I left to find Stella. So either a) something really was bugging him earlier and that's why he was acting so weird, or b) he knows I was with Stella and what was about to go down, and has an issue with it. I really fucking hope it's not the latter, because now that I've had a taste of her, I'm craving a whole lot more.

I find Dean in the back corner of my yard, poking around in the firepit. "Smithy said you were looking for me?"

He startles, and the look on his face is more like that of a kid caught with his dad's booze than a man stoking a campfire. There's definitely something on his mind. "Hey, yeah . . ." He clears his throat. "We need to talk."

Obviously. I shove my hands into my pockets. "I thought you might have something on your mind. What's up?"

He takes a stick from the pile and tosses it into the fire. "It's about Stella."

Well, fuck. I rock back on my heels, braced to defend myself. Or her. Or . . . I don't know what. I don't exactly want to explain that we were just going to hook up one time. Dean's pretty chill, but I'd fucking take issue if *he* had a one-night stand with *my* sister. Okay, I'm a hypocrite. "Are you sure you want to do this? Maybe it's better if you just trust that she's an adult and—"

"She is, but Mom doesn't see it that way, and she'll never ask her to leave."

"Wait. What?"

"A condo at Lakeview Acres is about to go on the market. You know I've been wanting to get Mom in one of those for years, and now that I finally have the chance, Stella's living with her. Mom won't move if she thinks she's putting Stella out." He frowns. "What did you think I was talking about?"

I shake my head. "No. Nothing. I . . ." I blow out a breath. "I see what you're saying. Isn't Stella apartment hunting?"

Dean puffs out a breath. "In theory, I guess? But it's more like she's keeping her eyes open for an affordable opportunity. She's starting nursing school at the Mountain Laurel Community College in the fall, so she doesn't have a lot of extra cash. She's looking for a roommate more than a place of her own. And since Brinley isn't living with you anymore, I thought maybe . . ."

I blink at him. I think I left half my brain in the bathroom with Stella, because it takes much longer than it should for his meaning to register. He doesn't want to kick my ass for hooking up with his sister; he wants me to let his sister move in with me.

He wants Stella to live in my house.

My feelings for her might be all over the place, but I know for sure I can't have her under my roof. Stella's brand of wild isn't something I want Hope exposed to on a day-to-day basis . . . which is just further proof that I'm a hypocritical ass. And hell, even though *I'm* the one who wants casual, I don't want to see the guys she brings home, couldn't handle overhearing her *being* with them. That level of casual isn't in my DNA. "Does she know you're asking?"

"What? No, man. I wouldn't make it awkward for you like that." He frowns. "You're not okay with this? You let Brinley move in back in April, so I thought . . ."

"It's nothing against Stella. The thing with Brinley was just a temporary situation and . . ." *And I don't want to bend Brinley over the bed and fuck her until she screams my name.*

Right. Maybe it's not the way *Stella* would behave in front of my daughter that I need to worry about.

I drag a hand through my hair and blow out a breath. "I want to help, but Stella deserves to come and go as she pleases without worrying about our schedules. I don't think it'd be a good fit."

Dean's gaze drifts to a spot over my shoulder, and I turn to see his attention on the pool house. "What if I helped you remodel the pool house? Once we knock it into shape, Stella could live in there and pay you rent. You wouldn't hear her coming and going."

Before we opened our construction company, Dean and I used to flip houses. We started in college and had no capital to speak of—just a couple of credit cards and the crappy little outdated three-bedroom by campus that Grandpa left me when he passed. Dean and I saw the potential and decided to fix it up and see if we could make some money. We did all the work ourselves for the first few years, so I know we could handle the pool house in a couple of weeks of evenings and weekends—if that. It's small, and most of the work it needs is superficial.

But do I want Stella to be my tenant?

"I know Stell is a little over-the-top and can rub you the wrong way, but—"

"What? No, that's not it." Fuck. The housing situation in Orchid Valley is a nightmare—the tourists and week-enders from Atlanta have driven the prices of everything so high that half the people who work in the OV live halfway to Atlanta. If Stella's going to nursing school and keeping a job at The Orchid, she doesn't need to be losing hours of her week to her commute. "She didn't tell me she was going back to school."

Dean nods. "Yeah. Turns out her English degree isn't producing the best job opportunities. Who would've seen that coming?" He rolls his eyes, just in case I didn't catch the sarcasm dripping from his voice. Dean's the opposite of his sister in so many ways. Stella's carefree and impulsive, and Dean's all sense and practicality. Stella's choice of major was the subject of *many* Dean lectures and rants, which only made Stella double down on her decision and refuse to explain what jobs she'd be pursuing.

"Would she really want to live there?" I ask. "It's five hundred square feet, and one whole wall is windows. Hope and I spend so much time in the backyard that she'd never have guaranteed privacy, and the bedroom . . . it isn't even a bedroom. It's just a loft big enough for a bed and a dresser."

"Stell doesn't need much. Hell, technically it's more privacy than she has at Mom's." He presses his palms together. "Please, Kace? This would take a whole load of stress off my shoulders."

47

"We don't know for sure that Stella's on board. Maybe we should float the possibility by her before we—"

"Stella!" Dean shouts, waving a hand in the air. "Come over here a minute."

I flinch. I didn't mean *right this second.* But when I turn, Stella's walking toward us, a fresh can of White Claw in her hand. She's put a cover-up over her bikini, for which I'm both grateful and disappointed. I lean into the grateful. Dean doesn't need to see me staring at his sister's tits . . . or see any marks my beard might've left on her cleavage.

"What's up?" she asks, standing between us. "You two look like you're trying to make a plan to eliminate the national debt."

I duck my head to hide my smile. I was nervous as fuck when I thought Dean might know what we'd been doing, but Stella's all casual. Her refusal to take anything too seriously is what I find most maddening and endearing about her. I'm self-aware enough to know I'm more like Dean and could use a pinch of carefree in my life.

"Kace was just saying there's no reason you can't live in his pool house."

My head snaps up, because that's *not* what I was saying. There are *lots* of reasons. I'm just not sure any of them are good enough for Dean to pass up a chance to get his mom out of that old house.

Stella coughs on her White Claw. "That's . . ." She pats her chest. "That's definitely unexpected."

"It's not the perfect situation," I say, cutting a look to Stella. "But what Dean's not saying is that he has a chance to get your mom into one of the Lakeview Acres condos, and he wants to make sure you'll have a place to stay."

Stella's jaw drops and she shakes her head. "You do?"

"I know you've had crap luck with rentals and awful landlords," Dean says, "and I didn't want to say anything until I'd found a safe place for you to live."

"So you asked *Kace?*" She turns to me, eyes wide. "I'm so sorry. Don't feel obligated."

"That's not why I'm offering," I blurt, even though a minute ago I'm not sure I was offering at all. I'd forgotten about her old, creepy landlord. Shit. I'm not going to be the reason Stella finds herself in a situation like that again. "Just take the pool house. It's fine."

Fine.

But when Stella's eyes linger on mine as she drags her bottom lip between her teeth, my gut clenches.

I'm screwed.

The woman I'm lusting after is moving in with me.

There's nothing *fine* about this.

CHAPTER FIVE

STELLA

*F*or twenty-seven years, I've been the mess that needs cleaning up, the problem child.

When I was eighteen, and Dean was off to college and Mom had the opportunity to travel to Europe for two weeks with her boyfriend, I was the reason she had to pass on the trip—*can't trust Stella not to throw a party.*

When I was in college, I flew to Naples for a week at a luxury beachfront resort, only to find the resort didn't exist and the Craigslist ad I'd bought it from was a scam. Dean was out of town, and it was Kace who had to drive down to rescue me.

When I was twenty-two and starting my first real job, I ended up with a landlord who used his key once (that I know of) to sneak in and watch me sleep while he . . . But I try not to think about that. *That* was a nightmare. The guy claimed I was lying and it never happened. Since he was a police officer, I was too afraid to report him. Then the ass refused to let me out of my twelve-month lease, and I had to mooch off my brother while I handed over most of my paycheck for rent on an apartment I wasn't using.

After all this time, you'd think I'd be used to my role as the damsel in distress—or rather, the hot mess in a disaster of her own making—but I'm not. It's a really shitty feeling, and I hope I never get used to it. Knowing I'm in the way of Mom making the move she's been dreaming of leaves me feeling small. "Dean, why didn't you tell me?"

My brother grimaces and shrugs. "I thought it'd be easier to work it out before I came to you."

So he asked *Kace*. Kace, who's looking at me like I'm a pair of unidentified dirty underwear he's being forced to deal with. I want to hang my head. To *disappear*. But I'm sick of letting guys treat me like I have a tiny brain and even less backbone, so I lift my chin. "I'm sure Kace is just being nice. He doesn't want me moving in with him."

"That's why this is such a perfect arrangement," Dean says. "You wouldn't be moving in *with* him. You'd be moving into the pool house."

I bite back my frown—because I don't want to seem like an ungrateful asshole—but I've just been inside the pool house. Aside from being crammed full of junk left behind by the previous owner, it's in rough shape. Kace literally has the path from the door to the bathroom roped off so people don't stray and hurt their bare feet on the cracked and chipped tiles of the main room. There are holes in the drywall, and don't even get me started on the cobwebs and creepy-crawlies.

"We'll fix it up," Kace says. "Dean and I will take the next couple of weeks to make it . . . livable."

I turn and stare at the tiny structure on the opposite side of the pool. From the outside, it looks fine. It has the same sunny-yellow siding as the main house, and the side that faces the pool is wall-to-wall windows. It was probably a gorgeous guest house once, and I have no doubt that Dean and Kace can make it gorgeous again. The guys specialize in taking the worst houses and turning them into the best.

I don't doubt their abilities, but I'm not buying into Kace's willingness. "I really don't want to impose. I'll find somewhere else."

Kace looks at Dean before turning back to me. "It wouldn't be an imposition, Stella. It's fine. You'll be safe here."

"Please, Stella?" Dean says. "Move into the pool house. At least while you finish school."

And have Kace look at me like I'm a charity case every time we cross paths? I'll take what's behind door number two instead, please. "Give me the week to find a place. If I come up empty-handed, I'll move into Kace's pool house until I can find something else."

Dean beams. He thinks this conversation is over and is probably ready to move me in at seven a.m. next Saturday, but it's not happening. I'm sure I can find another option somehow.

I excuse myself and find Brinley on the opposite side of the yard, playing cornhole with her husband, Marston.

"Stella, baby!" Brinley says, wrapping her arms around me and hanging on just enough to tell me she's not quite sober.

"Somebody's been drinking," I say, laughing. "What happened to the no-booze-until-the-vow-renewal diet?"

"I nixed that idea," Marston says, tossing a beanbag at the target. "She doesn't need to fit in a smaller dress. She's perfect the way she is."

"He thinks I'm perfect," Brinley stage-whispers, then gives a dreamy sigh.

Marston winks at her. "I *know* it."

My heart tugs. They're so freaking good together. Marston pulls her away from me and into his arms. He smiles down at her, and he *sees* her. It's always been that way with them—since they met as teenagers. Marston didn't see the spoiled little rich girl so many others saw in Brinley. He saw a girl who had her own heartaches and struggles, the girl he loved from that first moment and never stopped loving.

Someday I'm going to find that. But for now, I feel lucky to get one hot night with Kace.

The next three hours drag while I wait for everyone to leave. Normally, I'm the one trying to convince our friends to stay later. I'm the one who doesn't want to go home and never wants the night to end.

But normally, a naked Kace isn't waiting for me once all our friends find their way home.

Sure, the potential of me moving into his backyard could make this awkward—but that likely won't happen. And even if it does, it'd be for a month, maybe two. Surely one night together won't make that weird.

By eleven, Dean has said his goodbyes, along with Marston, Brinley, Smithy, and Savannah. It's just Kace, Abbi, and me sitting around the fire. Judging by the awkward glances Kace keeps sending my way when Abbi's distracted, my chances of getting him naked are falling lower and lower. I blame Dean and his terrible pool house idea.

Cockblocker.

Finally, Abbi stretches her arms over her head and yawns. "I should get going."

Kace practically jumps out of his chair, ever the smooth criminal. "Sure. Thanks for coming." He wraps her in a hug and kisses the top of her head. "Call me if you need help with the car tomorrow."

I frown. "What's wrong with your car?"

Abbi makes a face. "Nothing. Kace just wants me to get new tires."

"Your tread's nonexistent. It literally makes me lose sleep."

She grins at him. "How do you know I don't do this intentionally to make up for how much you tormented me growing up?"

"I wouldn't put it past you," he says, hands on his hips. "But seriously. You take it in, or I will."

She rolls her eyes. "I have an appointment."

"Good."

Abbi shoots me a look. "You wanna head out with me, Stella?"

No. I want to jump your brother. I hold up my nearly empty White Claw. "I'm going to stick around and finish this."

She turns to Kace. "You'll drive her if she drinks another one?"

I bow my head to hide my flinch. Even my friends don't trust me to make responsible decisions.

"Of course," he says, nodding. "Want me to walk you to your car?"

She waves him off. "Nah. I'm fine. See you at Mom's tomorrow night."

"Love you," he calls after her.

"Love you back." She pushes through the gate, and a few moments later, I hear her car heading down the street.

Kace settles back into his chair and rests his elbows on his knees. When he looks up at me, I already know I should've left with Abbi and saved myself the awkward rejection. "About what happened earlier . . ." He searches my face in the light from the fire. "I think maybe it's good we were interrupted."

I sigh dramatically. "I wait for twelve years, and all I get is one half-assed make-out session? Figures." I wink at him, but maintaining my smile is too hard, so I hide it behind my can.

He arches a brow. "Hey now, I wouldn't call it half-assed."

"Too short to call it anything else. Unless that's your . . . style?" I cock my head to the side.

"We already established how much I'd like to take my time with you, Freckles." He growls and mutters something that sounds like *"Fucking Dean."*

I concur but drain my drink and push out of my chair. "Don't stress, Kace. It would've been fun, but I get it. I'm Dean's little sister, and you're—"

"It's not that." He stands, reaches for me, then drops his hands awkwardly to his sides. "It *would* be fun. I really would've . . ." His smile's a little crooked and his eyes a little mischievous and *ohmygod* do I want him. "I think we'd have a good time."

I blink. "Wow. Didn't expect that."

He shrugs. "After earlier, I don't see the point in pretending otherwise. You know I'm attracted to you. You know what I want to do to you, with you." He pauses for a beat, and the way he swallows makes me think I'm not the only one imagining those things. "But I'm thinking past tonight—about the consequences of one night of fun if you end up needing a place to live."

"I'll find somewhere," I say with way more confidence than I feel. In preparation for *hopefully* starting nursing school in the fall, I've been training my replacement at The Orchid. My modest full-time salary will become a modest part-time salary beginning Monday. Even living at Mom's, the pay cut was a little scary, but if I have to pay rent, I don't know how I'm going to manage it. I'm not at all surprised that Mom refused to move. She's the one who encouraged me to go back to school and get a more career-focused degree. But I won't be the reason she doesn't get to sell that money pit and move into a lower-maintenance place.

"Dean's right, you know. The pool house could be the perfect solution for you. Let's not take it off the table just because your bikini made me . . . *thirsty*." He smiles and drags his gaze slowly over me. I'm not in my bikini anymore, but I feel naked. *And so thirsty.*

"Can I blame the bikini for my lustful thoughts too? Maybe we should send it to confession. We're both off the hook."

He laughs softly, eyes crinkling in the corners. "I'm trying to say that crossing that line tonight might set a bad precedent for us. I can't very well have a booty call in the backyard of the house where I'm raising my child."

Wouldn't stop your wife. I tamp down the bitter thought. "You don't need to explain yourself. We had a moment. It might've been something more if we hadn't been interrupted, but we were." I shrug with all the carelessness I don't feel. "Let's not make this a thing. I'll go back to fantasizing about you, and you can go back to seeing me as Dean's annoying little sister. We'll pretend our bathroom interlude never happened."

He drags a hand through his hair and stares up at the clear sky. It's a beautiful night. If things had gone differently, we could've stayed out here for hours under the stars. It would've been . . . Well, it didn't happen. Who's to say something else wouldn't have scared Kace off?

"I am sorry," Kace whispers, looking at me again.

I wag a finger at him. "If you're going to start using the tools of the modern hookup world, you need to learn the first rule: never apologize for changing your mind. You don't owe anyone anything and have every right to back out at any moment. Your body, your choice, et cetera, et cetera."

He blows out a breath. "That's good advice."

I shrug. "What can I say? I'm a font of wisdom."

He steps forward and slowly brushes his knuckles down my arm. "For the record, I'm apologizing to myself more than you. You're fucking beautiful, Stella, and last night wasn't the first time I noticed. And tonight wasn't the first time I wanted to act on this attraction."

I try to breathe, but air refuses to enter my lungs. "Yeah?"

He gives me a sad smile. "Come on. I'll walk you to your car."

I wince. "Could you not? I just . . ." I blow out a breath. "I've had my fill of awkward for the night."

He glances over his shoulder toward the gate. "Right. Good night, then."

I chew on the inside of my cheek, wishing I could say something to turn us back to the fun and flirty, if dysfunctional, dynamic we've settled into lately.

This is for the best.

Some part of my brain knows it's true. The same part knows that a quickie in the bathroom with Kace wasn't going to help me get over him or make him fall for me, but that reasonable thought is barely a whisper against my disappointment.

＆

KACE

Stella's wet bikini top sticks to her skin as I peel it away to reveal a perfect puckered nipple. She hooks a leg around my waist and rocks into me. "Please."

I want to give her everything she's asking for. I want to slide my hand into those skimpy bikini bottoms and feel the slick warmth I know is waiting for me.

I pinch her nipple, and she gasps. I need it in my mouth, to feel it go harder against my tongue while she shivers beneath me. I'm going to taste every inch of her.

"Are you seriously using my sister for sex?"

I spin around at the sound of Dean's voice. "What are you doing here?"

He scowls from the entrance to the pool house. "I thought I could trust you."

Suddenly, Amy's standing next to him, and she elbows him in the side. "Would you shut up? Kace needs this." She waves her hand toward Stella. "Go on. Fuck her. I'm so proud of you, Kace. Don't stop now."

Where the hell did they come from? I turn back to Stella, but she's sitting in the corner now, curled into a ball, arms wrapped around her knees. "I feel sick. I see it every time I close my eyes."

My eyes fly open, and my heart races.

A dream. It was just a dream.

A twisted, screwed-up dream that would better qualify as a nightmare.

Where the fuck did that even come from? Okay, I get the weirdness about Dream Dean thinking I was using his sister for sex. Part of me feels shitty about a just-for-sex hookup with anyone, but Stella? Fuck. There's a much larger part of my brain that knows that's uncool.

But what she said at the end about seeing it every time she closed her eyes—those were her words when we got her out of that apartment and away from her creep landlord. So am I the creep in this situation? Apparently my subconscious doesn't do subtle.

Yawning, I climb out of bed and head toward the bathroom to take a piss. The maneuvers I have to do to hit the toilet with this hard-on could land me a spot on *America's Got Talent*, but since I haven't had sex in going on two years, I'm getting used to the morning wood acrobatics.

After washing my hands, I stare at myself in the mirror and run a hand over my beard. It's gotten scruffy, and my hair's getting a little long. My sister calls this my lumberjack look. I'm tempted to shave the beard and start over, but any time I seriously consider it, Stella will make some comment about how hot she thinks it is, and I can't bring myself to do it.

And if that doesn't just sum up the clusterfuck my life's become, I don't know what does. I won't shave my beard because I don't want Stella to be less attracted to me, even though I'm trying like hell not to be attracted to her.

When I turn on the shower, the pipes rattle in the walls. I need to check for a clog in the plumbing vent—need to do about a hundred things where this old house is concerned.

To prepare for my day, I try to make a mental checklist of the house-related tasks I want to get through while Hope's with her mom. But as I step under the hot spray, my mind quickly wanders from what I *should* be thinking about to what my still-hard dick wants to think about. Those too-brief minutes in the pool house yesterday. The dream before it got weird. Stella in my arms, turned on and gasping, rocking against me. *"Please."*

I close my eyes as I focus on that one word, stroke my hand up my aching erection, and play that part of the dream on repeat—her perfect lips as she whispered, *"Please."*

I didn't want to send her home last night. I wanted to bring her into my empty house and strip her naked. I would've peeled off her cover-up and then taken my time with the bikini. She would've trembled beneath my touch as I slid my hands down her arms and kissed my way up her neck. Her skin would've been soft under my mouth, but her hand in my hair would've been a little rough, just like when I had her alone earlier in the day. I would've kissed my way down her chest and flicked my tongue beneath the cups of her bikini until her legs wouldn't hold her up anymore and I had to lead her to the couch. She would've held my gaze as she peeled my swim trunks from my hips, and when I tried to move to sit beside her, she would've given me that wicked, sexy smile of hers and guided me to stand.

I palm my balls and shudder as I imagine her pink lips grazing the tip of my cock. I've fantasized about that mouth countless times in the past few months . . . fuck, *years*. So often that it's second nature to conjure the image now. I grip myself tight and slide my hand up and down in long, slow strokes as I let the fantasy take over. Stella teasing my cock with her tongue. Her hands on my thighs then sliding around to grip my ass as she moves to her knees and takes me deep.

My strokes become shorter, my grip tighter, and I jerk into my hand at the mental picture. Her mouth would feel amazing, but I'd need more, so I'd pull away before I came, bend her over the couch, and drive—

My orgasm hits me like a fucking freight train, and I come all over my hand and stomach with a groan. I keep moving through the aftershocks, clinging to that image of taking Stella from behind, her knuckles white on the back of the couch as she begs me for more.

"Fuck," I mutter when the last of the pleasure is wrung out of me and the water's washing away the evidence. I needed that, but I already know it won't be enough, because no matter how many times I use my hand and vivid imagination to deal with these increasingly frequent Stella fantasies, it doesn't change that she's all wrong for me.

Didn't stop you last night, a voice whispers as I wash. If Smithy hadn't interrupted us, I wouldn't have stopped unless she'd asked me to. And if Dean hadn't suggested I give her a place to stay, I know exactly what would've happened after everyone left—or, at least, what I wanted to happen.

But now she might be moving into your backyard.

Do I really want to continue this unrelenting lust-fest when she's that close? Can anything good come of that? There are a thousand reasons why I should stay away from Stella and only one why I shouldn't. And since my libido isn't the greatest decision maker, I guess my decision's been made for me. Maybe I wouldn't be so fixated on Stella if I was dating around, like Amy suggested. I should use that damn app—find someone I can enjoy myself with, have sex for the first time in way too long. Then maybe Stella won't be the temptation she is now.

By the time I climb out of the shower, my mind's made up. I grab my phone and log on to Random.

There are a few potential matches waiting for me—women who've already indicated they're interested. The girl with the cleavage shot Amy swiped on left me a message last night, and I almost laugh when I see her username. I click to read what she said and—nope, make that *four* messages.

> Bambi: Hey, gorgeous. You want to meet up?
> Bambi: Hey, I'm still around if you're down for this.
> Bambi: Hello?
> Bambi: WTFever. Don't swipe on women if you don't have the balls to follow through.

I blow out a breath. Looks like I fucked up my first interaction on Random—not that I would've met up with her anyway. Do people really do this? *Hey, you looked hot in one picture. Let's fuck!*

Shaking my head, I close out the text stream with Bambi and scroll through the women who swiped interested on me since Amy set up this account Friday night. *LisaLuvs-Roosters* is a blonde with blue eyes who reminds me way too much of Amy, so she's out. *CarrieBerry* is cute. Her dark hair brushes her jaw line, and she has big brown eyes and a pretty smile. She strikes me as the kind of girl who smiles a lot, but she also looks like a *girl*. As in, I'm not even sure she's old enough to be on here. Her profile says she's twenty-three, but I would've guessed much younger. That "barely legal" thing has never been my fantasy.

Then there's *JimmysGirl*. Weird profile name, but she's . . . Okay, she's fucking hot. In her profile picture, a white dress hugs every inch of her body. She has full tits, curvy hips, a tiny waist, and long, dark hair that cascades down her back in soft waves. I'd bet she gets a lot of interest with that pic, but I try not to think about that as I click through to her profile.

28-year-old female. Pharmacist.

I'm Jimmy's girl, just like my username says, but Jimmy likes to watch. Wanna play?

Yeah, not my kink. *Pass.*

I've pulled up my texting app and started typing out a message to Amy before I realize what I'm doing. The fact that I want to talk to my ex about this experience says so much about why I haven't moved on. I delete what I've typed and head to the kitchen to make coffee.

Amy would love to hear about these early matches. She'd get a kick out of JimmysGirl and probably call me an old-man prude for my concerns over CarrieBerry's age. It'd be fun to laugh together, but that'd only set me back and . . . well, she's right. It's time to move on.

After my coffee's done brewing, I sit down with my phone and decide to try again. Just because those were the only women who swiped on me in the last fourteen hours doesn't mean they're the only ones on the app who might be interested.

My stomach sinks as I scroll through. I can't stop thinking about why these women are on here. Are they crazy? Desperate? And my awareness that I too am on Random and am a hypocritical asshole only makes me feel worse.

Every profile picture is an attempt to convey a message. *I'm sexy. I'm confident. I'm harmless.* In a space where there's so little opportunity to communicate, it'd be foolish not to use the avatar to say something about yourself, but the whole thing just feels so damn contrived.

Maybe that's why the sight of the Jessica Rabbit avatar has me grinning. The cartoon image from the movie *Who Framed Roger Rabbit* is a hypersexualized redhead in a tight red sequin dress that shows lots of cleavage and even more thigh. If a woman had posted an actual picture of herself dressed like this, I'd roll my eyes and keep scrolling, but the fact that this girl chose to use a cartoon instead of a picture of herself intrigues me. I tap through to her profile.

ItsyBitsy123. 27-year-old female. Wanderer.

I'm living my best life, and that means having fun. No cheaters, creepers, or trolls, please. I've had my share. Bonus points if you enjoy reading anything more advanced than your morning cereal box.

That makes me laugh. She's the most interesting person I've seen on here yet. So I swipe. And I wait.

CHAPTER SIX

STELLA

The banner hanging above the entrance of the Orchid Valley branch of Mountain Laurel Community College says, *Welcome, students!* And I can't help but think I wasn't the kind of person they were imagining when they hung that sign. The admissions office assured me that community colleges are full of nontraditional students of all ages, but every time I imagine a full classroom, I picture a bunch of eighteen-year-olds, fresh out of high school . . . kind of like the gaggle of laughing girls vaping together a few cars away.

This summer is all about general education for me. I already have a bachelor's degree, but I need to take chemistry and anatomy and physiology before I can apply for the nursing program. Since there are always more applicants than spots, I also need to do *well* in those courses—a prospect that was terrifying enough before I realized I don't know where I'll be living this summer or how I'll be paying the rent.

"Are you going in?"

I turn toward the voice and smile at the tall guy who's asking. He's in jeans and a polo shirt and has a messenger bag slung over his shoulder. Most importantly, he looks closer to my age than the posse of girls giggling a few yards away.

I adjust my own bag and step toward him. "Yeah. I guess so."

He beams at me, showing off his straight white teeth. *Not bad at all.* "First day?"

"Yes. And I'm totally nervous."

His gaze flicks over me in that way guys do when they're checking you out but trying to be quick about it so they don't come off looking slimy. I'm going to work a shift at The Orchid right after class, so I'm dressed professionally in a black pencil skirt and a flowy yellow tank. There's definite interest in his eyes when he brings his gaze back up to meet mine. "What department?"

"Oh . . . science, I guess." I take a deep breath. It's too easy to assume I'm going to suck at my science classes just because I struggled with them in high school, but I'm trying so hard not to let negative thinking drag me down. I'm older, more mature, and my study skills are way better than they were back then.

Beaming, he offers a hand. "Same here. You're a part-timer too, I assume?"

I shake my head. "Just for the summer. Full-time starting in the fall," I say with a confidence I don't feel. Need to ace a couple of classes first.

His eyes go wide. "Really? That's great. Maybe you can put in a good word for me."

What? "A word with who?"

He chuckles. "I know, right? I can't figure out who makes these decisions, and I ended up piecing together a full-time schedule from three different schools, but good for you. That's great."

I'm confused but too nervous to worry about it. "Hopefully it will be."

He offers a hand, and it's warm and a little rough against mine. "I'm Anderson. It's nice to meet you."

"I'm Stella."

"Listen, I have to meet up with someone and then I have class, but I'd like to buy you a coffee or something later."

I bite back a grin. Here I was worried I wouldn't have classes with anyone my age, and I've already made a friend before setting foot in the classroom. "Yes. That'd be amazing. I have a break at noon."

"It's a date. Meet me in the Starbucks in the Commons?"

A date. With a cute fellow student. *Eat your heart out, Kace Matthews.* "Perfect."

"I look forward to it," Anderson says. He heads toward the building, tossing me one final wink over his shoulder before he pushes through the doors.

A few deep breaths later, I muster the courage to walk in after him and find my classroom. Unfortunately, as I expected, the majority of the students around me look like they're fresh out of high school. There's an older man I recognize from The Orchid, and I wave to him as I enter.

"Stella," he says, smiling at me. "What are you doing here?"

"Same thing as you, Charlie." I nod to the open notebook in front of him. "Taking a chemistry class."

He taps his notebook and shakes his head. When he speaks again, it's in a low, conspiratorial tone. "I told my kids I'm too old to be doing this, but they said I might as well. Always wanted to go back to school, and I'm gonna be old whether I do it or not."

I slide into the seat next to him. "I was kind of figuring the same thing."

"Does Brinley know you're here?" Brinley's not only my lifelong best friend, but she owns The Orchid, where I'm a receptionist, and is therefore also my boss.

"She does, and she approves. I've already trained my replacement, and I promise she'll take good care of you."

He shakes his head. "Nah. Nobody can take care of me as well as you do. Always made sure to get me scheduled before my favorite massage therapist booked up. It won't be the same there without your smiling face."

"Well, I'll still be there on weekends and some evenings, so no worries."

He pats my arm. "Then I'll keep coming back."

"Good morning, everyone. I'm Professor Burns, and I'll be your chemistry instructor this term."

Our attention shifts to the front of the room and the man standing at the dry-erase board. My heart skids to a stop at the sight of him. *Anderson.* He wasn't a fellow student but a *teacher*.

His gaze lands on me, and the shock that rolls across his expression tells me he's as surprised to see me as his student as I am to see him as my teacher. *Fuck.*

He clears his throat and looks away, schooling his expression as he takes in the rest of the class. "This is Chem 101, and I hope you're ready to work, because this is a condensed term, meaning we'll be doing in six weeks what I normally teach in sixteen." He picks up a stack of papers from the corner of his desk and proceeds to pass them out. I sink down into my chair, willing myself to become invisible as he goes over the course requirements.

By the time class is over, my brain has shifted gears and instead of panicking about having a date with my *professor*, I'm spiraling into panic about the course requirements and how much we'll be covering this six weeks. I might be more mature than I was in high school chem, but the concepts still make my head spin.

"This should be fun," Charlie says when Anderson—no, make that *Mr. Burns*—dismisses us. "I always loved chemistry. It was my favorite in college."

I force a smile and hoist my bag onto my shoulder. "Maybe you can be my lab partner and teach me your tricks."

"Ms. Jacob," Mr. Burns says. "Could I see you before you leave, please?"

Charlie waggles his salt-and-pepper brows. "Uh-oh. In trouble already?"

I snort. He has no idea. "I'll see you tomorrow, Charlie."

He winks and heads out behind the other students.

Once everyone else is gone, I approach Mr. Burns' desk. "I'm sorry," I blurt at the same time as he says, "I owe you an apology."

We laugh, and he sighs, holding up a hand. "When we talked outside, I thought you were an instructor."

"And I thought you were a student," I say.

He runs a hand through his hair. "So you understand why I need to cancel our coffee"—he clears his throat, clearly unwilling to say the word *date*—"why I need to cancel our plans."

"Oh my God. Yes. Of course!"

"It's just that you're a student, and I . . ." He shakes his head, and his gaze briefly skims over my body before he brings it back up to meet mine. "I really am sorry."

"We both made assumptions."

He makes a face that seems to say, *Did we, though?* "I mean, I asked what department you worked for."

I frown. That's not the way I remember it, but what did he say exactly? "I guess I misunderstood."

Something about his expression makes me feel like a child who's just broken the rules and is trying to talk her way out of it. "Let's just not *misunderstand* anymore. Okay? Because I don't . . . I'm not interested in spending time outside the classroom with a student."

Yowch. Okay, I get it. "Understood." I back toward the door. "See you tomorrow."

God, it's going to be a long six weeks.

§◍

MY DAY CONSISTED of accidentally flirting with my chem professor, barely avoiding a panic attack in anatomy and physiology, a shift at The Orchid, and a futile search for a place to live. By the time I get home, I'm beat.

I still haven't talked to Mom about the available condo at Lakeview Acres, and I know she won't bring it up if I don't confront her. In fact, I know she won't *move* if I don't move first. I hope to avoid the conversation entirely until I can tell her I've found an affordable place to stay.

That won't be a problem tonight, since she's already asleep when I get home. I keep my steps quiet as I head down the hall to my childhood bedroom and change into my pajamas. Rusty, Mom's twelve-year-old golden retriever, meets me at my bedroom door, a pair of my underwear hanging from his mouth.

"Rusty!" I scold, yanking them away. "No!" But Rusty looks up at me with big brown eyes full of adoration, and I can't stay mad. "You're lucky you're the best guy in my life."

I pad to the bathroom to return the undies to the hamper, brush my teeth, and wash my face. By the time I'm in my sleep clothes and climbing into bed, my bone-deep exhaustion has shifted into a restlessness. *Damnit.* I just want to sleep for ten hours and try to start tomorrow with a good attitude.

I scroll through social media, smiling when I see Brinley's latest Instagram post. It's her and Marston, splattered in paint, with Cami's newly painted bedroom in the background. I give it a like and ignore that "some girls get everything" jealousy. Truth is, Brinley *deserves* everything, and she had to fight for it, so I refuse to resent an iota of her happiness or success. I also refuse to impinge on that happiness by asking to bunk with them. She'd say yes, and Marston would go along with it just because he'd do anything to make Brinley happy, but they've had enough come between them to get where they are. They deserve some peace and a chance to enjoy each other without me tagging along.

When Instagram no longer interests me, I open up Random for the first time in days, but when I see I have matches waiting, I actually groan. I clearly came here more out of boredom than actual interest. I don't have it in me to deal with the fuckboys from this app tonight. But bad habits must really die hard, because I'm already checking to see who's swiped on me.

My stomach lurches into full-on gymnastics at the sight of the bearded thirst trap in the avatar, grinning at the camera.

Kace is on Random. He told me this, didn't he? I'm not sure I believed he'd really use it, but that's not the real shock. The real shock is that Kace swiped on *me*. I couldn't be more surprised. I'm not qualified for much in this world, but I have the experience of a pro when it comes to being rejected by Kace Matthews.

The match is dated Sunday morning. The morning after sending me away on the worst kind of walk of shame, Kace got on Random, saw the picture of me in my cutest yellow sundress, and swiped. What kind of game is he playing? Did he change his mind? Is this his way of letting me know he wants to finish what we started?

The app is semi-anonymous; when you click on someone's picture, their basic profile pops up—username, age, and brief bio—but I don't need any more details beyond his picture to know that GoodHands69 is Kace. I click on the message box. It's ridiculous to talk here when we can just text each other, but if this is the game he wants to play, I'm down.

ItsyBitsy123: Well, hello, handsome.

I like to imagine he's settled into bed too. Shirtless— because that's my favorite way to imagine Kace—with one hand behind his head, the other holding his phone as he waits for a message from me.

> GoodHands69: Hey! I'd almost given up on you!
> ItsyBitsy123: Sorry about that. I haven't logged on in a few days. I would have, though, if I'd known you'd be waiting. You want me to come over?
> GoodHands69: Um . . . not yet??? Sorry, I have no idea what I'm doing right now. You cool with just talking?

Fuck, he's adorable. He could've texted me and gotten a response immediately. Or he could've hit up any other chick on here, but he got on a *hookup* app and swiped on me. And now he wants to use said hookup app to . . . *chat*. I'm not surprised, really. It fits Kace's MO—nothing impulsive, nothing risky. He'd be the type to make himself try out something like this, only to gravitate to the familiar face.

> ItsyBitsy123: Talking's good. I'm already in bed anyway and won't consider moving for anything short of the best sex of my life.
> GoodHands69: And is that easy to come by on here?

I actually laugh out loud. I've had so many bad experiences with Random that it's a wonder I haven't burned my phone to keep myself from going back for more.

ItsyBitsy123: I wouldn't know. I like to think I
   haven't HAD the best sex of my life yet.
So tell me what you're doing on Random.
GoodHands69: Grocery shopping?
ItsyBitsy123: Har-har. Don't be an ass.
GoodHands69: I'm in a weird place. Ready to
   move on from my marriage, but also not
   ready, because I have a daughter who
   matters more than anything. I'm trying to
   figure out a few things. Anyway, I guess I
   needed the distraction.

I roll to my side and consider how to reply. Should I
bring up what happened in the pool house, or do like we
agreed and pretend it never happened? If he wants to
pretend, why is he talking to me on here?

ItsyBitsy123: Do you want to talk about it?
GoodHands69: No. I'm . . . still processing, if
   that makes sense?

It does. I think I'm still processing too, but I'm not sure
how chatting with him is going to help me let go of all the
"what-ifs" our almost-hookup planted in my brain.

GoodHands69: What brings you to Random
   tonight?
ItsyBitsy123: I used to think I was here
   because it was fun. Lately, I suspect I'm a
   glutton for punishment, but maybe my
   luck has changed?
GoodHands69: What makes you say that?

ItsyBitsy123: Um, because you're here, Mr. GOOD HANDS. How long's it been since you dated? Be honest.

GoodHands69: Honest? I haven't dated anyone since my ex-wife. Some days I think dating might be good for me, but it's not the same as it was when I was in college. A friend suggested Random might be a good way to get started, but you're the only one I've been interested enough to swipe on. (You can thank your profile picture for that. It made me smile.)

I bite my lip. I wonder if Dean was the one who got him started on here. I can't imagine my brother intended Kace to hook up with *me* when he recommended Random. Then again, if Kace wanted that, all he had to do was let me stay on Saturday. I'm so confused and afraid that because of my lifelong crush, I'm making a mess of something that should be very clear. *Pretend it never happened. It was a mistake.*

ItsyBitsy123: Glad you liked my picture, but why did you swipe on ME?

GoodHands69: I'm . . . curious.

ItsyBitsy123: Well, damn. Don't be so giving with those compliments. Might go to my head.

GoodHands69: I mean, you're different. The other profiles . . . I don't know how to explain it.

ItsyBitsy123: Sure you do. You just don't want to admit it.

> GoodHands69: The other profiles felt too
> real, and I'm not sure I'm ready for that
> yet. This seemed safe.

I frown at my phone. On the one hand, this confirms my suspicion that he swiped on me because I was familiar. On the other hand, I don't understand how someone he knows in real life would seem *less* real than talking to a stranger. Or maybe he means there's no chance we'll end up hooking up, so it's like a practice run for using the app?

I roll to my stomach and bury my face in my pillow. Only Kace could twist me in overthinking knots like this, and I really need to walk away before I tell him how much I want him. And not just physically.

But my phone buzzes with a new alert, and I'm fucking weak when it comes to this man, so I look, knowing I'll chat with him all night if he wants.

> GoodHands69: Did that sound insulting? I
> didn't mean it that way. Tell me to go away
> if I'm bugging you.
> ItsyBitsy123: You can talk to me anytime.
> Sometimes I tease, but I can be serious
> too. And, believe it or not, I'm a good
> listener.
> GoodHands69: No, I can tell that about you.
> But I want you to have a turn. Tell me
> something.

Damn, he's sweet. Reason #23541 no one can blame me for carrying a torch for him. But in typical Stella fashion, I make it a joke.

ItsyBitsy123: I assume that's not an invitation
    to start sexting? You're not asking what
    I'm wearing?
GoodHands69: Ha! That's probably what I'm
    supposed to be using this message
    function for, but I'm not in the right
    headspace to go there—even as I type
    that, I hear my buddy in my head telling
    me I'm acting like a loser. I can't help it.
    I'm a connection-before-sex kind of guy.

I've had other guys on here say something similar, but with Kace, I know it's true. We might spend a lot of time in the same circle of friends, but I wouldn't call him *my* friend. He's never taken me seriously enough to try to *connect* with me—and maybe that's my fault, but having him try now makes me hopeful and vulnerable in the most extreme way.

As much as I flirt with Kace, the truth is I've never wanted *just* sex from him. Don't get me wrong—if he offered, I'd take it (as I proved Saturday), but it'd never be enough for me.

ItsyBitsy123: You're not a loser, and it's
    refreshing, so screw him. What do you
    want to know?
GoodHands69: Hmm . . . tell me something
    only your closest friends would know.

I stare at the screen for a long time before I finally settle on a response. What do I wish Kace understood about me?

ItsyBitsy123: I'm afraid I'm too much like my
mom . . . and I feel awful even thinking
that. My mom's an incredible woman.
GoodHands69: But there has to be a reason
you feel that way. In what way are you
afraid you're like her?

My stomach's in knots, and I actually back out of the
message function so I can stare at his avatar while I
consider my reply. How long have I wished Kace would just
talk to me? And all it took was connecting on a hookup app
that was never intended for talking.

Sighing, I click back into the messenger and frown. I
sometimes forget this app is set up to automatically delete
any messages—either sent or delivered—after you close out
the messaging function. It also gives you a black screen if
you try to take a screenshot. It's all supposedly for "privacy,"
but it's obviously a way to hide evidence for the cheaters
who live on here. I've never cared before, figuring karma
will get the jerks in the end, but I'm already disappointed to
have lost these exchanges with Kace. I wish I could keep
them for posterity. *Hey, a really great guy actually paid attention
to me once.*

It takes me a while to figure out how I want to reply, but
when I do, my thumbs fly over the screen. I'm anxious to
get out my thoughts.

ItsyBitsy123: Mom has rotten taste in men—
my father included—and instead of finally
finding the good guy who'd break that
cycle, she just . . . stopped trying. Some

days, I feel like I'm one more bad date
away from doing the same.
GoodHands69: But you keep trying.
ItsyBitsy123: Of course I do. I like sex. Even
the best vibrator is a piss-poor substitute
for the real thing.

I hit send and immediately flinch. I want to use this
conversation to open up and show him who I am under the
surface, but here I am, leaning on the same old defense
mechanism of being over-the-top about my sexuality, even
though I know that'll make Kace throw up walls. But he
surprises me.

GoodHands69: I call bullshit. Sex is great,
and I miss it too. That said, I bet your
fear has very little to do with physical
intimacy and everything to do with
wanting human connection. A partner.
Someone who understands you and will
be by your side no matter what.

I feel like he just crawled inside my chest and wrapped
himself around my heart. He's not saying anything ground-
breaking, but the idea that he feels like he knows this about
me? Maybe I'm the one who's been underestimating *him*.

ItsyBitsy123: You really see me. That's . . . I
don't know if it's comforting or scary. I
feel like you just stripped me naked.
GoodHands69: In my experience, being

vulnerable is like that. Comforting and scary. When it's good, it's both.

I wish we were face to face. Instead, I have to settle for closing my eyes and imagining the hug Kace might give me if we'd had this conversation around his firepit Saturday night instead of on an app. Although I haven't been the recipient of many Kace hugs, the ones I've gotten were spectacular. He's not a cologne guy, but he always smells clean—like Tide detergent and fabric softener, and maybe a little like whatever deodorant he uses. He's broad and thickly muscled, and when he wraps his arms around me, it feels like that strength is seeping into me.

> GoodHands69: It's late, and I should
> probably sleep so I'm not a zombie when
> I'm driving my daughter to school
> tomorrow. But . . . I'd like to message you
> again. If you wouldn't mind?

I grin. *Mind?* Is he nuts? I'd stay up until sunrise if he wanted to keep chatting. The idea that he wants to talk again makes me giddy.

> ItsyBitsy123: You prefer the app to texting,
> then?
> GoodHands69: If you don't mind. This feels .
> . . I hate to say it again, because I
> probably sound like a weirdo, but this just
> feels less intimidating. I'd like to keep our
> conversations disconnected from real life.
> For now at least?

I chew on the inside of my cheek. I'm not sure how I feel about that. I want him to want to connect with me in real life, not just on Random. But I know I never would've opened up about my fears if we'd been face to face, and I'm not sure I would've over text, either.

Maybe Kace is right, and there's something freeing about using the app. This way we can pretend we're meeting for the first time.

> ItsyBitsy123: I'll look forward to hearing from you. Sleep well.

CHAPTER SEVEN

KACE

*T*uesday morning, I'm dragging ass. For too many nights in a row, I've been stuck in my own head when it was time to sleep, and it's catching up with me. I dropped Hope off at preschool already, and instead of hitting the road for my typical Tuesday run with Dean, I'm relieved to be pouring my second cup of coffee after he stood me up.

My phone buzzes with a new Random notification, and I take a sip of the dark, piping-hot liquid as I open the app. The sight of a message from ItsyBitsy has me smiling wider than I have all morning.

> ItsyBitsy123: Good morning, handsome.
> How'd you sleep?

I'm not sure I want to answer that. After talking to her

on Random last night, I would've thought I'd be able to fall asleep without thinking of my best friend's little sister. I would've been wrong. I should never have touched Stella, because now I can't stop thinking about it.

I actually typed out a text to her last night. *Can't stop thinking about the things you need to learn.* I stared at it for a solid minute before I made myself delete it. If she finds a place to live that isn't within ten yards of my back door, I'll send that text and see what happens. Otherwise, I need to keep my thoughts to myself. I'm sure as hell not sharing them with another woman.

> GoodHands69: I haven't slept great lately.
>   But that's why God gave us coffee.
> ItsyBitsy123: I'm sorry to hear that. Too much
>   on your mind?
> GoodHands69: You could say that. But at
>   least I'm not losing sleep over my wife
>   anymore.

I flinch the second I send the last message. Crap. I don't want to sound like the bitter ex—especially since I'm really not. Losing Amy *sucked*, and some days are tough, but I couldn't make her happy. I won't resent her for being honest about her feelings.

> ItsyBitsy123: I'm glad to hear that. And I
>   know you probably don't want to hear
>   this, but Amy doesn't deserve you.

Whoa. *That* throws me. Did I tell this woman my wife's name? I remember talking about my divorce, but—

I scroll up to see the messages from last night, and nothing happens. It's like they were never there.

> GoodHands69: Why can't I find last night's messages?
> ItsyBitsy123: The app eats them the second you close out of the message feature.
> GoodHands69: Is it weird and old-fashioned of me to want to be able to revisit our conversations?
> ItsyBitsy123: Not at all! I feel the same way. The feature's annoying and inconvenient AF, not to mention likely enabling cheaters (though, really, if your guy has Random on his phone, that might be a good sign he's not faithful).

I chuckle. I never expected to enjoy conversations with anyone I met on here, which is shallow of me, but I guess I've heard too many horror stories.

I want to know this woman's name, see her face, but Orchid Valley is so small that there's a decent chance we've met or at least have mutual friends. I know myself well enough to know that the second this feels too real, I'll shut it down. Names and faces can wait until I'm sure this is something I'm willing to explore seriously.

> GoodHands69: What's the deal with your username?
> ItsyBitsy123: Itsy Bitsy. Like the spider in the song?

GoodHands69: Hmm . . . well, that clears up
    nothing.
ItsyBitsy123: That poor spider just keeps
    getting knocked down, but she never
    stops trying. You could say I can relate.
GoodHands69: Where are you now?
    Climbing or getting washed out?
ItsyBitsy123: Climbing, baby.
GoodHands69: Good. I'll be here cheering
    for you next time you get to the top.
ItsyBitsy123: I appreciate that.

My phone rings, and Dean's picture flashes on the screen. I swipe to accept the call and press my cell to my ear. "Morning, asshole. I thought you were going to meet me for five miles this morning." Not that I really care. I'm too fucking tired to run, let alone try to keep up with a former cross-country athlete.

"Sorry. I stopped by Mom's to help her with her computer and ended up getting sucked into a hundred other things over there."

I laugh, all too familiar with that experience when it comes to my own mother. "It's fine. I skipped out this morning, anyway. You get everything taken care of?"

"Not really." He sighs, and I feel a big ask coming. "I need to get that sink fixed before I have the real-estate agent out to Mom's. You know I'm shit with plumbing."

I was planning to sit down in my office and catch up on emails, but I already know how this conversation will end. "Barely worse than I am," I mutter. The last thing I want to do this morning is fix a leaky bathroom sink. When it comes to construction and home improvement, I can do a little bit of everything, but plumbing is my *least* favorite job. The rule of thumb is that the simplest plumbing job will require at least three unplanned trips to the hardware store, and I'd rather go in with a sharp mind. Never mind that the bathroom in question is right next to Stella's room.

"I know I'm asking all the favors lately," Dean says. "You know I wouldn't if—"

"If it wasn't for your mom. I know. And that's why I want to help." Sighing, I resign myself to a morning of cursing at pipes.

"Mom already left for work. You still have the key?"

"Yeah, but *you're* making the first hardware store run."

He chuckles. "Of course. I'm heading into an appointment, but I'll be your errand boy as soon as I'm out."

"You'd better. Does Stella know I'm coming? I don't want to freak her out."

Dean grunts. "Nah. I just left, and she was still in bed."

I swallow. That image isn't helping. At all.

"I wouldn't wake her, though," Dean says. "Let's just say my spidey-sense tells me she had company late last night."

This sends a flurry of different emotions through me. Jealousy, annoyance, frustration. And fuck, my *pride* feels battered. I can't stop thinking about her, and she's already dragging some other guy home?

I shouldn't care. This is Stella. She does what she wants. But I still hear myself mutter, "I can't believe she brings her hookups to your *mom's*."

"Right?" Dean laughs again, and I grit my teeth. The idea of Stella sleeping so close to where I'll be working was bad enough, but the thought of her sleeping off orgasms from some other guy? *Way worse.*

❧

I FREEZE HALFWAY up the walk to Dean's mom's when I realize I left my earbuds at home. *Fuck.* I was planning to distract myself from the sexy redhead sleeping on the other side of the wall by listening to music. *Loudly.*

Too bad. I just want to get this over with. At least it looks like her company already left—there's no sign of an unusual car in the driveway.

I use my key to let myself in, and Rusty meets me at the door, tail wagging wildly.

I stoop to my haunches to give him a good scratch behind the ears. "Who's a good boy?" I ask softly. His tail slaps the wall as he licks my face, and I grin. I should get Hope a dog. Amy was always opposed, claiming dogs stole any spontaneity from your life. *"You can't just run away for the weekend on a whim if you have a dog."* So we didn't get a dog. Never "just ran away for the weekend," either. Figures.

Rusty bores of me quicker than he used to and heads back to the living room for what I'd guess is his second morning nap.

I turn down the hall toward the guest bath when I realize even earbuds wouldn't have spared me from all the evidence of Stella's extracurriculars.

Her black skirt and yellow top are lying in the hallway between the door to her bathroom and bedroom, as if she—or someone else—stripped it off her there. A hot-pink lace bra is on the floor right beside . . .

I spin around and drag a hand over my face, but no. There's no unseeing that scrap of fabric, and now that my brain has latched on to the image, it's on a one-way track barreling toward the sight of her perfect ass framed in pink lace.

Fuck.

I don't *want* to want Stella Jacob. I don't want to fantasize about that perfect body or wake up with an erection that demands I think about her while I get myself off. I don't want to see her fucking panties on the floor and wish *I* was the guy who'd stripped them off her. And yet here we are.

Her bedroom door is cracked, and I resist the urge to peek inside. I bet her bedspread is as bright as her personality, and I can imagine the sheets crumpled and her pajamas tossed haphazardly on the floor beside it. Part of me wants to know how she keeps her most private space, but I'm not going to be some creep who peeks into bedrooms and stares at panties, like her old landlord. And I'm not going to let myself think about her bringing a guy here. She's a fucking grown woman with a healthy sex drive, and she's going to bring guys home from time to time. It's easy enough to imagine her stumbling in, tipsy from too many drinks at Smithy's, that smile stretching across her face as she drags—

I shut the thought down. Because there's no fucking reason for me to imagine some alternate timeline where *I'm* the guy Stella brought home from the bar.

Just do the job you came here for.

Ignoring the underwear and the cracked bedroom door, I step into the bathroom and stoop to look under the sink.

There's a red ceramic bowl under the plumbing to catch drips, and I put it in the sink, turn off the water supply, and then position myself on my back to track down the problem. I have the wrench in my hand and my head in the cabinet when I hear it . . . soft, barely audible whimpers. Sexy, needy, breathless.

Her hookup is still here.

I move to stand so fast that I hit my head on the pipe. "Fuck!" Too loud. That was too fucking loud, and I just want to get out of here. I'd rather drink paint thinner than listen to some random guy pleasure Stella. Would rather make it a double before *meeting* the asshole the morning after.

I scramble to get out from under the sink and stand. The room spins a little as I right myself, and I have to brace against the counter. My head pounds.

"Kace?"

I close my eyes at the sound of her voice. *Pass the paint thinner.*

"Jesus, are you okay?"

The soft fall of her steps grows closer, but I don't want to lift my head and look at her right now. I don't have any right to the jealousy she'll see in my eyes if I do.

So I keep them shut. Even as she steps close and the warmth of her body brushes mine. Even as her fingers skim my cheek and she smooths my hair back to examine my forehead.

"This is gonna be one hell of a goose egg if you don't get ice on it." She steps away, and I finally meet her green eyes and scan the freckles in the morning light coming in between the slats of her blinds. I'm *weak* for this woman. "Be right back, okay?"

Either she and her hookup were fucking half clothed, or she got dressed fast. She's in a baggy T-shirt that hangs off one shoulder and . . . well, I'm not exactly sure what she has on under that. Probably better not think too much about it.

She walks toward the kitchen, and I don't look away as her T-shirt shifts and slides against her simple black panties.

I'm really screwed in the head if I'm ogling a woman who was literally in bed with someone else less than a minute ago. I need to get out of here. I'll come back later after she's gone. "I can get myself ice at home," I say, following her down the hall.

She flashes me a confused frown over her shoulder. "That's dumb, Kace. I have it right here." She grabs a bag of peas from the freezer then strides back to offer it to me. My fingers brush hers as I take it.

I swallow. "I'll get out of here. I didn't realize you were still— I mean, that . . ." I clear my throat. *Fucking awkward.* "That you had company over."

Frowning, she guides my hand with the "ice pack" to my forehead. "I don't have company over."

I gingerly touch the bag of peas to the bump. God *damn,* that hurts. "It's fine, Stella. It's none of my business. I heard you two . . ." *You're making it worse. Abort. Abort.* I step around her, ready to run out the door. "Anyway, I'll be back later. Let me know when you're done—I mean, when he's gone. Or when I can come back."

She steps into the hall and grabs my wrist to stop me. Her smile is the picture of puzzled curiosity. "There's no one else here, Kace. What did you—" Her cheeks flame red with the speed of a struck match. "You heard *me?*" Her eyes dart to her bedroom and then back to my face. "From in there?"

"Yes, but it's fine, and I . . ." Then her words register. *No one else is here.* My eyes seem to have a mind of their own as they drop to the hem of her T-shirt again and then shift to the feminine fingers still wrapped around my wrist. She was in the bedroom *alone*. Oh, fuck me, but the idea of her lying in bed making *herself* moan like that? My brain might've decided against being a creep, but my dick is totally on board. My mind immediately flashes to my fantasy, to the vivid image of her gripping the back of my couch and the sound of her moaning as I— "I should go. You can get back to . . ." Yep. Every time I open my mouth, I make it worse. "I'll go."

She sidesteps in front of me. When she crosses her arms over her chest, her shirt creeps up, but I'm not going to look. I don't need a reminder of her soft thighs. The laundry-faded black of her panties will be forever imprinted on my brain. "Are you going to be all weird about this?"

I jerk my gaze back up from where it drifted to her bare legs. "Weird about what? There's nothing to be weird about."

"You look like you just caught me masturbating to *My Little Pony* or something."

I nearly choke on my tongue. "*My Little Pony?*" *What the fuck?* I shake my head. "You know what, I don't want to know."

"Oh, inside joke, I guess." She waves away my confusion. "Anyway, it wasn't anything freaky. Just . . ." She lifts her right hand and wiggles her fingers. "Normal, single-girl self-maintenance."

I cover my eyes with one hand. They can't be trusted, anyway. "It's like you're determined to torture me."

She tugs my hand off my eyes and drags me into her bedroom, where she kicks the door closed behind her and bites back her smile. A small lamp illuminates a room crowded with too much furniture, as if she moved her whole apartment in here, and there's no room to put space between us.

This isn't going to help anything.

"Sorry for my lack of filter," she says. "Under normal circumstances, I wouldn't have mentioned it, but you're so damn cute when you're flustered." She shrugs. "It's like putting an ice cream cone in front of me and telling me I can't lick it."

Lick it. I squeeze my eyes shut and wrestle my imagination back where it belongs. I should be thinking about *anything* but Stella's tongue. "Fuck, Stella. Don't say shit like that, okay? I'm trying to be a decent guy here."

Her gaze takes a leisurely stroll to my mouth then across my chest, tripping over my torso before landing just below my belt. Thank Christ I'm in jeans and not athletic shorts, but I'm sure she can still see quite clearly what's happening south of the border. "I think maybe you should sit. Can't be too careful with a head injury." She nods to the couch that's shoved into the corner. But the second my eyes land on her bed and her twisted sheets, I'm thinking about her writhing and moaning at her own touch.

"I can sit in my own house. Give you some privacy." Aaaaand now it sounds like I think she's going to masturbate when I leave. Or like I want her to. Or like I need to be alone so I can imagine her doing it . . . Okay, that last one has a ring of truth to it. "I mean, to get dressed or whatever."

She smiles. "I don't have to get dressed for another hour." She shrugs and steps forward, nudging me backward until I hit the couch. "Sit. Let me take a look at that bump."

I'm a masochist, so I obey and lower the ice pack when my ass hits the faded blue upholstery. She leans forward to take a closer look, and I have to close my eyes. She's definitely not wearing a bra.

Turning off one sense only heightens the others, and now I'm obsessed with the smell of the detergent from her shirt and the perfume she probably wore out last night.

This girl is everything I don't need in my life. She's wild and unpredictable with the priorities of a college party girl. I would've thought she'd outgrown that before graduation, but her time working at Allegiance with Amy proved otherwise.

When I date again for real—and I'm not looking to do that for a long fucking time—I want it to be with someone who's steady. Someone I can count on to be home every night and who will enjoy the simplicity of a life raising the coolest little girl around and making a home for her.

Someone who won't leave me because she's grown "discontent."

"Are you okay?" Stella's fingertips ghost over my head wound.

"I'll be fine." I fumble for the bag of peas and press it back to my head.

"Open your eyes and look at me," she says. I obey, and she studies each one. I follow suit and study her irises, the way the green darkens on the outside and is lighter in the middle. She sighs, and her breath floats across my forehead. "Just as I suspected."

"What?"

"Well, hell, Kace. This is a problem."

I arch a brow, then immediately drop it. *Ouch.* "I'm fine, Stella. No concussion. I promise." My voice sounds husky. It sounds like it would if we were in that bed together and instead of *her* hand between her legs, it was mine.

"Dilated pupils, accelerated heart rate, inability to focus on a conversation?" She keeps one hand in my hair and braces the other on the back of the couch. She leans forward, her lips brushing my ear. "It looks like you're turned on."

I bark out a laugh. *Not where I thought she was going with that.*

Climbing onto the couch, she puts a knee on either side of my hips, straddling my lap. "Aren't you?"

"I plead the fifth." I could recite the whole damn Constitution. I'm sure there's no amendment strong enough to keep her from feeling the bulge pressing against my fly.

"Stella." Her name is a desperate plea on my lips. I should ask her to move. Hell, I could pick her up myself and move her off me, but I don't want to. I've thought about her here too many times. My reason is losing to my lust. "Didn't you just have some guy in here with you last night?"

"No." She arches a brow. "Why would you think that?"

"Your clothes were all over the hall." I swallow. "Not that it's any of my business."

"You think I brought some guy home to my mom's and had him undress me in the hall?"

"I . . ." Obviously, *yes* is the wrong answer. "So you undressed yourself in the hall?"

"Rusty steals my clothes from the hamper."

"Oh."

"Would it bother you if I'd been with someone else?"

"Yeah." The word comes out rough, raw. Too much honesty, but I don't know any other way to do this. "I fucking hate the idea of anyone touching you but me."

Her green eyes flash. She shifts herself so her body's flush with mine and rocks against my hips. The movement is subtle. Nearly indecipherable. But it's there, and my hips lift off the couch, chasing that heat between her legs.

"We decided we weren't doing this," I say, but I've already gripped her hip with my free hand, holding her close.

"There are so many reasons we shouldn't. Then again, you got hard thinking about me touching myself, and now I really, *really* want to help you with that."

And Stella's the kind of girl who takes what she wants and says *damn the consequences*. That's exactly why I should stay away. Instead, I drop the bag of frozen peas so I can hold her with both hands. "How do you plan to help me?"

She grins and slides her hand between our bodies, stroking me through the thick denim of my jeans. It's so good and not enough. "There are a few effective treatment plans I could offer."

"Is there one without side effects? One that won't screw up our lives?" My words are breathless, and I'm already jacking up into her hand, looking for the pressure, for the relief. I slide my hands under her shirt, stroking the soft skin of her stomach. "The one where you don't hate me later." My voice sounds as tormented as I feel.

"We're good, Kace. We're just friends helping each other out. This is a mutually beneficial situation."

"So when you were alone in here, you didn't . . ." I swallow.

"Finish?" She shakes her head. "I was close, but then I heard something."

Fuck. I used to hate how blunt she was when talking about sex, but I was an idiot. It's hot. So fucking hot. She's not ashamed of liking sex or of having it often. Hell, after finding my marriage crumbling and our chemistry MIA, I should appreciate Stella's frankness like no other. "I'm sorry I interrupted."

She slides off the couch and onto the floor and looks up at me from between my knees, her eyes dancing with mischief. She tugs my hips forward, and I help, lifting off the couch so she can bring me where she wants me. When her fingertips brush the button on my jeans, I draw in a ragged breath and grapple for a hold on reason, but I'm already gone.

CHAPTER EIGHT

STELLA

*T*he master of mixed signals is looking at me with so much heat in his eyes that I don't think I could walk away if I wanted to. First he feels me up at his place and makes promises I still can't stop thinking about, then he slams on the brakes, only to find me on Random the very next day. And this morning, he thought I had some guy in here with me? Did he think someone was sleeping next to me when we were chatting this morning?

"You're a hot mess, Kace Matthews." I brush my fingers against the button of his jeans again, smiling.

He draws in a ragged breath. "Only with you."

I lock my gaze on his. "Tell me what you want."

His nostrils flare and his eyes go impossibly dark. "Judging by the way you're kneeling on the floor, I think you already know, Freckles."

My heart is racing so fast that I feel like I just finished

one of Savvy's spin classes. I pop the button on his jeans and slowly unzip them.

"Were you thinking about this while you were touching yourself?" he asks. He cups my face in one big hand then slowly slides it up along my jaw and into my hair. "Did you imagine your hand was mine, or were you thinking about some other asshole?"

"That's a dangerous question."

He wraps a lock around two fingers and tugs gently. "It's an important question."

I trap the moan in my throat. "I was thinking about you. It seems like I'm always thinking about you." I drag my bottom lip between my teeth and drop my gaze to his cock. I want it in my hands. Against my tongue. I want to feel him lose his control and fuck up into my mouth, pushing deep as he comes. "Do you think about me? When you're alone?"

"I can't fucking stop thinking about you. About that sassy fucking mouth of yours. If you knew the things I've imagined doing to that mouth . . ." His gaze drops, skimming over me. "The things I've imagined doing to every inch of you . . ." He shakes his head. "You might kick me out that door and lock it behind me."

"I doubt it." I curl my fingers beneath the waistband of his jeans and boxers. He lifts his hips as I tug them down. When his cock springs free, I moan. He's so hard. And thick. I flick my tongue against the tip.

He hisses. "Jesus, Stella." He shifts his hips forward.

I slide my hands up his thighs and push them farther apart before sweeping my fingertips across his balls.

He groans. "Are you just gonna tease me, or are you going to let me feel that mouth?"

My thighs clench at his unapologetic dominance. If I'd known Kace would be like this, I might've tried crawling into his bed a few more times.

I wrap my fist around his cock and guide the tip to my lips, sliding it against them. His hand tightens in my hair, and I meet his eyes. Opening my mouth, I take him in slowly. Inch by inch, I slide my lips down his shaft. His thumb brushes my cheek with the lightest touch, and I feel powerful and delicate in equal measure.

"Fuck." His eyes float closed. "So good. Your mouth is so fucking sweet."

Those words are my undoing, and I snap. I've fantasized about this—the taste of him, the shape and size. But the reality is so much better. He makes these tortured little grunts as I swirl my tongue around his shaft, and when I take him deep, his exhale is the sound of sweet relief. It's sexy and heady. *I'm* doing this to him. *I'm* the one he wants . . . even if it's just in this moment.

I've never *loved* giving head. Sometimes it's felt like a chore, a requisite part of foreplay, and sometimes it's been fun, but this is a whole new experience. A power trip. Kace might never give me his heart, and maybe I don't deserve it anyway, but right now he's mine. I want to make him feel good. I want to give him pleasure and release, and the fact that I can is a high I could ride for days.

I love playing with him, cupping his balls in my palm while I suck and lick, running my hands over the soft hair at the tops of his thighs while I let his hand in my hair set the pace. I want to memorize his response to every touch— every ragged inhale, every jerk of his hips as he gets closer to the edge and fucks my mouth.

"Stella . . ." His hand in my hair loosens and then

tightens again. "Fuck, Stella, I'm gonna come in your mouth, baby."

I moan—at the thought, at the promise—and take him deep, swallowing even before his orgasm hits. And during. And after. Until he's collapsed against the back of the couch, breathing hard and looking at me like I'm a goddess.

Heavy footsteps sound in the hall, passing my room. "Kace? Where the fuck are you?" Dean calls.

🐺

KACE

My gaze darts to the bedroom door—the still slightly ajar bedroom door—then to the beautiful woman on her knees in front of me. Her lips are swollen after giving me the blowjob of a fucking lifetime, and her brother is *right there*.

I stand, and Stella scrambles backward, eyes big. She bites back a laugh as I awkwardly shove my dick into my boxers and pull up my pants.

"Rule number two of hookups," she whispers, "is no freaking out after." Her gaze darts to the door, but Dean's footsteps are retreating. *Thank Christ.*

I button my jeans, then step forward and grab her hand to help her off the floor. She stands, and I pull her close. "I wasn't done yet," I growl into her hair.

Her silent laughter vibrates against my chest. "I can personally attest that you were, in fact, done." She licks her lips. "I can still taste you."

"Dirty girl. I mean *we* weren't done." I kiss her and slide a hand between our bodies, cupping her between her legs. She's wet enough that I can feel it through her panties, wet enough that if I could slam that door and press her against it, she'd be ready for me to slide in. *Aaaaand I'm hard again.*

I rub two fingers along the cotton between her thighs, and she bites back a whimper. "I guess you owe me, then," she says, breathy as fuck. I want to hear that voice in my ear as I drive into her. "But you should go before my brother comes back and catches us."

I stroke her again, considering this. Dean is out there, and I need to leave, but I don't want to. "How about we just lock that door so I can play with you for a little bit?" I slip a finger inside her panties, and *damn*. She's drenched. So slick it's impossible not to think about throwing her down on that bed and tasting her. "This for me?" I ask, my voice a husky whisper.

A desperate, barely audible cry slips from her lips. "Yeah. I guess I kind of liked giving you head."

"I changed my mind."

She swallows, eyes on mine. "About what?"

"I don't care if you're moving into my backyard. We need to do this the right way." I slide a finger into her, and she gasps and clenches hard around it. Slick. Wet. Tight.

Fuck Dean. I'm never leaving this room.

"You should've seen yourself," I say, my mouth against her ear. "The way you were moaning around my cock, the way you weren't afraid to take me deep. I almost came at the first touch of your tongue. If I had, I'd get more time to play with you now."

My phone buzzes at my hip, and I ignore it. Steps sound in the hallway again, but I hold Stella close. Right now, I don't care about a damn thing but the feel of her on my hand and the way her breath catches when I pump my fingers inside her.

Dean's voice echoes in the hall. "Kace, your truck's here, but you're not," he says, probably talking to my voicemail. "Where the hell did you go?"

Stella's eyes lift to mine. A little panicked, but a lot hazy with lust. She swallows and rocks against me, fucking my hand with the tiniest little thrusts, like she can't help herself. "The window," she whispers. Her eyes float closed, as if she's struggling to focus. "You could climb out there and go around back."

"In a minute." I take a handful of her hair in my free hand and gently tilt her head back. Slanting my mouth over hers, I slide a second finger inside her. Her knees buckle. I swing her around and pin her against the door, pushing it shut. Her pussy clenches around my fingers, and I know she's skating on the edge of coming. The lightest pressure to her clit, and I'd get to feel the spasms of her orgasm. She's barely holding on, and it's hotter than anything I've imagined.

"Please," she whispers, back arching, hips searching for that pressure where she needs it.

I don't give her what she wants. Not yet. "Can you be quiet for me? I'll make it good."

"Yes." Her hips jerk. "Kace."

I press my smile to her neck. I've imagined my name on her lips like that—breathy from pleasure and need—so many times. "You want my mouth on this pussy? I'd play with you so long, you'd beg to come."

"I'm begging now."

I'm vaguely aware of Dean working in the bathroom on the other side of the wall, of the sounds of wrenches clanking against pipes and his softly muttered curses. I'm in denial if I think anything I can do right now is going to leave either of us satisfied. "I've wanted you too long for a quick finger fuck to ever be enough, but I don't have time to do this right. I need to savor you, Stella. For hours, not minutes. I need you naked and moaning, need to know the taste of you coming on my tongue."

Another thrust of my fingers, and she throws her head back in pleasure and frustration. "Please."

I flick my tongue across her earlobe. "Only because you asked nicely."

I shift the angle of my hand and press my palm against her. It's like flipping a switch. She clenches around me, and her nails dig into my back, and I watch her face as the orgasm washes over her—the way her head tips back and her mouth opens before she snaps it shut again and bites back a moan of relief. And now I know what I'll be seeing in my dreams tonight.

So. Fucking. Beautiful.

Slowly, she relaxes in my arms and opens her eyes again. "Holy shit," she breathes. "I can't believe that just happened."

"You and me both, Freckles." I kiss her once, hard on the mouth, before making myself drop my hands and back away. If I stay in this room any longer, I'll be searching for condoms. "Consider that a teaser. We're not done here."

She leans against the wall then sinks to the floor, a satisfied smile on her face. "I'll believe it when I see it."

I open the window and let myself have one last, long look at the sexiest woman I've ever met. "Is that a challenge?"

She shrugs. "Maybe. Are you gonna take it?"

"You can count on it."

CHAPTER NINE

STELLA

*M*y apartment/roommate hunt hasn't been the smoothest, but I am *highly* motivated by this morning's unexpected interlude with Kace. *Damn*, that was hot. I could barely focus on the lecture in chemistry. I was so distracted, in fact, that I nearly forgot I almost accidentally went on a date with my professor. I've wanted Kace for a long time, but now that I know how it is between us, I'm crazed for more. And I think he is too. I messaged him on my break, using Random, since that's what he said he wants me to do. *Can't stop thinking about you.* But he's either busy or wigging out, because he hasn't replied.

All the more reason not to screw up whatever this is by becoming his tenant.

When I pull up to my next potential home, I feel like the universe may finally be on my side. This place is blocks from downtown Orchid Valley—meaning it's walking distance from Smithy's and The Orchid—and it's beautiful if a little run-down. I'm supposed to meet Kat, one of the girls who lives here. If I move in, I'd be the fourth roommate, but the colonial-style house certainly looks big enough.

I park my car, but I'm a few minutes early, so I pull out my phone to see if Kace has messaged me. Sure enough, the notifications light is flashing, and I can't click it fast enough.

> GoodHands69: I've been thinking about you too. But listen . . . this is awkward, so I'll just say it. I'm also talking to someone else. I realize you are too—maybe several other guys. That's how this works, right? But I've never done anything but serious and exclusive. Since I'm not looking for either of those things now, I find myself in new territory.
>
> GoodHands69: Honestly, I don't know what the rules of casual dating are—or if you'd even call this dating. I do know I can't play games and pretend I'm someone I'm not. So, I want you to know I'm involved with someone else. It's just physical and temporary. But I don't feel like that gets me off the hook for not telling you about her, either.

I press my hand to my chest, but it doesn't ease the ache there. *Kace is seeing someone else.*

I'm an idiot that I didn't see this coming. He's on

Random. He's looking to get back out there. Hell, I'm the one who's supposedly "teaching" him how to do casual, and I should probably be feeling all warm and fuzzy that he wants even that from me. But it still burns like hell. I want to be enough. Enough that he doesn't need to mess around with a physical relationship with some other girl. Enough that "serious" and "exclusive" are things he wants now—with me—not at some potential moment in the future.

I know I should be thanking my lucky stars that he's even offering me this much. But is it better to go hungry, or to pretend you don't need anything more than scraps?

I bite my lip and type out a reply.

ItsyBitsy123: You like her, then?

He must be on his phone already, because a reply pops up fast.

GoodHands69: Yeah, but I can't see us together in any meaningful way. This is just a fling. There's no substance, just physical attraction.

Hot with no substance. Poor girl. I know what it's like to have Kace see you that way.

GoodHands69: I sound like an ass, but she'd probably tell you the same thing. She's all wrong for me.

And your thing with me? I type. *Is THIS a fling?* I stare at the words, then delete them. Don't ask a question if you can't handle the answer.

I shove my phone into my purse and head up to the house.

The front door opens before I can knock. "Hey! You must be Stella! I'm Kat." Kat's willowy and tall, with a dark braid that hangs to the middle of her back and tattoos up and down both arms. She told me on the phone that she's my age, which is a bonus, since the majority of people looking for roommates are college students. I might be returning to college, but I can't return to the college-party house life. Been there, done that, got the medical bills to prove alcohol poisoning isn't all it's cracked up to be.

"Thanks so much for letting me take a look at this place," I say, peeking over her shoulder. "It's beautiful."

"We like it, but it has its flaws for sure." She smiles, waves me inside, and proceeds to show me around the house.

I love the hardwood floors and high ceilings. I'd never be able to afford a place like this on my own, but as one of four people splitting the rent, it's doable.

After we look around upstairs and I've checked out the available bedroom, Kat takes me back to the main floor and pushes open a swinging wooden door off the dining room. "This is the kitchen," she says. "Obviously, it's tiny and needs updating, but the appliances all work. We use the closet back there for a pantry, so there's plenty of room for our food."

"I don't cook much anyway," I say, flashing her a smile before I peek into the pantry. Each of the shelves is labeled with a different name. "Does everyone buy their own food?" I ask, returning to the kitchen.

Kat makes a face and nods. "Yeah. We tried the whole split-the-grocery-bill thing, but it's not a good fit for this group. I'm a vegan," she says, pressing a hand to her chest. "Jay eats like a teenage boy, and Danika eats out constantly." She shrugs. "It works better this way. I hope that's not a problem."

"Not at all. I've split groceries with roommates before, and it was always a nightmare." I smile.

"Right? This is so much better." She returns my smile, and I feel hopeful about my living situation for the first time since Dean admitted he needs me to get out of Mom's place.

"I really love this place," I admit. "When can I meet the roommates?"

"Well, Danika's out of town, so she said she trusts us to pick without her, but Jay's just out back if you want to meet him now." She points over her shoulder toward the yard.

"That'd be great. Thank you." I follow her through the pantry and to a back door with crumbling concrete steps that lead to a cracked patio. It's not a problem for me—this is the typical condition of these historic homes before guys like Kace and Dean get their hands on them—but I can't help but compare it to Kace's backyard, which was like this when he bought the house and now looks almost new after only a couple of months of his hard work.

"We have a potential roommate," Kat announces, pulling my attention off the patio and toward the guy lounging in the lawn chair.

He turns to me, and I freeze. Kat's roommate is Jared. My disastrous date from Friday night. And he's looking at me like I'm an obsessive stalker he can't escape.

ಕ⬮

KACE

Tuesday passes in slow motion. Despite giving Dean what I thought was a pretty damn believable excuse about searching for plumbing parts in his mom's shed, he acted weird as fuck the entire two hours it took to fix that stupid leak. I got so sick of him giving me sideways stares that I was ready to lecture him about Stella being an adult who can make her own choices. But I'm still ninety percent sure he doesn't know there's anything happening between me and her, and rather than open that can of worms, I kept my mouth shut.

By the time we were done, Stella was gone. It was for the best, maybe, since I had my own shit to do. Unfortunately, counting her freckles with my tongue wasn't on the list. If she'd still been home, I might've kept her from class so I could make good on some promises.

As it is, I don't think I've gone sixty seconds without thinking about her. That mouth. The sight of her on her knees. The heat between her legs. The sounds she made when she came. I spent most of my day hard and obsessing about sex, and now I remember what it's like to be sixteen again. Then Itsy messaged me on Random, said she couldn't stop thinking about me, and I felt like an ass.

I've never played the field before, and even though Stella and I are just casual, just blowing off steam with no promises or strings, it was strange to have one woman admit she'd been thinking about me while I was busy fantasizing about someone else. I know I'm not doing anything wrong, but it doesn't sit right. I wasn't sure if I needed to tell Stella about Itsy and vice versa or if that was completely unnecessary, but then I realized it doesn't matter if it's necessary or not. I'm not the kind of guy to omit information like that—even if nothing serious is happening with a woman.

So I told Itsy—that was the easy one—and now I need to tell Stella, who I'm pretty sure is going to laugh at me. I'm so anxious to get this over with that I came to The Orchid with the flimsy excuse of needing to check in on the new steam rooms my guys are installing, even though they have it covered and sent me photo updates yesterday.

As expected, the tile guys are still on track. *Just like they were yesterday.* But I play it cool and check in with Brinley to make sure she's happy with the progress and doesn't need anything else. She is. And doesn't. *Just like yesterday.*

Only then do I allow myself to head up to reception to look for Stella. I don't even know if she's working today, and if she is, it's not like I can pull her away from her post to fuck her on a massage table. Though the idea of Stella, massage oils, and an adjustable table holds enough appeal that I file the idea away. Just in case the opportunity presents itself . . .

I push through the swinging door between the staff hall and reception, and my heart sinks at the sight of a young woman at Stella's regular post.

She smiles brightly. "Hi! Can I help you?"

"Um." I shift and shove my hands in my pockets. "Is Stella working today?"

The girl shakes her head. "No, but she's in the back with the chef. Want me to page her for you?"

"No, that's fine. I'm—" *Her fuck buddy? The contractor for a renovation she has nothing to do with? Dying to get her alone again?* "I'm Abbi's brother. I'll just head back and find them."

"Oh! Well, it's nice to meet you, Abbi's brother. I'm Holly."

"Nice to meet you, Holly."

She beams and sweeps her pretty brown eyes over my chest. I almost laugh. Dean tells me I'm oblivious when women flirt with me, but maybe I'm starting to pull my head out of my ass, because this one is definitely interested. Not that I reciprocate. I have enough on my plate, *thank you very much.*

She waves toward the entrance opposite the one I just came from. "They're in the kitchen."

"Thanks."

When I get to the kitchen, Stella's in there with Abbi, as promised. She's in a black tank top and tight white cotton shorts that lead my gaze right to her ass.

"You're kidding me," Abbi says, sliding a tray of cookies into the oven.

"Unfortunately not." Stella tugs on her ponytail and groans. "He literally pushed out of his chair, folded his arms, and said, 'This has gone too far.' He made it sound like I was only interested in the house because he lived there, and of course Kat just met me, so she didn't know any better."

"What a dick. How were you supposed to know he was one of the roommates?"

"Right?" She rolls her head from side to side, stretching out her neck. "What a nightmare. Imagine if *he'd* been the one out of town, and I'd agreed to move in."

Abbi shudders. "Always a silver lining."

I clear my throat, realizing I've probably already eavesdropped on an inappropriate amount. "Hey, Abs. I'm headed out and just wanted to say hi before I go." This would've been a great cover if I hadn't told the receptionist I was looking for Stella. I suck at this cloak-and-dagger shit.

Stella spins around, looks me over, and swallows. "Hey, Kace." Usually, she's all cocky self-assurance, like she's inside my brain and knows just how hard this attraction is for me to ignore, but tonight there's something different about the way she's looking at me. It's as if she's suddenly become shy or . . . regretful? Fuck. I hope it's not that.

"What's up, Stella?" I ask. Cool. Casual. But when her gaze drops to my mouth, all my blood rushes south of my belt, and the silence stretches on too long.

"How's the project going?" Abbi asks, oblivious, thank Christ. "Brinley will be high-strung until those steam rooms are fully functional again. You'd better know what you're doing."

Eyes off the sexy redhead and her talented mouth. I shift my focus to my sister. "Believe it or not, I do. Everything's fine and on schedule." I wander over to the counter, where dozens of cookies are cooling on racks, and snatch an oatmeal chocolate chip. "What were you two talking about?"

Stella cuts her eyes to Abbi then back to me. "Um. Not much. I was just telling Abbi about my adventures in roommate hunting."

Abbi grunts. "She's going to need that pool house."

I nearly choke at the reminder of why I shut down this thing between us on Saturday. But that ship's sailed. It seems so obvious now that exploring this attraction, indulging it a little, was inevitable. We're adults. We can handle this. "The guys are coming over tomorrow afternoon to get started. Dean wants to move you in next weekend so he can rip up the old carpet at your mom's."

Groaning, Stella covers her face with her hands. "You shouldn't have to do that. If I find a place, all that work will be for nothing."

"Nah, it needed to be done anyway." I shrug. "Do whatever works for you, but if you haven't found a place by this weekend, we can work out a month-to-month lease on the pool house, and you can keep looking."

"That's really sweet, Kace," she says softly, but when she meets my eyes, she looks more vulnerable than I've ever seen her.

I swallow. She promised me Saturday and again this morning that we could do this without screwing everything up, but I can't tell if she's changed her mind. Never mind that those conversations didn't account for whether or not we'd be seeing other people.

We really need to talk.

"I'm headed out," I tell Abbi. "Can I walk you to your car, Stell?"

"Crap!" Abbi squeaks. "Stella, if you're gonna make it to Butts and Guts, you need to hustle."

Stella glances at the clock and sighs. "Right. I'm here for exercise, not for cookies." She wanders toward me, then slides an arm through mine. "You can deliver me to Savvy's torture chamber on your way out."

I laugh as she leads me toward the door.

"Bye, you two," Abbi says.

"Bye," we chorus as we push out of the kitchen. We stroll down the hall through the treatment suites and toward the group fitness room. I wouldn't call Stella's pace a "hustle," and I wonder if she's as reluctant to walk away from me as I am to go home without touching her again.

Talk first.

"Why are you going if it's torture?" I ask. Okay, I'm dodging the point of my visit.

"Because it's worth it." Stella smacks her ass with her free hand and grins up at me.

"You're killing me." I pull her into the first dark room I see, press her against the wall, and kiss her. I intend to make it quick and then have a conversation about Itsy, but her lips are soft and silky beneath mine. *Quick* was never a possibility. She threads her fingers into my hair and moans into my mouth. My hands roam down to cup that ass and give it an experimental squeeze. "So worth it."

She runs her fingertips over my beard and down my neck, and I shudder, remembering how those fingers felt unzipping my jeans, wanting that again, needing more. "I've been thinking about this all day," she whispers, and my ego grows two sizes. Along with other things. "I think you've ruined me."

I lift her, positioning her between the wall and my body to give me better access to her neck. I trail my lips along her jaw, nip at her earlobe, and suck at the sensitive spot where her neck meets her shoulder. *Christ, she smells sweet.* "I've barely gotten started."

She bites back a groan and wraps her ankles behind me. I press between her thighs, cursing the man who invented denim. When she pops the button on my jeans, I remember where we are and why I pulled her in here.

Reluctantly, I lower her to the floor. Even in the shadows of the empty treatment room, I can see her swollen lips and the flush on her cheeks. "Sorry about that. I actually brought you in here to talk."

She leans against the wall and blows out a long breath. I can practically see her steeling herself for rejection. "Okay . . ."

I probably shouldn't touch her again until we talk this out, but I find myself brushing a knuckle down the side of her neck anyway. For so much of my life, Stella's been off-limits—forbidden fruit—and now that I've crossed the line and had a taste, I want more.

I trail my finger over the swell of her breasts and across her nipple. I can't stop touching her. I don't want to stop. I can't stop thinking about Itsy making me laugh and how I keep imagining Stella's smile when I read her words.

God, it's crazy to think, but what if Stella *is* Itsy? It's probably wishful thinking, but . . . "What picture do you use for your profile on Random these days?"

She frowns at me. "You've seen it already, haven't you?"

I want to say, *"Not that I know of."* I shake my head instead.

"The one of me in the yellow dress? Ring any bells?"

Disappointment is a heavy rock dropped in my stomach. "Right, that one." *Not Jessica Rabbit.*

"You came in here to ask about my profile picture?"

"No. Actually . . ." I shake my head, feeling foolish. "Before we do anything else, I want to make sure you're okay with this not being exclusive." Fuck, this is awkward. In writing or in person, it's just a weird conversation to have.

"Don't obsess." She smiles, but it doesn't reach her eyes. "You've been honest about what this is from the start."

"I want you, but if you decide you can't do this casual thing with me, then there's no pressure to—"

"Kace." She laughs, and the sound makes me feel a hundred pounds lighter. "I was ready to have you take me against the wall in the room where they do laser hair removal. It's safe to say I'm still on board."

"Right. Shit." I blow out a breath and drag a hand through my hair. "You probably think I'm a freak now. I just don't . . ." I swallow. "I want this, but I don't want you to end up hurt."

Something changes in her expression for a beat, but it fades away before I can read it. She steps forward and presses her lips to the center of my chest, right at the solar plexus. "I don't think you're a freak. I think you're sweet. Maybe the sweetest guy I've ever known." She pulls back, tugs the band from her hair, and redoes her ponytail. I must've messed it up without realizing it. "I've gotta get to class, or Savvy's gonna kick my ass."

Right. I was so focused on getting my mouth on her again that I totally forgot she was on her way somewhere. "Come to my house tonight. Hope's with her mom, and I . . ." I drag my gaze over her. Her nipples have pebbled under her tank top. *Don't obsess?* I already know I'll spend the next hour obsessing over how they'd feel against my tongue. "Just come over?"

She licks her lips. "I have to study. I'm sorry."

Something in my chest sinks, but I shrug. *Casual.* "Just tell me when."

"Sure thing." She backs toward the door, that carefree

smile I saw after we kissed gone, replaced by something more cautious.

"You okay? Are *we* okay?"

"I'm fine. Just *late.*" She winks at me then calls over her shoulder, "We'll talk later."

CHAPTER TEN

STELLA

I can't decide if I'm the world's biggest coward or if I actually made a smart decision for the first time in my life. I could be at Kace's house right now. Naked, with his head between my legs, or maybe in his shower with my breasts pressed to the tile and his hard chest against my back. Or curled up together on the couch . . .

So many possibilities. An opportunity to fulfill *years* of fantasies. And I said no.

"I want this, but I don't want you to end up hurt."

Kace isn't looking for a happily-ever-after. He wants *one thing* from me . . . and has been honest about that from the start. But when Kace said he didn't want me hurt, it made me realize there's no other destination for me when it comes to him. If I let myself enjoy him for as long as that lasts, it'll break me when it ends. If he tells me he can't do serious and then gives some other woman that chance, it'll shatter me. And I know he will. *Eventually*, he'll let someone in his heart and life again. But if I shut this down now, I'll always ache with the what-ifs.

There's no win here for me. Just a bunch of different roads that lead to the same broken heart. A little voice inside my head says maybe, just maybe, if I take what he's giving, he'll eventually see me as more than the party girl who's only good for a fling. Maybe he's already seeing more of me, and maybe I could be the one he opens his heart to. That's dangerous thinking. And yet . . .

I pull up the Random app on my phone and stare at his profile picture for a long time. *Maybe* I have a way to make him see me.

I click into the messaging feature and decide to shower him with honesty.

> ItsyBitsy123: I could be in bed with the
> hottest guy I know right now, but I
> decided to spend my night alone instead.
> All because I don't trust myself not to
> catch feelings. Am I crazy?

I wish this app would let you know when someone has read your messages, but the only way you ever know is if they reply. I'm highly suspicious that the person behind this design feature didn't want any accountability. I'm also highly suspicious it was a man.

When there's no reply after a few minutes, I pull out my textbooks and a notepad and start reading. Surprisingly, I actually *like* anatomy and physiology. It makes sense to me and is interesting. But chem? Not so much. I get through my A&P homework first and am slowly working my way through another chemistry chapter when my phone buzzes with a Random notification.

> GoodHands69: Sorry about the delay. I was linking my account to my computer. My friends would laugh and call me an old man if they heard me say this, but sometimes messaging on a phone is frustrating for me. I have no patience for how long it takes to type anything of substance. Luckily, it turns out you can log on to Random from a computer and it'll let you message from here. In case you're like me and ever want the ease of a keyboard.
>
> GoodHands69: To answer your question . . . no, I don't think you're crazy at all. You need to know yourself. Are you the kind of person who can explore physical attraction without the emotional stuff coming along for a ride?

I grab my laptop and look up Random. Sure enough, they have an actual website. It's pretty basic, and it makes the rudimentary app look high-tech, but when I log in, I can click on Kace's avatar and access the messaging function.

> ItsyBitsy123: Thank you so much for the computer tip. No joke, this is way easier.
>
> ItsyBitsy123: As for whether or not I can handle a physical relationship, I thought I

could, but maybe I've been lying to
myself. My emotions always get tangled
up with the physical, and it's not fair to
wish that went both ways.
GoodHands69: You should give yourself
some credit. You're pretty awesome, and
I'm sure this guy's at risk of catching
feelings too.

My stomach is suddenly occupied by riotous butterflies, and I reread the message three more times. I can't decide if he's just being nice or if he means it, that this is more than just sex to him too. I want to be mature about this—tell him all my feelings and my fears, and ask him to dig in a little more to his—but the truth is I never believed I'd get a shot with Kace. Now that I have it, I'm scared to lose it.

Before I can figure out what to say, another message comes through.

GoodHands69: I realized I should tell you
that Who Framed Roger Rabbit was my
favorite movie when I was a kid. My
parents had this old VHS tape, and my
sister and I watched it, like, ten times one
summer. Okay, I watched it way more
than ten times. I'll admit to you—and
only you—that I had a serious crush on
Jessica Rabbit.

I laugh and roll over in bed, stretching. He can be completely random, and I had no idea he was so funny. If I don't get back to my chemistry homework soon, I'm going to need an extra shot in my Starbucks in the morning, but how can I shut down this conversation when Kace is telling me about his favorite childhood movie and his crush on an animated sex symbol? It's kind of sweet, actually.

> ItsyBitsy123: You have a thing for busty redheads?
> GoodHands69: Shh! It's my secret weakness.

My stomach floods with butterflies, and every single one of those bitches is flailing like a Harry Styles fan at a meet-and-greet. It's too late. I'm already a lost cause. This guy is going to destroy me.

I imagine Kace relaxing in his living room, beer in hand, eyes on his laptop, smiling. *That smile.* Kace isn't all that generous with his smiles, and I spent the years he was married to Amy jealous as hell that she could elicit them so easily. I want to be the one who makes him smile. The one he wants to share *all* his silly childhood stories with.

> ItsyBitsy123: Your secret's safe with me.
> GoodHands69: What was your favorite childhood movie?
> ItsyBitsy123: Nothing that unique. Disney princesses as a kid, then later, I was obsessed with Harry Potter, just like everyone else. Oh, and then the Twilight movies, because Jacob is haaawt.
> GoodHands69: I thought the vampire's name was Edward.

I gape at my phone. I'm practically *giddy.*

ItsyBitsy123: YOU KNOW HIS NAME?

GoodHands69: I mean, my sister was
obsessed, so . . . yeah. Are you going to
revoke my man card?

ItsyBitsy123: Never! Real men aren't afraid to
watch Twilight. Or read it, for that
matter.

GoodHands69: Hmm . . . so I guess now I
need to read and find out who this Jacob
is. I'm curious enough that I might.

ItsyBitsy123: Seriously? You'd do that just
for me?

GoodHands69: Why not? I like to read. I
have to keep myself busy when my
daughter's at her mom's. I hate an empty
house, and I can only spend so many
hours renovating before my body reminds
me I'm not twenty anymore.

My heart tugs hard at the image of Kace keeping himself distracted when he's home alone. Dammit. I should've gone over there tonight. But if I had, we'd be fooling around instead of having this conversation, and as much as I'd enjoy that, this is nice too. Better than nice. Heart-to-hearts with Kace are revelatory.

ItsyBitsy123: Do you miss being married?

He doesn't reply, and I worry I've crossed a line.

ItsyBitsy123: You don't have to answer that if
you don't want.

No reply. Did I screw up? Maybe he just closed down the app and went to bed.

I force myself to walk away from my computer. I change into my PJs, wash my face, and brush my teeth. When I return to my laptop, he's replied, and it feels like Christmas morning.

> GoodHands69: The truth? Yeah. I really do. I miss my wife. I miss sleeping next to her and talking about my day with her. I miss laughing together. Sometimes I feel like this divorce would've been easier if things had been obviously bad between us. Instead, it was like sitting outside on a sunny day and watching lightning take out your whole house. Our marriage wasn't perfect, but it was GOOD. I'm guilty of being so busy wanting that back that I forget I need to think about a future that doesn't include her. Everyone who cares about me wants me to move on. I want that as well—and, fuck, maybe this is too much honesty—but how can I search for new love when I still don't understand what I did wrong to ruin my marriage?

My heart cracks a little. Kace never ruined his marriage, and if I had any guts at all, I would've made sure he understood that years ago. My fingers hover over the keyboard for a long time before I type.

> ItsyBitsy123: You can't blame yourself for the

end of something that requires two
committed participants. You should be
proud that you were willing to fight for it,
and proud that you were willing to let her
go when she needed that. That's all
anyone can ask for.

I reread my reply. I'm not sure it does any justice to
what I so desperately want him to understand.

ItsyBitsy123: BTW, don't ever worry about
being too honest. There's no such thing.
And anyway, I like getting a look inside
that big heart of yours.
GoodHands69: Thank you. For that, and for .
. . just listening. It means a lot.

I can hardly swallow around the lump in my throat. This
guy has no idea, does he? I'd listen anytime, anywhere.

ItsyBitsy123: Absolutely any time. I mean
that.

CHAPTER ELEVEN

KACE

"*M*r. Matthews? This is Janie from Little Angels Preschool. Today's Hope's share day, and she said she forgot her stuffed friend on the breakfast table." The woman lowers her voice. "I'm sorry to bother you in the middle of the workday, but she's taking it pretty hard."

Instead of show and tell, Hope's school does *share day*. They each get one day a month to bring in something special from home and share it with the class. Hope looks forward to her share day only marginally less than Christmas. "It's no problem. I'm on my way now."

"Oh, thanks so much!" Janie says.

We say our goodbyes, and I head out to my truck while calling Amy. It's not like her to forget Hope's things, but our lives have become a little more chaotic since we started this shared-custody thing, and details slip through the cracks sometimes.

When I get her voicemail, I try her work line, but that goes to voicemail too. Figures—she's always in a meeting or on her way to another. "Hey, Ames. Hope left her share-day toy on the table. I'm just going to swing by your place and grab it for her. Talk to you later."

Within five minutes, I'm pulling into Amy's driveway. The sight of her house makes my gut twist. This little bungalow is the physical embodiment of my divorce. It's weird that a house could upset me more than any of the other thousand things that changed when she left, but this place has always made me sad. Home was supposed to be where we were all together. Now that doesn't exist.

Pushing aside my angst, I climb out of the truck and use the key she gave me to let myself in.

The foyer looks right into the living room, where Amy's straddling someone on the couch, her head thrown back, wild blond curls everywhere, tits bouncing as she moans.

Why didn't I knock?

"Shit!" I turn around and walk right back out the door, slamming it behind me.

"Kace!" she shouts, but I'm already heading to my car.

I yank my door open, throw my phone in the passenger seat, and slide in. Squeezing the steering wheel, I force myself to draw in a deep breath. It takes every ounce of my will not to storm in there and start swinging my fists at whomever she had beneath her. It's not my right. *She's not my wife.* But, fuck, it's like my heart never got the memo, because it's pounding so fast, so hard, and it just *hurts* so fucking much I have to shut my eyes.

The rap on my window has me opening them again. Amy's standing outside my truck in her fluffy pink robe. My first thought is surprise that she still has it. I bought it for her at Christmas a few years ago, and when she opened it, she made a comment about nothing saying *the spice is gone* like a terry cloth robe instead of lingerie. The off-hand remark pissed me off, but it wasn't until after we'd tucked our exhausted toddler into bed that she said she needed me to at least *pretend* I still thought she was sexy, even if it wasn't true. I told her she was being ridiculous and that I'd never stopped finding her sexy, that *she* was the one who'd been pulling away when I tried to touch her, that we hadn't had sex in months. She said she couldn't be the woman from my fantasies when she was busy being the mother to our child.

She slept on the couch that night, and even though she came back to our bed after that, our sex life never improved. But apparently *hers* has since she left.

Her face is screwed up in a frown. "Kace, I'm sorry. I didn't hear you knock."

I should step out of the truck and have this conversation somewhere other than the middle of her driveway. I should give her a chance to change out of that fucking robe, but I don't trust myself not to go after the fucker inside, so I roll down my window. "I didn't knock," I say, shifting my gaze back to the house. I can't look at her without seeing her as she was when I walked in that door. The ecstasy on her face. When was the last time I made her look like that? "I thought you were at work."

"I took the day off." She gives a tentative smile. "That was super awkward, so I'm guessing I don't need to tell you it's best to *knock* in the future?"

"No shit," I mutter, jaw tight. "Who is he?"

"What?"

"The guy who was just giving my wife a *ride*." I look at

her now, needing to meet her eyes, even though I know my anger and this feeling of betrayal in my gut are equally irrational. Her eyes are wide. "Who. The fuck. Is he?"

"It doesn't matter." She shakes her head and looks away for five aching thumps of my heart. When she turns back to me, her face is hard, her expression pained. "Kace, I'm not your wife. And I haven't hidden the fact that I've moved on —emotionally *and* physically." She swallows. "I wish you would too."

I look out my window toward the house. The asshole's still in there. Is it serious? Will he want to marry Amy? Will Hope call him *Daddy? Fuck.* "Hope left her share-day toy on the table. I was here to take it in for you, but it looks like you're available and can do it yourself."

Amy's eyes fill with tears. "Don't act like I just cheated on you. That's not fair."

"I know." I turn the key in the ignition, and the engine roars to life. "That's why I need to get out of here."

❧

AT THE END of the day, I collapse into bed and stare at the ceiling. I'm exhausted but wide awake. I'm pissed at Amy for bringing her boyfriend—or whatever—into the house where my daughter spends half her nights, and I'm even more pissed at myself for caring. I knew she'd been dating, figured she'd had sex since she moved out. But there's a big difference between *knowing* and *seeing* it.

I pull my phone from my pocket and open Random. Maybe Itsy's around. A chat with her might clear my mind.

129

GoodHands69: I walked in on my ex-wife
fucking someone else today.

I send it before rereading the words, then flinch when I realize I can't take it back. I close my eyes and drop my phone to the mattress. I am officially the clichéd divorced guy who obsesses over his ex's new life. I don't want to be like this, but I need to talk about it.

Abbi would rant and rave and get in a huff about how I should've fought for primary custody, and I'd end up having to defend Amy. I could call Dean, and he'd listen and make all the right sympathetic noises, but he thinks I should've moved on by now. He's second only to Amy in how much he's been pushing me to "get back out there" and "leave the past in the past." But I don't want to resent him for trying to be a good friend and tell me to get the fuck over it. So here I am, confiding in my match on a hookup app.

When my phone buzzes, I'm almost afraid to look at it. What's she going to think of the fact that I still *care* about Amy sleeping with someone else?

I make myself look.

ItsyBitsy123: I am so sorry. Did you
immediately start drinking? I think I
would have.

A weight lifts from my shoulders as I read and reread the message. God, I needed this.

GoodHands69: Thank you for not judging
me. I know I shouldn't care, and I'm
trying not to, but it turns out that's way

easier on an intellectual level. Actually
seeing her with someone else? Well, I
could've happily died without that.

ItsyBitsy123: No shit. She was your WIFE.

GoodHands69: Exactly. It's like I need to do
a factory reset on my brain.

ItsyBitsy123: Are you okay? Want to meet up
for a drink or something? I'd be drinking
the shit out of my feelings right now if I
were you.

I hold my breath as I consider this. Hope is already in
bed, and I could get Abbi to come over to babysit. She's
always offering.

I try to imagine what it'd be like to meet up with Itsy.
I'd get to see what she looks like, see if there's any spark
between us in person. I have to admit I'm curious, but I
can't start a physical relationship with this girl while I'm
still messing around with Stella. I don't have it in me.

GoodHands69: Do you mind if I take a rain
check? I'm not in the right headspace for
a meetup tonight, and not big on drinking
my feelings to begin with.

ItsyBitsy123: That's very mature of you.

GoodHands69: Nice of you to say. Everyone
else in my life seems to think I'm reacting
to my divorce like a heartbroken
teenager.

ItsyBitsy123: I think you're reacting like a
man who loved his wife with everything
he had. Maybe she didn't deserve that

love, but that doesn't mean you didn't
feel it.

I shake my head. As good as it feels to talk to someone
who assumes I'm the good guy, I can't do that to Amy.

> GoodHands69: Amy deserved it. She
> deserved more. I just haven't figured out
> what that more is yet. I wish someone
> could show me a map of my marriage and
> point to the place where I made the
> wrong turn. I fucking tried, and it wasn't
> enough. If I understood, maybe I wouldn't
> be so afraid of trying again with someone
> else.

૪૱

STELLA

I might not have the map to Kace's marriage, but I know
more about where it went wrong than he realizes. I'd
assumed that, as they worked their way through the
divorce, Amy would've admitted the truth about her
mistakes, but the poking I've done and the things he's said
about the marriage he misses so dearly have led me to
believe he still doesn't know the truth. Now, I'm sure of it.

"You're glued to your phone tonight," Savannah says as
she hands me a full glass of wine from the opposite side of
her big kitchen island.

I smile. "Sorry. I promise I'm almost done."

> GoodHands69: I'm sorry to go on like this.
> I'm sure I sound like another pathetic
> divorced dude who's hung up on his wife.

I shake my head and tap out a response.
"Take your time," Savvy says, pulling out her own phone.

> ItsyBitsy123: I don't think you're pathetic for
> being hung up on Amy. You were in love
> with her, and you had plans for your life
> together that you don't want to give up. I
> only wish she deserved your devotion.
> More soon. Having an impromptu girls'
> night.

I darken the screen and slide my phone back into my purse. "Now I'm done with that and can give you my full attention. How's Alec?" I should probably be home studying right now, but when Savvy found me at the end of my shift at The Orchid and asked if I wanted to come to her place for a glass of wine, I jumped at the chance. And then Kace started messaging me the minute I parked, and now I wish I were at home so we could message back and forth all night again.

She shakes her head. "Nuh-uh. Don't dodge. I want to know who just had your attention so completely that you didn't even notice when I pulled out the wine. New guy in your life?"

I bite my bottom lip. "Not exactly."

Savvy arches a perfect blond brow. "Explain, please."

I take one gulp of my wine and then another.

"*Stella.*" She folds her arms. "Spill."

"I've been talking to someone on Random," I say.

"I thought you were swearing off that app," she says, but her tone is curious, not judgmental. Savvy's a bit like me in that she struggles in the relationship department. That was until last October, when she went with Brinley to Vegas and hooked up with Marston's best friend and business partner, Alec. There's no way anyone could call a night with a guy like Alec *unlucky*. But Alec's based in L.A. and Savvy doesn't want to do the long-distance thing, so despite him calling her regularly and sending her flowers, she insists they're just friends and going to stay that way.

"I got on Monday night out of habit more than anything, and I almost got right back off, but then I saw Kace had swiped on me."

Her eyes widen, then she blinks. "Kace *Matthews?*"

"Yes."

"You're sure?"

"Yes."

"It's not some guy using his picture or pretending to be him."

I shake my head. "No. It's definitely Kace, and I already knew he'd been using Random. He told me he was going to give it a try."

She sips her wine. "Wow. Go, Kace. I rescind my previous criticism. I guess decent guys do occasionally use that app." She smiles slowly. "And good thing, because now he's finally giving you a chance. Sweet Lord, it's about time."

I swallow hard then swirl my wine. "Whatever this thing is between us, it started before we connected on Random. We . . ." I blow out a breath. "We were going to hook up at his party, but then Dean asked if I could move in, and Kace shut it down, which was understandable. I was ready to let it go until he reached out to me on Random and said he wanted to connect on there because it's less intimidating somehow." I shake my head, not sure how to explain why that made so much sense to me at the time. "And we just *talk* on there, and it's good. And yesterday morning, he was at Mom's to do some work, and I pulled him into my bedroom and we . . . did stuff."

"Get it, girl!" She beams as if she's been on a personal mission to get me into Kace Matthews' bed. "And was that good?"

I bite my lip, but a pathetic whimper escapes anyway. "So good. The man has a *mouth* on him, and I'm not just talking about his spectacular kissing skills."

She grins, but it falls away. "Why do I feel like there's a big *but* coming?"

I wrap my hands around my glass. "Savvy, it's like he's really seeing me as more than this space-case party girl for the first time. He's been opening up to me, and I've been opening up to him. This is becoming more than the physical fling we planned."

Savvy sighs. "But?" she asks softly.

"But he's seeing someone else."

"Oh, shit. I'm sorry. How'd you find out?"

I laugh. "He told me. Twice, actually. He was so sweet about it too. Like, *hey, I know this is supposed to be casual, but I wouldn't feel right if you didn't know*."

"That doesn't surprise me at all. He really is one of the good ones." She grabs the bottle of wine and tops off my glass, even though I've barely sipped at it.

"As much as I want to be the kind of girl he'd choose, part of me knows that's a pipe dream."

"You don't know that."

But I do. If *Bobby* couldn't handle the skeletons in my closet, then Kace never will. My eyes flare hot, and Savvy becomes a blur as tears well. "I'm gonna get hurt, but I've never had anything like this, and I . . ." My throat feels too tight to finish.

"You think he might be worth getting hurt for," she says.

I nod. "I want to know what it's like to be treated right. Even if it's temporary."

She cocks her head to the side. "Maybe he'll want to treat you right for longer than that. Maybe this is a piece of good that'll stay in your life, Stella. Kace is smart. Give him a chance, and he'll see you're worth it."

CHAPTER TWELVE

KACE

*D*ean turns in a slow circle in the middle of the pool house. "Jesus, maybe I should let Stella have my place and I can move in here."

"You'd really give up your house to live in a tiny pool house? In my backyard?" I arch a brow. "Because Stella might take you up on it." *And that might be for the best.* As much as I enjoy talking to Itsy on Random, the Stella fantasies are still coming at me full tilt.

"Nah. I love you and Hope, but this is a little too close. It'll be perfect for Stella, though."

Dean, Smithy, and I have been working the last two days to clear out the old stuff that was stored in the loft and main room. Some of it needed to be donated, some organized and moved to the main house, and some just needed to be pitched. Why was I saving the box full of Amy's college essays? Right, because she always wanted to keep them, but once it came time to find a space for them in her new house, she didn't want them anymore. She told me to throw them out, and I just . . . couldn't. Today, I did, and I'm going to call that progress. I think Itsy would be proud of me. Maybe I'll tell her . . . if she ever responds to the message I sent this morning. It wasn't much—just asking how she slept and thanking her again for last night.

"Why would you want *Dean* back here?" Smithy asks, eyes wide. "Fuck, man. Stella in a bikini every time you look out your window? Sign me up."

"Smithy," Dean says, "just because someone lives in a pool house doesn't mean they're out at the pool all the time."

When Smithy turns to me, it's with an expression so tragic that you'd think someone just told him he has testicular cancer and is going to have to forfeit his balls. "Bummer, man."

Sometimes this guy makes my brain hurt.

My phone buzzes, and I dig it from my pocket and grin when I see I have a new message on Random. Maybe I didn't scare her off, after all.

> ItsyBitsy123: Hey, handsome. Sorry I didn't reply this morning. I overslept and had to hustle out the door. So, to answer your question, I slept great—too great, apparently. What about you?
>
> GoodHands69: Like the dead . . . well, maybe not the dead. I had dreams about Jessica Rabbit last night. Which was . . . different. I hope you're proud of yourself.
>
> ItsyBitsy123: Jessica Rabbit, huh? And was

she animated in the dream? Did you play PATTY-CAKE? (Omg, I can't even type that without laughing. That movie is too much.)

GoodHands69: I guess you could call it that. Ahem . . .

"Who is she?"

My head snaps up, and Dean and Smithy are both staring at me like I've grown a second head. "What?"

Dean waves to my phone. "Dude, you're grinning like Selena Gomez just sauntered in front of you buck naked. Who are you talking to?"

I close the app and shove my phone back into my pocket. "Just . . . someone I met on Random."

Dean smiles bigger than I've seen him smile in weeks. "Fucking seriously?" He smacks my arm. "Good for you, man. It's about time. What's her name?"

I shrug. "I don't know."

He chuckles. "Kinky. She hot? When did you hook up with her, and why didn't you tell your best friend?"

"I don't know, and I haven't *hooked up* with anyone," I say, then cringe, because that's only half true. I'm not sure if what happened in Stella's room or this pool house counts as a hookup, but they weren't nothing.

Dean scrunches his brows together in confusion. "I'm sorry. What?"

"We're just talking." I shrug. "I've waited this long to move on. No need to rush it now."

"Okaaaaay." Smithy holds out a hand. "Lemme see her. I've gotten good at spotting the crazies."

Dean snorts. "Sure you have."

"No, man, I mean it. You can see it in their eyes." Smithy circles a finger at his temple.

"Well, this girl has a picture of Jessica Rabbit as her avatar, so save your superpowers for another time."

"Ooh," Dean says. He pulls a face and rocks back on his heels. "Shit, man. My condolences."

He and Smithy share a look, then Smithy nods and says, "Right?"

"What? Why?"

Laughing, Smithy drops the broom he was holding then bends at the waist as he laughs harder.

Dean points to him and nods. "He gets it."

"Gets what? What are you idiots talking about?"

Smithy straightens and shakes his head. "She's . . ." He gasps before he belly laughs. "She's ugly."

"What the fuck? Why would you assume that?"

Smithy looks to Dean, who just shakes his head. When Smithy turns to me, he swallows back his laughter and holds up a hand. "Listen, maybe she's hot. It's possible."

"Totally possible," Dean says, but then he ruins it by grunting out another laugh. "But Random is a hookup app. People aren't on there because they want to find their soul mate. They're on there for some—"

"*Random*," Smithy says. "It's about attraction and . . ." He curls his hands into fists and draws them back as he thrusts his hips a few times. "I guarantee she'd post a picture of herself if she was hot."

"Attraction can be about more than appearance." I grab a bag of trash in each hand and head out into the summer heat to the dumpster. The guys do the same. "I'd rather be turned on by a woman's mind than her cup size."

"Kace," Dean calls, following behind me, "we're not

saying personality doesn't factor into chemistry, but have you ever *tried* to have sex with someone you don't find physically attractive?"

That's a fucking stupid question, so I don't dignify it with a response. "I'm saying physical attraction can grow from intellectual attraction. And anyway, maybe she uses that avatar because she looks like Jessica Rabbit." I hoist the bags into the dumpster with a little too much aggression. Are my friends really this shallow?

Smithy tosses his in then wipes his hands on his jeans. "Is Jessica Rabbit even hot?"

"Fuck yes, she is." The words are out of my mouth before I even think it through, and then I wish I could snatch them back. *Maybe she looks like Jessica Rabbit.* I direct all my attention to the bags in Dean's hands, taking them from him and tossing them into the dumpster.

If anyone could be the real-life Jessica Rabbit, it'd be Stella Jacob, and I don't exactly need her brother knowing how hot I think she is, *especially* since we're messing around. Double especially since she's moving in here.

"Sorry, man," Dean says, "but I think your wishful thinking has gone a little too far."

I risk turning back to my friends, but there's no sign either one is thinking about Stella. Dean's got that amused smirk on his face, and Smithy's fucking around on his phone.

"I haven't seen that movie since I was, like, six," Smithy says, tapping on the screen. "Is that the one with the human-size duck?"

"I think that's *Howard the Duck*," Dean says.

Smithy grins. "Right. *Howard.* Watched that after eating some of my mom's special brownies once, and *damn*, it was a trip." He giggles. Yes, *giggles*. "Why does 'Mom's special brownies' sound like a euphemism for some seriously hard-core kink?"

Dean cringes. "Because you're messed up."

"Oh, *hell*," Smithy says, nodding at his screen. "Jessica is *fine*. I'd plow that. Think animated pussy is softer?"

"You're disgusting," I mutter, but I really don't care if Smithy's busting out the locker-room talk about a child-hood animated favorite. Really, I'm just relieved Dean isn't giving me the protective big-brother glare I probably deserve.

"So, when are you going to meet up with your Jessica Rabbit?" Dean asks.

I shrug. "Like I said, I'm not in a hurry." Honestly, I'd rather wait until Stella and I have worked whatever we have going on out of our systems. Tuesday's little taste of "dating other people" transparency was more than enough for me.

Dean sighs and shakes his head.

"What?" I ask.

"Nothing."

"It's not nothing." I use the hem of my shirt to wipe the sweat from my forehead. The heat is making me fucking irritable today. "Tell me."

"No name, no real-life picture, and, let me guess, no personal details?" Dean asks.

I shrug. "I mean, we've been talking. She hasn't been *hiding* anything."

"How do you know you're not being catfished?"

"What?" I snap. Why do they assume that's what's happening here? But hell. Honestly, I'm embarrassed. I should've known a cartoon avatar was a red flag, but I'm so fucking bad at this dating thing that it didn't cross my mind.

Smithy shoves his phone back into his pocket. "Catfished. It's when you fall in love with a gorgeous chick online but it actually turns out to be a middle-aged sociopath who lives in his mom's basement and sells Canadian pharmaceuticals on the dark web."

Dean narrows his eyes at Smithy. "Weirdly specific example, as always."

"That happened to Tom Brady once—before Giselle. He fell hard for this chick online, talked about her constantly, sent her extravagant gifts. Turns out it was his great-aunt trying to swindle him."

"That didn't fucking happen," Dean says. "You never even played with Brady."

"Fuck you. I was on their practice team one season, and I watched the guy have a total meltdown when he found out he'd been sexting his aunt."

Dean shakes his head. "Didn't happen."

Smithy frowns. "Or maybe it was the backup QB?"

My phone buzzes again, and I really want to look, but I'm not interested in sharing my conversation with these idiots, either.

I wait until the guys have left for lunch and I'm alone on my porch before I read the latest message from Itsy.

ItsyBitsy123: Well, now I'm jealous.

Thanks to the disappearing messages feature, it takes me a minute to figure out what she's talking about, but then I remember we were talking about "patty-cake" and laugh.

GoodHands69: Don't be jealous. She was you.
You were her.

ItsyBitsy123: I guess dreams are weird like
that. But . . . if she was me, I think I need
details.

I stare at the screen for a long time, trying to think of some hot but not embarrassing detail to give her, but honestly, I shouldn't be having this conversation at all. I didn't lie. I *did* dream about Jessica Rabbit, but at some point in the dream, she became Stella. It feels wrong to feed one woman dirty details of a dream that also involved a different woman.

GoodHands69: Nope. Can't do it. I'm not a
sexting kind of guy, I guess. But maybe
one day I'll show you. If you want . . .

ItsyBitsy123: I'm going to hold you to that.
Unless you're going to ask me to suck you
off behind the Dairy Queen . . . while
your dad watches.

I bark out a laugh and shake my head. The guys are totally wrong about this girl. She's legit. I can feel it in my bones.

GoodHands69: Please tell me that didn't
really happen.

ItsyBitsy123: Oh. It did. And then I had to
block him because he wouldn't stop
messaging me dick pics. And they were
DEFINITELY not all the same dick.

shudder I try not to think too much
about that . . .

GoodHands69: Jesus. I'm sorry.

ItsyBitsy123: I've had so many bad
experiences with guys lately that I'm
afraid I'd punch the first one to approach
me. With my luck, he'd turn out to be one
of the good guys—like a pediatrician who
has a great relationship with his mom,
loves to read, and gets off on giving
orgasms.

I laugh again. I really want to meet this girl.

GoodHands69: I'm not a pediatrician, but I
just so happen to tick a few of those other
boxes.

I debate some sort of corny emoji at the end of that for
so long that by the time I hit send—no emoji—her next
message is already coming through.

ItsyBitsy123: Does that last part make me
sound sex-obsessed? Because I'm not . .
.well, maybe I am in some people's views.
It's all relative. I consider sex a healthy
part of life, and I want it in a romantic
relationship, but I also want mutual
respect, understanding, and emotional
connection. Am I asking too much?

ItsyBitsy123: Don't answer that. I splurged on
a therapist once, and she said I need to

work on RAISING my expectations, not
lowering them. This probably doesn't
surprise you at all, but that doesn't come
naturally.

I grin down at my phone. From my dreams, to wanting a
guy who gets off on giving orgasms, to talk about her therapist. This girl's all over the place. She makes my head spin
and . . . I like it. I haven't had someone I could talk to so
freely in a long time.

It's ironic, really. The whole point of this app is to
match people up so they can have no-strings sex. In all like-
lihood, the messaging function is meant for coordinating
meetup spots, not heart-to-heart conversations.

ItsyBitsy123: Not all guys are good like you. In
fact, some days it seems like you're the
only good one left. And don't freak out on
me. I know you're not ready for anything
serious and you're seeing someone else. I
just really enjoy talking like this.

I swallow hard. I don't know what the fuck I'm doing
here, but I'm not ready to give up talking to this girl or
touching Stella. And I don't know where that leaves me.

GoodHands69: Don't you dare lower your
expectations. You deserve everything you
want and more.

CHAPTER THIRTEEN

STELLA

*W*hen I get home from my shift at The Orchid Thursday night, I've spent so much time clutching my phone to my chest that I've practically become one with it.

Don't you dare lower your expectations. You deserve everything you want and more.

Yes, I'm pretty much floating on cloud nine after a few sweet messages from Kace. Maybe Savvy's right, and this thing with Kace can become something more. I want to believe it.

Either way, if I didn't know tonight was one of his nights with Hope, I would've surprised him at his house after work. But since part of what makes him so irresistible is that he's a good dad before all else, I drove home. It's for the best. I need to spend every moment until bed studying for tomorrow's chemistry exam—because apparently, when you only have six weeks of class, your first exam comes during week one.

"Stella, baby, come in here, please?" Mom calls as I walk in the door.

I cringe at her tone. That's her you've-been-keeping-secrets tone. The one she'd use when she caught me sneaking out at sixteen.

I drop my purse onto the entryway table and kick off my shoes before plodding to the kitchen.

Mom's sitting at the table with a cup of coffee. I get my brew addiction from her, but I can't drink caffeine at all hours of the day like she can. I like my sleep too much, whereas Mom can mainline it twenty-four seven and sleep like a baby. I suppose I'm not just like her *yet*. "Hey, Mama. How was your day?"

She wraps her hands around her mug and studies me. Mom has an easy smile. Only when it's missing am I reminded just how much it hides the sadness in her eyes. Is this what I'll look like in twenty-five years? Sad and lonely from years of falling for the wrong guy and beating myself up about it? "Your brother told me you've been apartment hunting." She sighs. "And even though he denies it, I'm guessing you made that choice so I can move?"

"It's fine, Mom. I really don't mind. I *want* you to move to Lakeview. It's perfect, and you have friends there."

"And I want to support you while you get your nursing degree."

I force a smile. I can't bring myself to tell her that if I can't pass chemistry, there'll be no nursing program for me, let alone the degree, and the accelerated pace of the six-week course means I'm far enough in after a few days to know I'm in way over my head. "You do support me. Every day. Always have."

"You know what I mean. Can you afford this?"

I shrug. "I can afford some. Not a lot. I'm looking for a roommate rather than my own place."

She sighs. "Better than rooming with your old mom, I'm sure."

"Psh! Are you kidding? You're the best roommate. You always keep the coffee pot fresh."

She bows her head and studies her coffee, and dread swells in my chest.

"What is it?"

"I can't afford this place anymore, sugar bean. My mower broke, so the neighbor's been letting me use his, but I also need a new roof, and I'm a little behind on the taxes." She rolls her eyes. "I thought it was supposed to be a good thing when the value of your home went up, but it's not been so great for me. I was a little irresponsible and refinanced a couple of times when I needed money for this or that, and the mortgage kept creeping up along with the taxes, and . . ." She blows out a breath. "It just all feels like too much these days, but luckily, selling could solve a lot of my problems. Dean thinks he could flip it fast for me, so I'd get enough to put fifty percent down on that condo—that's the only way the bank's gonna give me the loan, ya know."

I cover her hand with mine and squeeze. "Then sell. I'll be okay. I won't be homeless."

"I don't want Dean to do anything until you have a place to stay."

I force a smile. "I already have a place." I won't allow her to continue struggling just because the timing is inconvenient for my love life. "Kace has that guest house he's been wanting to rent out, and I'm planning to stay there until I can find something else."

She lifts her head, and relief washes over her face. "Yeah?"

I nod. "It's all good. You don't need to worry about me."

She grins. "Oh, I won't worry about you if you're with Kace Matthews." She winks. "He's one of the good ones."

I swallow hard. I want to spill everything right onto the kitchen table, to tell her it's supposed to be a fling, that this all started with me telling him no-strings hookups are possible, but I'm falling for him and I'm giddy and excited and afraid all at once because it feels too good to be true. I don't tell her any of those things. It's one thing to tell Savvy, but it feels cruel to get Mom's hopes up. She might've given up on finding her knight in shining armor, but I know she still wants that for me.

"He is a good guy," I say, "but he's still in love with his ex-wife."

"He'll move on eventually." She sips her coffee. "And if it's not happening fast enough, you could tell him the truth about her."

I tense. "Mom . . ." She's the only one who knows what I saw, and on more than one occasion, she's tried to convince me to tell Kace. But what's the point now?

Mom shakes her head. "No, I know you don't want to do that. You're a better person than I am, Stella Elaine."

"No one's better than you, Mama." My phone buzzes, and my stomach flips when I see it's a message from Kace—and not a Random notification, but a text. I wonder if he just wasn't thinking or if he's decided we can make this "real" by texting now. "I need to go study. I'll talk to you tomorrow?"

She smiles, and I kiss both of her cheeks before grabbing my bag and heading to my bedroom.

I barely get the door closed before I'm unlocking my phone to see the message.

> Kace: Tell me I'm not the only one who's
> been distracted all day. All week.

I grin so big my face hurts.

> Me: Definitely not. So distracted.
> Kace: Can you come over before class
> tomorrow? I'll be back from taking Hope
> to preschool at 8:15. I want to show you
> what the place looks like now that it's all
> cleared out. New cabinets are on order.
> Me: I hate that you're doing that! What if I
> find somewhere else to live?
> Kace: Sorry, Freckles. I'm a little rusty. Let
> me restate that—I want to get you alone,
> and I'm using my progress on the pool
> house as a flimsy excuse to get my hands
> on you. And my mouth . . . if you're
> interested.

I bite my lip. This guy makes my stomach flip-flop so much. Talking to him like this is like being at the top of the first big hill of a roller coaster—all exhilaration with a dash of terror. I was going to wake up early and go straight to campus, but I do some mental calculations to figure out how to squeeze a little time with Kace into my day.

Me: I can give you thirty minutes before I
have to meet my study group. Big test
tomorrow.

Kace: I'll take it.

Eep.

And I'm supposed to study tonight, knowing this is happening in the morning? I'm supposed to *sleep*? How exactly?

Me: What happened to needing HOURS to
savor me?

Kace: Oh, I still do, but with my custody
schedule, I don't see that happening for
another week at the soonest. So in the
meantime, it's a beggars-can't-be-choosers
situation.

Me: And which one of us is begging in this
scenario?

Kace: Right now, it's me, but tomorrow
morning, it'll be you.

Me: Hmm . . . we'll see.

Kace: Go study before I have to climb into a
cold shower.

Me: Sweet dreams.

☙

KACE

By the time eight fifteen hits on Friday morning, I'm on my second cup of coffee and have already adjusted my expectations from *get Stella naked* to *find a private corner and kiss the shit out of her.*

I'm an early riser. I've always been that way. Days just feel better in general when I get a few miles in before the sun's up. Today, that meant the treadmill, since Hope was still sleeping, but I prefer the road, the rising sun on the horizon. This way I was able to get my run done, shower, and answer a few emails all before seven. I was getting Hope ready for school when the doorbell rang, and I found Smithy waiting on my front porch with a grin and a crowbar.

"Let me at those cabinets," he said. And there went my plans for thirty minutes of alone time with Stella.

Eight seventeen.

She's late anyway, so Smithy probably didn't spoil anything, but the anticipation is making me crazy. I'm distracted as hell. I feel like I'm in high school again with my first serious girlfriend.

I sink onto the porch swing with my coffee. I check my phone and smile when I see I have a new Random message from my favorite animated text buddy.

I'm not sure what to think about this tug I feel in my chest every time I hear from her. I never expected to connect with anyone on this app, but I actually look forward to talking to her.

> ItsyBitsy123: Good morning, handsome. I'm running late today, but I logged on here anyway. What can I say? You've made a monster out of me. Anyway, I'm sitting here in PJs, still half asleep, and instead of finding a sweet message from you, I see

this message from some other dude:
"S'alright if you're ugly, darlin. I won't be
looking at your face when I slide it in your
ass."

If you weren't gracing my account with your
sweetness, that might just be it for me.
Messages like that are the reason hetero
women adopt thirteen cats and swear
off men.

Don't get me wrong. I'm all for couples
communicating their sexual wants and
needs, but "you're ugly but I'd still fuck
your ass" seems like a strange jumping-off
point. Whatever happened to the old-
school romantics? You know—the ones
who buy you a drink and lie to you about
your beauty before informing you which
holes they plan to stick it in. I know, I
know, picky bitch.

Heading out now. Xoxo

Heading out where, I wonder. I don't even know where
this woman works or what she does for a living, but I'm not
ready to make it real by asking. For all I know, she could be
Hope's preschool teacher or the barista who always remembers my order at the café by the office. I'd rather we remain
anonymous until this fling with Stella runs its course.

I want to say the right thing in my reply. Sure, Itsy was
sharing to give me a good laugh, but she was also showing
me this vulnerable part of her. Telling me about the jerk
who messaged her could've been her way of explaining she's
been hurt before.

I'm still grinning at my phone and contemplating my response when Stella pulls into my driveway. I stand and wait on the front of the porch to greet her as she climbs out of her car. It's twenty past eight, and she looks like she can barely keep her eyes open. She's in frayed jean shorts and a wide-necked black T-shirt that falls off one shoulder. Her red hair is piled into a messy bun on top of her head, and yesterday's makeup is smudged around her eyes. *She's so fucking beautiful.*

Guilt is a wrench tightening my gut. I'm staring at her, *wanting* her, right after Itsy shared something private with me. I'm not sure I'll ever be comfortable talking with one girl while messing around with another. Being honest isn't enough. I'm going to have to figure out what I want, and fast.

Stella yawns as she climbs the front steps. "I would do dirty, dirty things to you for a cup of that coffee," she says, and all thoughts of guilt fly from my mind as I bite back a groan.

After all, "dirty things" was the plan until Smithy showed up on my doorstep at seven a.m. "No dirty favors necessary." I open the front door for her and nod toward the kitchen. "Help yourself."

"You sure?" She waggles her brows. "Give me cream and sugar, and I'd even play *patty-cake*."

I freeze. *I'm going to kill those fucking assholes.* "Do I have Smithy or Dean to thank for that little jab?"

"Only yourself, *GoodHands*." She winks at me. "Give me some credit. I can be clever."

Nope. Murder is too kind. Whichever one of my dickwad friends is responsible for this deserves torture.

I follow her inside and watch as she pours herself a cup

of coffee and doctors it with cream and sugar. The contents of her mug are a light beige by the time she brings it to her lips. She moans around the first sip, and then the second.

My breath hitches. *Pull it together, Matthews.* "Good news or bad news first?"

"Good, please."

"I have an extra set of hands helping me today, meaning the pool house will be that much closer to finished by the weekend."

She narrows her eyes. "And the bad news?"

"Kace!" Smithy calls from the back door, as if on cue. "Get your ass out here."

I grimace. "Smithy is that set of hands, and he's already here. So plans have changed a little."

She takes another sip of her coffee then sweeps her tongue across her bottom lip in a way that makes all the blood rush south of my belt. "No begging?"

Slowly, I trail my gaze down her neck, over her bare, freckled shoulder, and down to her thighs. "I didn't say that."

"Oh, hey, Stella!" Smithy says, strolling into the kitchen. "Damn, girl, you look like you were ridden hard and put away wet."

Stella's jaw unhinges. "Smith! I was up late *studying*, asshole."

Smithy chuckles and winks at her. "I'm just jealous I wasn't the one doing the riding, is all."

An unexpected surge of protective jealousy swells in my chest, and I fix him with my glare. "She looks great. Don't be a dick."

Smithy's eyes go wide before ping-ponging between us. "Okay, then, my apologies."

Stella nudges me with her elbow. "It's fine. Smithy, I'm here to see my future abode." She grimaces, leaving no doubt how she feels about this arrangement, then checks her watch. "And I need to leave in twenty minutes, so we should move quickly."

✌

STELLA

Kace and Smithy lead the way out the back door and around the pool. The sliders on the front of the pool house are standing open, and Taylor Swift's "Shake It Off" is playing from a wireless speaker.

"We cleared everything out," Kace says, motioning for me to step in ahead of him. "Then patched the broken tiles with the extras we found in the loft. Today, Smithy and I will be pulling out these old cabinets and prepping for the new ones, which should be delivered on Monday."

"I think these fuckers were hung with Super Glue," Smithy says, reaching for the crowbar.

I flinch and step forward. Seeing Smithy with a crowbar is like watching a child pick up a semiautomatic. "Careful, Smith."

Kace touches my arm and shakes his head. "It's fine."

My eyes widen. "Really?" I'd be uncomfortable with Smithy holding a butter knife.

"I've worked on hundreds of remodels with him, and he's surprisingly competent with tools."

Smithy grins. "Funny—your mom said the same thing," he says, then he adds in a couple of hip thrusts for good measure.

A cackle rips from my chest, and I smile and feel lighter for the first time all morning. In truth, I've been in a shit mood since getting that rude message on Random. Some guys know just what to say to make you feel like trash, and I attract them by the dozen for whatever reason. I turn to Kace. "You've done so much work. This is nuts."

"It hasn't been as much as you'd think."

Of course he'd say that. "I have tomorrow off. Tell me how I can help."

He shrugs. "We were going to paint this weekend, but—"

"I'll be here. I can't let you do all this work for me without pitching in a little."

Kace nods toward the stairs. "Let me show you what we're working with up here."

I follow him up, making an effort not to stare at his ass, though if this world were fair and just, I'd get a view of his ass on a daily basis.

Smithy starts singing again, but the lyrics are muffled by the time we reach the landing of the loft. Suddenly, I'm all too conscious of being alone up here with Kace. I should be looking at the wood floors or noticing how big this area feels now that it's not piled with boxes. I should be appreciating the skylights and imagining what it'd be like to sleep here.

Instead, I'm trying not to stare at Kace and obsessing over what's happening between us and how it might change when I move in.

"I know there's not a ton of space up here, but you could easily fit a queen-size bed against that wall, and I'm going to pick up some IKEA closet units to install over there." He points to the opposite side of the space. When he turns to me, his eyes are bright, and he looks hopeful. "What do you think?"

Flames of embarrassment lick my cheeks. I need to be practical, but I hate that he's had to do so much just so I won't be homeless. I want Mom to live comfortably for the first time in her life, and Dean's plan can make that happen.

My sigh gets caught in my throat as Kace spins me around and presses his mouth to my neck.

"What do you think?" he asks, but before I can answer, he has me pressed against the wall, his hands on my waist, his teeth scraping lightly across my bare shoulder. He drops his voice to a whisper, and the words are a sensuous tickle against my ear. "I've wanted to do this since I saw you standing on my front porch this morning."

Tilting my head to the side to give him better access, I loop my arms behind his neck. He sucks my earlobe into his mouth, and I bite back a whimper.

"You should probably say something." He's still whispering. I swear he's doing it more to torture me than to be stealthy. "Otherwise, Smithy will get suspicious." He slips one hand under my shirt and glides his knuckles across my belly.

"I like it," I say, too loudly, and my voice hitches a little. Because, fuck, I *do* like it. I like his hands and his mouth and the way his fingertips skim the waistband of my shorts.

Pulling back, he grins and studies my face. His hand dips lower, his knuckles grazing the fabric between my thighs. "Me too," he whispers.

I dressed for comfort, but if I could have a redo, I'd put on skimpy lace panties and a skirt. I adjust my stance, shifting into his touch.

"Tell me you've thought about me this week. About this."

So much. *Too much*. "Maybe a little."

His grin turns lopsided, cocky, but his words are loud enough for Smithy to hear when he says, "I'm thinking gray on the wardrobe." He turns his hand and slides it into my shorts, hovering just above the spot where I ache for him. "Would you like that?"

"I might." I thread my fingers into his hair and watch him through my lashes. "I guess it depends on the execution."

"I think I've proven I have skills in this area." He finds my center, then draws light circles. "I promise you'll be satisfied."

Downstairs, Smithy's singing along with Britney Spears and probably completely oblivious to everything we're saying, even the part of this conversation we're having for his benefit.

"I guess we'll have to wait and see," I say, but I ruin my bravado with a gasp when his fingers slip inside my panties. He holds my gaze as he glides his fingertips over my slick flesh. Kace's eyes are dark, and his pulse thrums wildly at the base of his neck.

"Stella, didn't you need to get moving?" Smithy calls from downstairs.

Shit. "Study group," I blurt, trying to get my brain working again. "I have study group."

Kace lowers his mouth to mine and sucks my bottom lip between his teeth. When he steps back, his eyes are dark and all over me. "Think about me," he whispers. "Then keep next Wednesday night free for me."

I swallow. "I work until eight on Wednesdays."

"Then you'd better prepare yourself for a late night." He brings his fingers—the fingers that were just touching me so intimately—to his mouth and sucks them clean. Winking, he turns toward the stairs. I want to yank him back and beg him to finish what he started, but I have study group at nine and a chemistry test I need to ace, so I've no choice but to follow on trembling legs.

CHAPTER FOURTEEN

STELLA

*A*s fun as this morning with Kace was, my day went south pretty fast when I proceeded to bomb my first chemistry test, then struck out again on the roommate hunt. Meanwhile, Mr. Mixed Signals hasn't messaged me via text or Random all day, and I feel a little weird about it, even though the rational part of my brain keeps reminding me that I saw him less than nine hours ago.

Luckily, Smithy's is my favorite place in the world, and the second I walk in the door on Friday night, I feel lighter.

"Stella!" Smithy calls from behind the lacquered walnut bar. I remember when Dean and Kace helped him refinish and install that piece. Before that, a Formica counter stood in its place. "Whatcha drinking tonight, beautiful?"

I force a smile for the sake of my favorite bartender and slide onto a stool, hanging my purse on the hook beneath the bar. "Vodka soda?" It comes out like a question. The truth is, this week's been a great reminder that I shouldn't be wasting money on drinks, but roommate hunting in Orchid Valley is worse than dating here, so I've earned it.

Smithy prepares my drink and drops a lime in without asking. He knows me well. "What's bringing you down, beautiful?" he asks, leaning on the bar. "Did you get stood up?"

I take a sip from my glass, and my eyes go wide. *Hello, vodka,* and God bless Smithy for making this one so strong. "Nope. I'm still looking for a place to stay."

"I thought you were moving in with Matthews."

I frown. Pool-house life is looking more and more likely. "I'd rather not take advantage of his generosity for longer than necessary, but I don't know if I'll have any other options."

Smithy bobs his head. "Apartment hunting's a bitch if you're on a budget."

I grunt at the understatement of the century. "I've been looking all week with no luck." That's not one hundred percent true. Someone named Taylor ran an ad looking for a roommate, stating "only females need apply." The place was great and the price reasonable. Except "Taylor" was a middle-aged balding guy who barely looked away from my tits the entire time I toured his apartment. *Hard pass.*

"You could move in with me," Smithy says.

I laugh. Smithy lives in a gorgeous condo with a view of Lake Blackledge, but it's a one-bedroom. "And sleep where?"

His grin slowly transforms his stoner stare into a face that could star in female fantasies all over the world. "My bed's a king. There's *plenty* of room."

Laughing, I shake my head. "Dream on, my friend."

"Oh, I will." He winks at me, then heads down the bar.

Smithy's offer to share his bed is still less creepy than Taylor's offer to give me a discount on the rent, *"Since I can tell you're a sweet girl."* I shudder. I went back to Mom's and showered after that one, but even the hottest water wasn't enough to wipe the slime off.

I pull out my phone and nurse my drink as I scroll through social media. I want my girls to come join me and tell me everything's going to be all right, but Brinley and Marston are spending the night in Atlanta, Savvy has a date with someone who's not Alec, and Abbi said she'd be working late prepping food for tomorrow's wedding at The Orchid.

I sit, stew, and wish I was in the right mindset to drink my feelings, but I'm not. When I can't handle it anymore, I open Random and stare at Kace's profile picture. It's most likely because the messaging feature was never intended to be used extensively, but I wish they'd update it so I could see his picture and not just his username. I want to see his face when we chat.

After sitting on my hands all day, trying to resist the impulse to message him, I finally convince myself to stop being a coward. I've just sent, *Hey there, sexy, why so quiet?* when Smithy calls, "Kace!"

I instinctively jerk my head toward the entrance. Kace strolls toward me. He's rocking his lumberjack-hottie look today—jeans faded from wear and not a designer, and a Georgia Tech T-shirt that stretches snugly across his chest, shoulders, and biceps. His jaw is covered with his usual dark stubble, and his hair is wet and combed back from his face like he just took a shower. All in all, he's still the sexy motherfucker I've wanted since I was fifteen. Sexier, honestly. Fifteen-year-old me would've been totally unimpressed by the scruffy facial hair look, but twenty-seven-year-old me wants to climb him like a tree.

"Smith," Kace replies with a nod. He leans over the bar, and he and Smithy do a weird handshake-knuckle-bump combo. Guys are so lucky. They get to be weirdos and it's just cool, but it'd be laughable if two women greeted each other that way.

"Glad you're here," Smithy says. "Stella needs cheering up."

Seven days ago, I would've made a smart-ass comment about how Kace has never been interested in cheering me up, but the surprising reality is he's been the best part of my week.

But Kace frowns and turns to me like he's on the case. "Why? What's wrong?"

I shake my head and slide my phone back into my purse. "I'm fine. What brings you here?"

"Hope is with my mom, and I have a meeting. You didn't answer my question. Why do you need cheering up?" He's got that puffed-chest protective thing going on. As if he wants me to point him in the direction of the person who's responsible for my mood so he can take a swing at them.

"Roommate hunting is . . . challenging."

His eyebrows disappear into that sloppy mop of hair. "*Roommate* hunting? I thought you were moving into the pool house."

"Just thinking of the future and hoping I don't have to mooch off you for more than a month or so." I shake my head. This is too embarrassing. I'm a grown woman and should have my shit together enough that I can afford a place of my own. Alas, student loan debt is my nemesis, and who can afford inflated rent prices when their monthly budget includes paying the equivalent of a hefty mortgage on their liberal arts degree? "I've been meeting up with people all week, but nothing's worked out."

Kace's expression softens as he slides onto the stool next to me. He leans forward, and when he speaks, his voice is so low I can barely hear him. "I'm nervous about this too, okay? So if you're worried about what happens when this"—his gaze drops to my mouth—"when this thing between us ends? You're not alone. I'm kind of freaking out here."

He just tore off a chunk of my heart. He's worried what happens *when* it ends, and I'm worried that it'll end at all. And that right there tells me all I need to know about where I stand with Kace. Not that it should come as a surprise.

"But we're adults," he says, his warm eyes sweeping over my face. "We can figure this out."

"Is that why you haven't messaged me today?"

His eyes flick up to meet mine and go wide. "I . . ." He shakes his head. "You wanted me to message you?"

I snort. "Yeah. I kinda like your little notes." I lower my voice. "They tell me you're thinking about me."

He swallows and looks away. "I *am*. All the time. But Wednesday feels so far away, and I guess I thought texting might make it worse."

There are those mixed signals again. Except I know he's being honest. He plans on this ending, *and* he's thinking about me all the time. Which makes me, what? A fun diversion? I feel like I'm more than that when we message back and forth. Like he's open to us *becoming* more. "You make me crazy. You know that?"

The corner of his mouth hitches up in a crooked grin. "I've barely gotten started, Freckles."

A hot shiver rolls down my spine. "So many promises, so little follow-through."

"What are *you two* talking about?" Smithy asks, propping his elbows on the bar across from us and resting his chin on his hands.

"Sex," I answer, giving him my biggest smile. I feel more than see Kace stiffen beside me. And, okay, *somebody* isn't comfortable with our little fling becoming public information.

Smithy's eyes go wide. "Are you telling her about that girl you're talking to?" He turns his head in my direction and stage-whispers, "Take my advice. If you want him to clam up about her so he'll stop talking, suggest she's . . . *unattractive*."

I blink, trying to make sense of the thoughts scrambling my brain. I dismiss Smithy implying my competition isn't pretty—that's subjective, and really, what Smithy thinks is irrelevant. But it's the *other* part that gets me. Kace has told Smithy about the other woman he's seeing, yet he clearly doesn't want Smithy to know he's also kind of seeing me.

Someone down the bar calls for a drink, and Smithy straightens. "Duty calls."

When I turn to Kace, he's squeezing the back of his neck. "I'm not sure I'm cut out for this 'dating around' thing. It's brutal."

I jab my elbow into his side—*hard*.

"Ouch!" He scoots away from me and rubs his injury.

"You don't get to complain to the girl you're messing around with that it's so challenging to be seeing someone else at the same time. Dick move, Matthews."

He blows out a breath. "Sorry. It's just . . . it's really easy to talk to you."

That helps a little, and part of me wants him to talk. I have questions. *Is she nice? Would your mom like her? Have you texted* her *today? Do you tell her she should never lower her standards or that you can't stop thinking about her? What does she have that I don't?* "No. I don't think I want to know anything, actually."

"I'm not trying to be a jerk. I'm just trying to be honest."

"I know." I reach for my drink and take a sip. *I'm fine. This is fine. Everything's fine.*

He studies me for a long beat then pushes off his stool. "We were going to start painting at seven tomorrow— unless you have plans tonight and that's too early?"

I laugh. Right, because in Kace's mind, I spend every Friday night partying and every Saturday sleeping it off. "No plans."

He nods and points to the back of the bar, where my brother is scowling at a pool table. I've been lost in my pity party and didn't even notice he was there. "I've gotta go talk to Dean. We had our foreman convince a client to reconfigure her kitchen mid-install, and your brother's ready to fire him. I'd rather not lose one of my sharpest employees, so I need to smooth some feathers. I'll see you in the morning."

❦

DRINKING ALONE SUCKS, but I don't leave. Every once in a while, I look over my shoulder to check on Kace, but I must've missed him pulling out his phone, because I'm surprised when I have a notification about a new message from him.

> GoodHands69: Sorry. I've just been busy. I'm
> doing some big renovations on top of
> work and my daughter and . . . it's just
> been a busy week, and I guess I have a lot
> on my mind.

My cheeks heat. He's been extra busy because he's preparing the pool house for me, and instead of being grateful, I'm whining about him not messaging me.

> ItsyBitsy123: When you put it that way, I'm
> thinking I owe you. Want to find a dark
> closet somewhere so I can show you just
> how grateful I am?

I sneak a peek over my shoulder to see Kace staring at his phone, but instead of meeting my gaze or coming over, instead of showing me any of that dirty-talking man who had me against the wall this morning, his fingers teasing between my thighs, he stands and heads for the door. The ass doesn't say a word—just lifts his hand to wave goodbye, then leaves.

Am I supposed to follow him? Does he *want* me or not?

I wave at Smithy for my check, but before I even get my credit card out, my phone is flashing with a notification.

> GoodHands69: Maybe another time.

"Still sad?" Smithy asks, dragging my attention away

from those three words that feel way too much like a rejection.

I shrug. "I guess. Guys suck."

"Who made you sad?" Dean asks, taking the stool next to me. "Point me in his direction so I can kick his ass."

I almost laugh at the image, then immediately sober. Dean probably *would* kick Kace's ass—not for touching me or talking to me, but for leading me on. "Why do guys only treat girls good until the girl's on the hook? Do we suddenly become toxic once we're interested?"

Smithy props his elbows on the bar and leans forward, meeting my eyes. "Good guys," he says, "don't play games."

Dean nods. "Fuck anyone who doesn't know what he's getting with you, Stellabean."

My eyes prick with tears—maybe because my brother hasn't used that nickname in years, or maybe because it feels good to know both Smith and Dean mean what they say, or maybe just because Kace is one of the best guys I know, and if even *he* can't treat me right, why the hell am I even trying? I grab my drink and drain it. "Fuck him."

But then my phone buzzes, and I prove to myself and anyone paying attention that I don't mean that.

> GoodHands69: It's not that I'm not
> interested. The timing's just not right. If
> it feels like I'm stringing you on and you
> want to kick me to the curb, I wouldn't
> blame you.

I stare at my phone for a long time, then shake my head.

> ItsyBitsy123: I guess I'm a glutton for

punishment, because I'm not going
anywhere.

"Who are you texting?" Dean asks, grabbing for my
phone. "Is that the jerk who's practically making my sister
cry into her vodka?"

I quickly lock the screen and shove my phone into my
purse. "Nope. It's nothing. I'm fine."

He grunts. "You're not fine at all, but I won't push. I get
it. Sometimes we hang on to people even when they keep
knocking us down. Love's a bitch."

I frown. "Who's knocking you down? I didn't even know
you were seeing anyone."

He waves a hand as if to say, *likewise.* "We all have our
secrets, baby sister. But I'll be here if you ever need to talk
about yours."

"Same." I hesitate, not wanting to push, but . . . "*Do* you
want to talk about yours?"

Dean takes a long, slow pull from his beer then shakes
his head. "Nah. I'm good."

"The offer stands." I slide off the stool and kiss his
cheek. "Thanks. I'll see you in the morning." I turn to the
bar. "Bye, Smithy!"

Then I head out to my car and sit in the driver's seat,
staring at my phone.

Be careful with me, I type, *because I've been in love with you
since I was fifteen and I really want this to work.* Then I hold
down the backspace key, put my phone away, and drive
home.

CHAPTER FIFTEEN

KACE

*B*etween Dean, Smithy, Stella, and me, we managed to get the main room and loft of the pool house painted before lunch, and now Hope's roped Stella into making slime with her.

"Squeeeeeeeze," Stella says, grinning. She watches my daughter empty the bottle of glitter glue into the bowl where they're mixing their most recent creation. This is their third batch after making fluffy slime and unicorn slime, neither of which I'd heard of before. Stella has a smudge of baking soda on her nose and bits of dried glue all over her hands. Surprisingly, she doesn't seem to mind.

"Hurry! Get the shaving cream!" Hope says, practically bouncing in her chair.

Stella grabs the can of shaving cream and squirts it on top of the glue. "Tell me when."

"When! When!" Hope squeals.

Stella grabs a Popsicle stick and hands it to Hope. "You know the drill."

Hope uses all the strength in her tiny arms to stir the thick concoction. She groans and grunts, making a show of how hard it is, but my girl's on cloud nine. And Stella is . . . fuck, she's having a good time too, and I can't quite reconcile this version of her with the party girl who'd jump from one guy to the next, who'd lie and cheat to get her way to a promotion at work. I hadn't ever seen them together one on one before today. Usually, the only time Hope gets with Stella is when she's doing a sleepover at Brinley's or all our friends meet up for a cookout.

I knew my daughter loved her, but I never really understood why. Now it's obvious. Stella's really good with kids. Or, at least, really good with *my* kid, and that makes this thing between us way more fucking complicated. I can't let Hope know we're involved, or she might get attached to the idea of Stella being a fixture in our lives. Then, when Stella drops me for the next guy, which I figure will happen—it's just a matter of time—Hope will be crushed.

No, it's better not to put any ideas in her head at all. We have to be careful. The smartest thing would be to end things now before they go any further, but I'm feeling really fucking selfish because I don't want to. And it's not just about sex. If it were just about sex, I would've taken Itsy up on her offer last night when, in truth, I wasn't even tempted. I like talking to Itsy. We have the kind of honesty and connection I'd look for in a relationship, but Stella's the one I want in my bed. And the more time I spend with her, the more I think I'd like her out of it too—in my arms, in my home, in my life.

But I'm not sure what that would look like for us. Not

that it matters. Stella's not looking for more, and I'm not ready, either.

"Mommy!" Hope hops off her stool and runs across the kitchen, and I turn just as Amy sweeps Hope off the ground. What's she doing here? And why is it okay for her to roll into my house without knocking when she just gave me shit for doing the same at her house?

"Your hands are *messy*," Amy says, her eyes bright and smiling.

Hope giggles. "Me and Stella are making slime."

Amy's smile falls away as her gaze meets Stella's at the kitchen table.

"Wanna see?" Hope asks.

"Sure, baby." She carefully puts Hope down and follows her. She nods politely at each variety of slime, giving appropriate oohs and aahs when necessary, but her worried gaze keeps flicking back to Stella.

My ex-wife hates Stella Jacob. Hell, half the incriminating shit I know about Stella came from Amy. Stella worked as a receptionist at Amy's investment firm for a couple of years. Amy was never at a loss for stories featuring an irresponsible, unreliable, dishonest Stella. It made me really uncomfortable, hearing over and over again what Amy thought of her, and judging by the look on Amy's face right now, I'm about to hear more of it.

"Why don't you go get cleaned up so I can talk to Daddy alone for a minute?" Amy asks when Hope's done showing off her slime.

"Okay!" Hope grabs Stella's hand and leads her out of her chair. "Come with me, Stella. I'll show you my birthday list."

"Clean up first," Amy says.

"I'll show you *after* we clean up," Hope adds.

Stella looks back and forth between me, Amy, and Hope. "Actually, kiddo, I should get going. I need to study, but you can show me your list next time I'm over."

Amy's eyes go wide, then she turns her glare on me. "Next time?"

Stella rolls her shoulders back, and I have to resist the urge to pull her into my arms and tell her to ignore Amy's . . . what is this? *Jealousy?*

"Hope," I say, "what do you say to Stella?"

"Thank you for making slime with me today," Hope says. "I'm so happy you're going to live in the pool house!"

Amy flinches, but somehow manages to bite her tongue until Stella's out the door and Hope's upstairs washing her hands. Even then, all she gives me is a whisper. "I can't believe this is happening."

I sigh. "What brings you over, Amy?"

She folds her arms, and her eyes are full of indignant rage as they meet mine. "*Stella* brings me over. What the hell do you think you're doing?"

I arch a brow and lean back against the counter. She's ready to fight, but I'm not in the mood. "You'll have to be more specific."

"I was talking to Dean just now, and he mentioned you've all been busting your asses to remodel that pool house for Princess Party Girl. Really, Kace? You're moving another woman in with my daughter and didn't even think to consult me about it?"

"I'm not moving anyone *in* with Hope." I was going to talk to her about it next time we had a minute alone, but I haven't been real keen on spending time together since Wednesday's awkwardness. "Stella's going to rent out the pool house, which, as you've noticed, is an entirely separate structure."

"Are you fucking her?"

She didn't. I straighten, glad now more than ever that we sent Hope upstairs. "Excuse me?"

"You know she's been trying to get in your pants for years. She doesn't even try to hide it. When you move a slut into your backyard—"

"Don't call her that."

"—I have to wonder if it's because you're *fucking* her. Is driving across town too much of an inconvenience?"

"Enough." My jaw aches from clenching it. "You need to leave."

"And now you're picking her over me."

"I'm telling you to leave because you're throwing around insults about my *friend*." I lead the way to the door, and after a few steps, I hear Amy behind me.

"You know her history, Kace. She isn't a good person. Sex is a tool to her, and if she's fucking you, she wants something out of it." She snorts. "Probably a place to live, so it looks like you've already been played."

I don't stop until we're outside and Amy's pulled the front door shut behind her. Only when I'm sure Hope can't hear any part of this conversation do I finally look my ex-wife in the eye and call her on her shit. "Which is it, Amy? She's going to seduce me into giving her a place to stay, or she's wanted me forever? It can't be both, can it?"

"You can't trust her. I told you what she did at Allegiance." She fists her hands then releases them. "And there's more you don't know, too."

Amy told me Stella seduced the boss and then quit when she couldn't talk him into giving her a promotion. It was a bunch of hearsay and made my wife seem like the kind of gossip she's never been about any other woman. "What is it about Stella that makes you act like this?" I shake my head. "You didn't used to mind her at all, then suddenly, you couldn't stand her. For the last four years, you've gone out of your way to trash-talk her. Why?"

She opens her mouth then snaps it shut again. "I don't trust her and wish you wouldn't, either."

"Amy . . ." I blow out a long breath. "Are you worried I'm going to replace you with Stella?"

She studies her feet. "No."

"Do you think Hope is going to stop loving her mom just because Stella lives out back and can play with her occasionally?"

She shakes her head but still doesn't look at me.

"Listen . . ." I rub my neck. I don't know how much I want to tell her about what's going on with me and Stella. Is there any point when it won't last? Why upset Amy more than she already is? I look out at the road. A few cars roll by, and the neighbors across the street wave from their porch. I wave in return then laugh softly. "A few months ago, I would've relished seeing you act this jealous, and then it would've fucked me up for weeks while I waited for you to come home."

When she lifts her head, there are tears in her eyes. "I'm sorry. I never wanted to hurt you."

I swallow hard. "You did anyway, but I'm done waiting, Amy. And now I'm ready to . . ." I fold my arms. Just a few days of talking to Itsy, and I've completely shifted my position on what exactly I'm ready for. "I'm ready to try moving on. In whatever way feels right. I need to know if *you're* ready for me to move on, or if seeing me date other women is going to make you lash out like that again."

"Are you and Stella in a relationship?" She swallows. "Are you considering something serious with her?"

An image of Stella grinning at Hope flashes in my mind, and I shove it aside. Stella might be beautiful and fun, but what she and I have isn't about building a future. Our deal was a fling. Stella's looking for pleasure, mutual release, fun. "I have no plans to have a serious relationship with Stella, but that doesn't mean you can call her a slut or imply she's some sort of evil influence on our daughter. I won't let you treat her like that—whether she's my friend, my girlfriend, or my tenant."

Amy hugs herself tightly. "Okay. I'm sorry. I just panicked, and then I came here to talk about it and saw her with Hope and . . ." She tilts her face up toward the sky, and tears roll down her cheeks. "The thing about divorce is that even when you're the one who wants it, you're still giving up so much you'd rather keep."

Then why did you want it? I want to ask, but the question isn't the loud clanging in my mind that it used to be. Now it's less of a desperate cry and more of a curious whisper. I may never fully understand what happened in my marriage, but it's good to feel like I can finally let it go.

"So she's moving in?"

"Next weekend."

"Okay." She doesn't meet my eyes. "For how long?"

"I don't know." I shrug. "As long as she needs."

She nods a few times, as if she's forcing herself to accept this information. "I'm going to say bye to Hope, and then I'll get out of your hair."

I frown, thinking of the look on Stella's face when she

left. "Actually, can you hang out for a little bit? I think I need to go talk to Stella."

Amy holds my gaze, and the sadness in her eyes is undeniable. "Yeah. I can do that."

ૐ

STELLA

I might be older and more mature than I was in high school, but I still hate chemistry. I've read the first page of this chapter three times, but nothing is sticking.

I saw the look on Amy's face when Hope mentioned me living in the pool house. I know it's just a matter of time before Kace tells me I'm no longer welcome. I'm trying to be positive, to tell myself I'll find something, that this is better anyway, but what I'm feeling right now isn't really about where I'll be living. It's about the way Kace looks at me and the fact that Amy has the power to make him pull away from me completely. She wouldn't, would she? Not when I've kept *her* secret.

The doubt gnaws at my concentration, so I sit in my mom's living room, staring at the chemistry equation, and wait for the guy I've loved half my life to break things off or to ask me to find somewhere else to live or both.

The best part of my day was making slime with Hope. She smiled, giggled, and thanked me a hundred times. Every once in a while, I'd catch Kace watching me, some unidentifiable emotion twisting his face. It made me appreciate Hope that much more. At least an almost-five-year-old will tell you what she's thinking.

A knock sounds at the front door, and Rusty jumps off

179

the couch and rushes to greet our visitor with a wagging tail. I follow reluctantly, but Kace lets himself in before I get far.

He stoops to his haunches to scratch the dog behind the ears. "Hey, buddy. Are you hanging out with Stella? Are you the luckiest boy?"

Rusty responds by licking Kace's face.

Kace chuckles and gives the dog one final butt pat. Standing, he studies my face, worry creasing his. "I'm sorry about earlier."

"It's not your fault." I shrug. Like it's no big deal. Like Amy's hatred doesn't bother me at all. In truth, I want to scream that *she's* the one who did something wrong. It's not fair that she treats me like I'm toxic when my only crimes were being a naïve college student and knowing her secret.

"Amy is . . ." He shakes his head. "Can I come in? I'd like to sit and talk this out."

By all means, let's get comfortable before you break my heart. I wave my arms toward the living room. "After you."

Kace takes in my chemistry book waiting on the couch and lowers himself into the love seat. "First of all, the pool house is yours if you want it. That hasn't changed."

I brace myself, waiting for the other shoe to drop. "I'm shocked Amy's on board with that plan."

He sighs. "She's not a huge fan, but it's not her choice." He waves to the couch. "Will you sit before I pull you onto my lap and forget why I'm here?"

Oh. I bite my lip. Giddy relief bubbles through my veins. "What if I'd rather be on your lap?"

The corner of his mouth hitches into a smile. "We both know there won't be much talking if I get my hands on you."

"Huh. I recall you doing *quite a bit* of talking every time your hands have been on me, actually."

"That's it." He wraps his arms around me and sweeps me off my feet. I squeal and wiggle as he settles me onto his lap. He studies me, then his smile falls away. "You do something to me," he whispers. "I cannot stop thinking about you."

There's a balloon in my chest growing fuller and fuller. "I think about you all the time too."

His gaze drops to my mouth. "If I start kissing you now, I'm not going to want to stop."

I thread my fingers through his hair, toying with the ends of it. "We're on my mom's couch."

"I know."

I hold on to his shoulders and shift on his lap until I'm straddling him, and we're face to face. "What did Amy say about me taking the pool house?"

He groans. "I'd rather talk about the things I could do to you right here."

"That could be fun, but then I'd need a demonstration, and that's pretty risky if we don't want Mom knowing about this." It's a veiled question, and I regret it the minute it slips out. *Am I your dirty little secret?*

He cuts his eyes toward the dark hallway that leads to her bedroom. "She's here?"

"Not at the moment, but she has the day off work. I don't know when she'll be back."

"Shame." His gaze dips to my mouth for a beat, then drops to sweep over my breasts. I swear, a visual perusal by Kace is better than the touch of any guy I've ever been with. My skin tingles. "Then again, this couch isn't nearly big enough for me to do all the things I've been thinking about."

God, I want to kiss him. Instead, I lean my forehead against his. "You're avoiding the question."

His hands slide down my back. "Hmm?"

"Amy?"

He closes his eyes. "Right. She's not happy, but she'll get over it. I just wanted to apologize for the way she acted today." When his eyes open again, he frowns. "Did something happen between you two?"

I stiffen. "I just rub her the wrong way, I guess."

"I get that you've made some mistakes, but . . . she's irrational when it comes to you."

Mistakes. Of course I've made some, maybe more than my share, but I hate feeling like those mistakes define me with Kace. Especially when he doesn't even know the worst of it.

He pulls a face. "I've never understood why she dislikes you so much."

I grunt. "*Dislike* is such a nice word. Amy *hates* me."

"Why?"

The image of her pressed against the elevator wall with my boss's hand up her skirt flashes in my mind. But I shrug. "Vinegar and oil?"

He shakes his head. "I know you made a bad impression on her when you had an affair with Clint, but—"

I shove myself back and hop off his lap. "What?"

He flinches. "Shit. I probably wasn't supposed to know that."

"She told you that?"

Slowly, he pushes up off the couch. "I'm sorry. It's not my business, but she'd vent at the end of the day and—"

"Kace." I take his hands and look into his eyes. "I did *not* have an affair with that man."

He shrugs. "Okay, then Amy misunderstood. I don't want to get in the middle of that."

"I left Allegiance because Clint wouldn't stop coming on to me. He was an entitled creep, and he thought that because he signed my paycheck, I shouldn't object when he put his hand up my skirt in the break room. I didn't feel safe after that, so I left."

"Did you report it to HR? That's not okay, Stella. There are laws—"

"There are laws that allow women to fight against this shit only when we can afford a drawn-out court battle that'll flash the worst pieces of our past in front of the world." I shake my head. I couldn't risk that, and I made my peace with my decision long ago. While I'd like Kace to understand, I have no regrets. But the idea that Amy told Kace I had that affair? That she painted me as the one guilty of her transgressions? "There *were* employees who had affairs with him. Employees who played the *quid pro quo* game, reluctantly or happily—it wasn't my place to judge their decisions."

"Then she mistook someone else for you."

Or maybe she wanted to discredit me. "What else did Amy tell you about me?"

"I don't want to do this, Stella. I don't know why she thought that, but I need you to understand I have to have a good relationship with my wife."

Ex-wife. Say she's your ex-wife. The words are on the tip of my tongue, but I swallow them back.

"It matters to me that there's not anger and resentment between us. Don't make me get in the middle of this."

"She *lied* about me, Kace."

"Maybe she saw or heard something and misinterpreted it."

Like I "misinterpreted" Clint's hand up her skirt at that conference? "Like what?"

"You spending lunch hours in his office. You two leaving together." He turns his palms up. "Does it matter?"

"Yes!" My eyes burn. Fuck. It's one thing to make me carry around this secret, one thing to blackmail me with my own mistakes so I wouldn't share it with Kace, but to know she was planting lies about me at the same time? I could scream. "I never took lunch in his office, never left with him." But she did. She *really* did. "The only time that man ever touched me was the day I quit. If she'd walked into the break room when he put his hand up my skirt, she would've seen me jerk away and tell him not to touch me again. If she overheard us talking alone in his office that afternoon, she would've heard him offer me a promotion and fat raise for, and I quote, 'just a little time on my knees.'" My face is so hot and my eyes are burning, but fuck it, I'm not going to cry about that asshole.

"Stella . . ." He shakes his head, but fury lights his eyes, just like it did that night I was out with Jared. "Fuck." He drags a hand through his hair. "Now I wish he still worked there so I could go give him a piece of my mind."

"I took care of it in the only way I could, Kace. I got the fuck out of there."

He studies me for a long, quiet moment. "I'm sorry I believed everything Amy said to me."

The front door groans as it opens. "Stella?" Dean calls. "Is that Kace's truck out front?"

Kace's eyes go wide, and he stands. "It is," he says as Dean enters the room.

Dean grins. "What are you doing here?"

Kace shoves his hands into his pockets and shrugs, looking as nervous as if we'd just been caught doing something way more scandalous than talking. "Um . . ."

I'm definitely still his dirty secret. "Amy freaked out about me moving into the pool house," I say, coming to his rescue, "and Kace came over to apologize for how she acted."

Dean shakes his head and looks at the ceiling. "What's her deal with you?"

Can we please stop talking about this? I sweep my books and notes off the couch and clutch them to my chest. "I need to go study." Then I take slow and deliberate steps toward my bedroom, trying to hide that I'm running away.

CHAPTER SIXTEEN

STELLA

*K*ace left not long after I escaped to my bedroom, and I didn't message him all afternoon or evening. I'm trying not to be clingy, and I recognize my impulse to need extra attention when I'm feeling insecure. But I've checked my phone no fewer than five hundred times just to make sure I haven't missed a message from him. At nine, when I know he's had a chance to get Hope in bed and decompress for a bit, I finally message him. I open Random, since that's the place he seems to open up to me the most.

ItsyBitsy123: You up for chatting?

His reply comes almost immediately.

GoodHands69: I can for a bit. How was
    your day?
ItsyBitsy123: Okay, I guess. My eyes are
    crossing from studying for so long.
GoodHands69: What are you going to
    school for?

I frown. Haven't I told Kace I'm going back to be a
nurse? Or maybe he just knows I'm going to school but
doesn't know what for. I don't remember what I told him,
and I actually wish I hadn't told so many people I was going
for nursing. It's going to be that much more embarrassing
when I can't get into the program.

ItsyBitsy123: The plan was nursing, but I'm
    not sure now.

I quickly type another message, wanting to change the
subject.

ItsyBitsy123: What'd you do this afternoon?
GoodHands69: Hope and I went to our
    favorite trail with a picnic dinner. She
    can't go far yet, but she loves hiking. I
    think her favorite part is stomping in the
    creek and finding the perfect rock (she
    always wants to bring them home, but we
    follow the rules—take nothing but
    pictures, leave nothing but footprints, etc,
    etc).
She fell asleep in the car on the way home, and

then bath, snuggles, and story time filled the
rest of the night. It was a good day. Damn
near perfect, and one thing I've learned in
the past year is that the most perfect days
are the ones we make for ourselves. I've
been pretty good about making memories
with my daughter, but I'm realizing I haven't
made much of an effort in my personal life
outside of that. Which... makes me want
to talk to you about this other girl I've been
seeing, but I've been told that's rude.

I cringe and laugh at the same time.

> ItsyBitsy123: Damn right it is. I seriously
> don't want to know about her.
> GoodHands69: Got it.
> ItsyBitsy123: I hope that doesn't sound bitchy.
> I just know I'll make myself crazy
> wondering if she's better than me.

I chew on my bottom lip while I wait for him to reply.
I'm flirting with the edge of revealing too much about my
feelings for him, and I don't want to scare him off.

> GoodHands69: I'd never compare. But I can
> say I've really enjoyed talking with you.
> It's been good for me.

My heart feels too full.

> ItsyBitsy123: I like that we've connected in a

deeper way on here.

GoodHands69: Me too, but . . . fuck, if you
had any idea how many times I've typed
something about the other woman I'm
seeing and then deleted it, you'd think I
was a complete ass. I will refrain. I
promise.

I stare at the screen, trying to convince myself to ask
about her, to tell him we can talk about anything. But I'm
already racing my way to a broken heart, and I don't want to
make the inevitable crash any more painful.

He ends up messaging again before I can figure out
what to say.

GoodHands69: You ever get lonely? Not like
bored-and-want-company lonely, but that
bone-deep need for connection?

GoodHands69: Fuck. I feel guilty even
saying it. My life is good. My friends are
awesome. But I always imagined my
days would include a partner who'd see
me on a deeper level. Someone who'd
keep the loneliness at bay. If I'm
honest, I hadn't even felt that with my
wife in a long time. If I'm honest,
maybe I just WANTED to feel it with
her and was willing to pretend things
were better than they were. I'm not
sure why I'm dumping this on you
tonight—except for the obvious. I'm
lonely. And I'm starting to think that

maybe my ex was never going to be the
one to fix that.

My heart aches as I reread Kace's words. This strong,
steadfast man is lonely, and if anyone deserves the kind of
connection he's talking about, it's him. And maybe he isn't
looking for that connection from me, but . . . maybe I can
chase away the loneliness for the little time we do spend
together. Without thinking too much, I slide on a pair of
flip-flops and grab my keys.

❦

WHEN I PARK at Kace's house, the lights are on in the
backyard, so I go straight to the gate. He's out at the pool,
sitting on the patio and staring at his laptop, a baby
monitor humming from the side. On the other side of the
water, a small fire snaps at the night air.

I hesitate right inside the gate, suddenly unsure if
inviting myself over to heal his loneliness was the best plan.

Drawing in a deep breath for courage, I wander toward
him. I was already in my pajamas when we started messaging, and I didn't bother changing. My shirt is light pink and
says, "Zzzs for Dayz," and the tiny matching shorts are
barely visible beneath it.

When Kace catches sight of me, his eyes go wide, then a
grin slowly stretches across his face. He closes his laptop
without taking his eyes off me. "Hey, you."

I pull out the chair next to him and plop myself into it.
"Hey."

"I thought you'd be out tonight," he says, searching my
face. "It's Saturday."

I laugh and fold my legs under me. "I love that you think I'm hitting up the clubs every weekend, but it's more a rare treat than a regular hobby." I shrug. "And anyway, I'd rather be here with you. If you don't mind an uninvited visitor, that is."

"Not at all." He glances at the baby monitor, still humming softly. "Hope's sleeping, but we could . . ." He waves to the pool, which is open, the underwater lights making the water glow blue. "I don't get in without Hope very often. It might be nice."

"I didn't bring a suit."

His eyes light up before flicking over me. "That's a shame. I guess you'll have to swim naked."

My stomach flutters. If I get naked in that pool with him tonight, I know exactly what's going to happen, and nervousness sizzles in my blood. About letting him see me entirely naked. About crossing that final line with him. But I muster all my bravado, stand, and wiggle out of my sleep shorts.

Kace watches my every move as I drop them into my chair. I reach for the hem of my shirt, and his nostrils flare. His eyes glued to me, I slowly pull it off over my head and drop it with my shorts. My nipples pucker in the cool evening air. Kace stares at me and swallows. I'm frozen in place but melting under the heat of his gaze. "Stella, you're perfect."

He pushes out of his chair, but before he can reach for me, I jog away, tossing him a smile over my shoulder. I climb onto the diving board, run to the end, and swan-dive into the pool.

The water's warm after so many hot Georgia days, and when I surface, the night air feels cool on my face.

Kace stands at the edge of the pool, barefoot, arms folded, smiling down at me.

I look him over, staring meaningfully at his jeans and T-shirt. "You gonna take those off so you can join me?"

He licks his lips and shrugs. "I don't know. The view from here is damn sweet."

My cheeks heat, but I splash him.

With a soft chuckle, he shakes his head, and a second later, he's removing his shirt with one rough tug then peeling his boxers and jeans from his hips. He steps out of them and right into the pool. When he resurfaces, he treads water and tips his head up to the clear night sky.

"What are you thinking about?" I ask, treading water and inching closer.

Sighing, he shakes his head. "I'm just . . . Nothing."

"Liar," I whisper.

He swallows. "I think too much, honestly. I get so damn busy thinking that I miss out on good stuff that's within arm's reach." His gaze drops to my lips, and my breath catches. "I want you so much that I hardly know what to do."

I close the distance between us with two easy strokes and loop my arms behind his neck, pressing my naked breasts to his hard, bare chest. "You could try kissing me and see what happens then."

The corner of his mouth hitches into a crooked grin as he slowly lowers his mouth to mine. Every second I wait for our lips to meet, my heart beats faster. Then he's there, and we both sigh into the kiss, as if we've been holding our breath all day and we're finally able to breathe normally again.

He spins me and pins me between his body and the wall

of the pool, caging me in with his arms. When he breaks the kiss, his eyes peruse my face, my lips, then dip down to my collarbone and the swell of my breasts. "Still thirsty?" His lips quirk into a lopsided smile.

"Only when you look at me like that." I wrap my legs around his waist and draw in a sharp breath at the hard length of him against my center. Flesh to flesh. The air crackles between us—a blend of electric pulse and magnetic pull that has me leaning into him, silently urging his lips to connect with mine.

"How am I looking at you?" he asks, but his hands answer the question, squeezing my butt before his fingers trace the path up my spine.

I shiver. "Like you want me in your bed."

He lowers his mouth until he's a breath away, and it takes everything in me not to close that distance. I'm starved for his touch. "I think you're misreading me."

I roll my hips slightly to rub against him. "Really?"

"I want you right here," he says. His hands slide around to cup my ass, and he kisses me. He curls his fingers into my flesh and holds me until we're fully flush. The slightest shift from either of us, and he could slide inside me. His lips tease and part, his teeth nipping and tugging. He sucks on my bottom lip, and I whimper. Slanting his mouth over mine, he kisses me fully, his tongue rubbing against mine. I thread my fingers into his hair and melt into this kiss. This moment.

I love the feel of his hard chest cradling me, the way the water moves around us as our bodies rock together, the cool night air on my skin, and the crackling fire in the background.

He kisses his way along my jaw to my neck. "Do you

know how fucking sexy you are? Do you have any idea how many times I've thought about doing this? How many times we've been surrounded by our friends and family, and I couldn't think about anything but tasting you?"

I tip my head back as his mouth skims across my collarbone. He lifts me, propping me higher on the wall and exposing my breasts to the cool air. I open my eyes in time to see his go darker. He lowers his head and flicks his tongue across the hardened pearl of my nipple, and I have to bite my lip to keep from crying out. His mouth is hot on my breast. He teases with the tip of his tongue then sucks until it almost hurts and pleasure ignites my blood. He sucks and licks and bites my breasts, and need floods low in my belly, an ache building between my legs. I want deeper and faster, but I also want time to slow down so I can relish each touch.

"Kace." I gasp as his teeth sting. "God, I need . . ." I don't even know how to finish that. I need him, and this, and more, and promises I can't ask for.

"Shh," he whispers, flicking his tongue to soothe the spot he just bit. "I'll get you there, Freckles. I promise." He kisses his way back up my neck. "It's like you read my mind tonight. I was sitting out here thinking about right after I bought this place, and you and the girls came to check it out."

He licks the column of my neck, and I tangle my hands in his hair and lean my head to the side to give him better access.

"Do you remember that night?" He pulls back and studies me.

"Before you moved in?"

"Yeah."

He'd shown us all around, and then, when everyone was chilling with beers in the empty living room, I'd wandered out to the pool to get some air. The guy of my dreams was divorced and moving on with his life, and it was all I could do to maintain a modicum of dignity and not beg him to see me, to give me a chance. "You found me out here. With my feet in the water."

"Yeah. You looked so beautiful in the moonlight, and I had this image of having you in the pool." His hand skims down my side, then to my ass, where he squeezes. "Like this."

He wanted me even then. My heart squeezes with the realization, and I tug on his hair and bring his mouth to mine, kissing him with all the longing I've been trapping inside me for years. All the hope I feel at learning he wants this too.

He wraps his arms around me. We kiss, and he carries me into the shallow end to the steps, holding me tighter as we emerge into the cool air. His kisses are like a drug that make me want more and more until I don't remember where I am or what I'm supposed to be doing. I'm intoxicated and barely aware of anything but his mouth.

He guides me onto the top step, and when he releases me and steps back, my body is too cold everywhere he'd been pressed before.

"Do you have a condom?" I whisper. I want him completely, and the building ache between my legs is making me impatient.

"I don't need one," he says. He skims one finger down between my breasts and over my stomach.

My back arches, and I'm not sure if I'm going to melt or combust or both, so I have to hold myself up, bracing my hands behind me. How can one simple touch make me feel so much? "You're sure?"

He sinks to his knees a few steps down, smiling as he places both hands on my knees and spreads my thighs. "I have everything I need right in front of me," he murmurs, sliding his hands up my inner thighs. Lowering his head, he kisses just below my navel, then lower, just above my aching and exposed sex. "Let me kiss you here?"

Melting. I'm definitely melting. "Yeah," I manage, but it sounds like a desperate gasp.

It must be all the answer Kace needs, because he nudges my thighs wider and buries his face between them. He doesn't even kiss at first. It's more like a nuzzle—his lips barely brushing that sensitive bundle of nerves, his beard scraping my thighs.

He draws back just enough to look at me and whispers, "I thought of you like this that night. And I imagined what it'd be like to taste you here." Then his mouth and tongue and lips are everywhere. Licking and sucking and stoking a fire I didn't think could burn any hotter. He slides one hand up to palm my breast, and the other goes between my legs, one finger plunging inside me as he latches his lips around my clit.

I cry out, the sound echoing into the night, and he moves his finger inside me, in and out, before adding a second and—

I combust. My hips buck up and I'm undone, fucking his hand, writhing against his mouth, and his low grunt of approval is the final push over the edge.

He stays right where he is, coaxing every last wave of my orgasm over and through me until I'm wrung out. Only then does he crawl up my body, wrap his arms around my waist, and swing us both around so I'm sitting sideways in his lap. He's hard, and it takes all my self-control not to straddle him and take him inside me.

He kisses me, and I taste myself on his lips, and when he pulls back there's heat and something more in his eyes. "I'm so glad you came over," he whispers, cupping my jaw.

"Me too." And I am, but I'm also worried it was a mistake. How can I be so satisfied and happy yet discontent at the same time?

"I'll go get you a towel."

My eyes widen, and my lips part. "You're ready for me to leave?" I try not to sound defensive, but the hurt comes out in the sharp edge to my voice.

"Hell no." He pulls me tight against him, and his erection presses into my stomach. "I'm ready to take you to my bed."

CHAPTER SEVENTEEN

KACE

I grab a couple of towels from my stash on the patio and wrap one around my waist before taking the other to Stella. Water rolls down her curves in rivulets as she steps from the pool.

Kace, meet your walking fantasy.

If she wasn't shivering, I'd probably take a few minutes just to appreciate how fucking hot she is. Instead, I pretend I'm a gentleman and wrap the oversized pool towel around her shoulders.

"Thanks," she whispers, clutching it closed and smiling.

I drop a kiss on her forehead. "Anytime." Her lips tremble as she stares up at me, and I rub my hands over her towel-covered arms. "Are you okay? It's not that cold, is it?"

"I'm nervous." She laughs softly. "Go figure."

Emotion swells in my chest, and I swallow hard. I'm nervous too. About what we're about to do, about what happens after, about how I'm ever supposed to keep this casual when I can't stop thinking about her. "We don't have to do this if you're not—"

She lifts onto her toes and presses her mouth to mine, cutting me off. "I want to," she says against my lips. "I'm nervous because I want it so much."

I nod and take one of her hands to lead her inside. I never intended to have Stella in my room while my daughter was upstairs, but I can't wait until Wednesday, and Hope's a good sleeper. She'll never even know Stella was here. Even so, when we step into the bedroom, I shut the door behind us and lock it just in case. Then I pull Stella against me, her back to my front. She melts into me and releases her grip on the towel. I shift so it falls to the floor then slide my hands down her body, across her belly, and between her legs, where she's still slick.

She spins in my arms and runs her palms over my chest. "My turn," she whispers. She yanks at the knot in my towel, and it falls away, and then she's wrapping her fingers around my cock and stroking, her gaze locked on my dick as she works me over.

"Careful," I murmur. "Do that too much, and this'll be over before we begin."

Her eyes flash up to mine. "Yeah?" She smiles but doesn't stop stroking.

"I was already so close in the pool." I jack up into her fist. *Fuck. So good.* "The taste of you on my lips and the feel of your body clenching around my fingers when you came against my mouth? So fucking hot, Stella. I was a few seconds away from embarrassing myself."

She circles her thumb around the slickness gathering at my tip. "You want to finish like this? I don't mind."

I cup her face in both hands and kiss her hard. "On the bed, woman."

She leans toward me, chasing my mouth. "Bossy. I like it." But she doesn't move, and her hand doesn't stop stroking.

I smack her ass, and she squeaks. "You like that too?"

Her green eyes are dark and full of mischief when she looks up at me. "I like making you come. I've thought about it a lot this week."

"Not as much as me." I take her hand from my cock before lowering my head so my mouth is right by her ear. "But the next time either one of us comes, I'm gonna be buried so deeply inside you you'll have to bite your lip to keep from screaming my name. Got it?"

She moans and sways toward me. She kisses my shoulder then backs up to the bed, holding my gaze as she lowers herself.

I walk to the bedside table and grab the box of condoms. She turns to her side and reaches for me, but I dodge with a sidestep, smirking. "Hands on the headboard, naughty girl."

She licks her lips and obeys, moving to her back and gripping the rails of the headboard but never taking her eyes off me. I tear open a condom and roll it onto my shaft. When I climb onto the bed and over her, she whispers, "I need you."

I hook her knee with my elbow, spreading her wide as I settle between her thighs. "I know. I need you too." And the words resonate through me in a way I don't want to analyze right now. So I kiss her softly and slowly slide inside. I tear my mouth from hers because I have to see her face. Her green eyes open and meet mine, and an electric connection snaps between us.

She gasps, eyes fluttering, and drags her bottom lip between her teeth.

I smile down at her. "You feel good. So fucking good. Can you hold on there? I need you to come before I do, but I won't last long if those hands of yours are all over me."

She nods, and, fuck, she looks as vulnerable as I feel right now.

I draw up onto my knees so I can drive deeper and get a better view of this stunning woman beneath me. I shake my head. "So fucking beautiful."

And I'm close. Too fast, and this is going to be over way before I want it to be, so I slide a hand between our bodies and circle her clit with my thumb.

She arches off the bed, knuckles going white as she grips the headboard like it's the only thing keeping her tethered to Earth. I stroke her faster and pump my hips harder. She's close too, and with every thrust she makes more and more quiet sounds—moans she's trapping in her throat and biting back. Then, with one measured press of my thumb against her clit, she comes, pulsing around me so hard that I lose it. I grip her hips in both hands and watch her tits bounce as I slam into her again and again, chasing my own release. When it hits, it about knocks me over—pleasure so intense it whips like lightning down my spine and obliterates me from the inside out.

I collapse forward, and she releases the headboard and strokes my back. She wraps her legs around my waist and holds me close. I'm shaking. Because it was that fucking good. Because it means so damn much to me that she's here and this finally happened with her. And because I don't want her to leave.

And that thought scares the hell out of me.

❧

STELLA

I know I should leave and go back to my mom's. If this is just sex, just a fling, then this isn't the time for cuddling. But he's warm and solid, and I feel so safe curled into him.

Kace sighs, then rolls to his side and looks me in the eye. "You okay?"

I have to laugh. "Yes, Mr. Orgasms. I'm more than okay."

He grins. "Mr. Orgasms?"

"Anyone who makes me come so hard twice in one night should get a superhero nickname for it."

His eyes dance with amusement, and he runs the back of his hand over my cheek. "I like making you come. It kind of makes me feel superhuman." It should be a joke, and maybe he meant it that way, but there's something like grief in his eyes.

"Why do you seem sad, then?"

He hesitates a beat. "I haven't been with anyone since Amy."

He's told me that, and yet being here with this amazing man, knowing I'm the one he decided to change that with —it's humbling. "You waited because you thought she'd come home." It's not a question—I get it—but he shakes his head.

"I wanted her to come home, but that's not the real

202

reason I didn't get involved with anyone *physically*." He sighs. "The truth is in the last couple years of my marriage, we had sex twice—once on my birthday and once on an anniversary. Both times were . . ." He rolls to his back and stares at the ceiling. I snuggle closer to his side and put a hand on his chest, listening if he wants to say more, but not pushing for it. "Those two times, I learned sex can be lonely. It was as if she was checking a box—something she felt like she needed to do. And let me tell you, getting pity-fucked by your own wife is a hundred times worse than celibacy. It's lonely and soul-sucking."

"I'm sorry." I press my palm to his heart, feeling the steady beat there, the strength of it. "It wasn't you, Kace."

He shrugs. "Maybe it was, maybe it wasn't. That doesn't change the way it fucks with your head. I had a business meeting in Atlanta a couple of months after Amy moved out. A woman picked me up in the bar, and we went back to her room. I *wanted* to have sex with her, but as soon as we were naked and in bed, my brain latched on to those last couple of times with Amy and . . ." He winces. "It was a no-go."

"Ouch." I press a kiss to his shoulder. "I'm sure that happens a lot."

He snorts. "Yeah, maybe, but . . ." He grabs my hand, brings it to his mouth, and presses a hard kiss against my knuckles. "None of that's in my head when I touch you. You make me so crazy, make me feel so damn good. There's no room for it." He cups the back of my neck in one big hand, then rolls us over so he's on top of me. I draw up my knees, letting him settle between my legs. He's hard again, but there's nothing sexual about this position right now. He frames my face with his palms and looks into my eyes. "I don't ever want to get out of this bed."

I hook my feet behind his back, wrap my arms around him, and pull him closer. "Then don't."

He smiles against my mouth and kisses me. Kace's kisses are the stuff of legend—the sweep of his mouth, followed by parted lips and low groans as he touches his tongue to mine. I've never had a single kiss with him feel like he was going through the motions and trying to get something better. Kace kisses like a god because he *loves* kissing. I could get used to this.

He buries his hands in my hair and slants his mouth over mine. "I wish I didn't have to wait until Wednesday to have you under me again," he murmurs against my lips. "But I don't want to make a habit of sneaking you in and out of my house while Hope's here."

I'm not sure what to think about that, so I try not to think too much about it at all.

He kisses his way to my neck, and his beard tickles my neck as he suddenly chuckles.

"What?" I ask. He laughs harder, and I poke his side. "What are you laughing about?"

He lifts up, bracing a hand on either side of my head, and smiles down at me. "Amy accused me of moving you into my backyard because driving across town to fuck you was too inconvenient."

I flinch. "Wow."

He hangs his head and laughs again. "I was thinking about how I can't wait until you're that close all the time, and I realized just now that maybe she's a little right."

I pinch his arm. "Excuse me?"

"Should I apologize about this? Do you hate that I can't

wait to get you moved in so I can touch you?" He sweeps his lips over mine. "Kiss you?" He dips his head and flicks his tongue over my peaked nipple. "Taste you?"

"I'm not your fuck toy, Kace." I mean the words to come out teasing, but they reveal way too much of what I'm feeling, and he frowns at me. I swallow. "I mean, even flings should have some . . . substance." I practically choke on the word, remembering what he said about the other woman he's seeing—*physical attraction, no substance.* It might destroy me if he ever said that about me.

"I don't think of you as a toy." He presses a kiss to my solar plexus and then shifts down the bed to press another on my stomach. "I think of you as the sexiest woman I've ever met." He kisses just below my navel. "If you were a toy, I wouldn't be so obsessed with making you come."

He licks my clit gently, as if he knows I'm a little tender from the pool and the sex. "If you were just a toy," he says, looking up at me from between my legs, "I wouldn't be so tempted to keep you here all night."

I'm not sure that's true, but his mouth is toying with me again, and I can't puzzle out anything more complicated than biting back my moans of pleasure.

CHAPTER EIGHTEEN

STELLA

*W*hen I leave The Orchid after the evening shift on Wednesday, I'm so excited to get to Kace's house that I practically race to my car.

He's texted me a few times this week, but we seem to have abandoned Random, which is for the best, since the long heart-to-hearts with Kace are impossible to resist.

I really needed to put some extra time in with my chem study group. I scored a sixty-five percent on the first test, and the only way I can get a B or better in this class is if I get a ninety or higher on everything from here on out. In truth, the nursing program is so competitive that I'm not even guaranteed a spot with a B.

I've earned this night with Kace, though, and I can't wait to see his face when he strips me out of this dress and sees the black lace underwear I bought for the sole purpose of making him drool.

But all thoughts of seduction flee from my mind when I see my brother waiting for me at my car. My first sign that something's wrong is that he's here at all. The second is that he looks upset. He's a happy-go-lucky guy who doesn't get rattled easily, and who rarely shares his troubles the rare times he has them.

"Is Mom okay?" I ask, practically running to his side.

He blinks at me. "What? Yeah. Why?"

I wave a hand in front of him. "I don't think you've ever surprised me after work. Or school. Or . . . anything. What's going on?"

He swallows. "I need to talk."

My stomach knots. Does he know about my thing with Kace? Did Kace decide to tell him? I can't imagine he'd do that without warning me first. Maybe Dean figured it out on his own. "Okay. Wanna go to Smithy's?"

He shakes his head. "Nah. I don't want to talk about this in public."

The knots tighten. "Okay. You're making me nervous," I whisper.

He grunts. "You think *you're* nervous? Fuck, I can hardly sleep."

Okay, that's . . . dramatic. "Why?"

He shakes his head. "Not here." Turning, he opens the driver's-side door for me, then jogs around to the passenger side.

"You're not driving?" I ask, climbing in. Because there's red flag number three. Dean *hates* riding with me. Since I was sixteen, anytime we've gone somewhere together in the same car, he's insisted on being the one behind the wheel. The only exceptions are when— "Are you drunk?"

Dean leans his head back and closes his eyes. "Li'l bit."

I look at the clock, just to make sure I'm not confused. "You're drunk. At eight on a Wednesday?"

"Yup." He doesn't open his eyes. "Drive, please?"

Sighing, I start the car and drive to his newly remodeled craftsman home. I've barely stopped the car when Dean throws open his door and vomits in the grass. *Nice.*

Drawing in a deep breath for patience, I turn off the engine and walk around to his side to pat his back. "Tell me what's going on, Deanie."

Red flag four: he doesn't object to my childhood nickname for him. "I fucked up," he says. "I fucked up so bad."

I help him out of the car and put my arm around him. We walk into his house, side by side. I lead him to the kitchen, where he immediately collapses onto a chair while I get him a glass of water and pop bread in the toaster.

When I clunk the glass down in front of him, he hangs his head like a chastened child. *What did you do, Dean?* "I'm listening," I say softly.

"She broke up with me."

Am I the worst, most self-involved sister in the history of the world? He told me at the bar that he's been seeing someone, but I haven't thought about it since. "Who?"

He swallows. "I've always had feelings for her." He holds up a hand, as if I'm going to object when I don't even know who he's talking about. "I never *wanted* to. It was just there. And I didn't want this thing to be a secret, either. I understood why she didn't want to tell him. I didn't like it, but I understood."

"Who?" I have a sinking feeling I already know. *Damn it, Dean. You know better.*

"Then last week, Kace fucking *walked in* on us."

"You were the one Amy was with when Kace walked in on her?"

"Yes, and we were almost caught, so I was pushing for her to let me just tell him already, and I don't know, maybe I should've backed down, but he's gonna find out eventually." He groans and tugs at his dark hair. "Then she broke up with me."

"She dumped you today." It's not a question. This explains why my brother's trashed on a Wednesday evening.

He squeezes his eyes shut. "I didn't mean to fall in love with her. It was supposed to be a one-time thing. But we were drunk and it just sort of *happened,* and then—" His words are slurred and he looks so fragile, like he'll break if I say the wrong thing. "Before you judge me, you've gotta understand that when she and Kace were a couple, she became this extension of my best friend. You should judge me if I *didn't* care about her."

Jesus. I knew about Clint, but I never knew Dean was involved with her too. That cheating bitch—and I thought Dean was better than that. "You had an affair with Amy? You slept with her while she was married to *your best friend?*"

He jerks back as if I smacked him. "What? No. Never. I didn't touch her when she and Kace were married. It started at Smithy's five weeks ago. We closed down the bar and . . ."

"And you decided you were going to fuck your best friend's ex-wife? The same ex your best friend wants back? And then, what? You *kept* fucking her?"

"I know it sounds awful, but dammit, Stell, we're *good* together. I've never felt like this with another woman. She's the most beautiful woman I've ever seen, and she makes me laugh, and she's *such* a good mom."

I've tried to keep my feelings about Amy neutral, but in

this moment, I hate her. Not only did she betray Kace and hurt him, now she's hurting Dean . . . and she's likely to destroy a lifelong friendship. "What the hell was she thinking?"

He scowls at me. "Thanks, sis, but I'm not that bad."

"That's not what I mean." Taking a deep breath, I sink into the chair beside him. "I'm sorry. I just . . ." I swallow and grapple for empathy. I want to shake him until he comes to his senses and realizes this will only end badly. "I had no idea."

"No one knows. We've been keeping it quiet. I knew Kace would freak out, and I didn't want to upset him."

My phone buzzes.

Kace: I'm making you dinner. Pasta or steak?

I study Dean's face. Has my brother ever fallen in love before this? He's had a couple of long-term girlfriends—if you'd call less than a year long-term—and I'd bet he's said those three words, but I never saw him with someone I believed he'd be willing to make sacrifices for. "Does she feel the same about you?"

He hangs his head and shrugs.

There's so much heartache in that gesture that I want to track Amy down and make her listen as I enumerate all the ways she isn't worthy of the men in her life. "Don't let her play you."

"She cares about me. The thing with Kace just spooked her, and today, I said I wish he'd seen us so we could quit sneaking around, and she . . ." He swallows and turns away, looking out the window. "I know this would change every-thing. I know it could screw with my friendship with Kace and possibly fuck over our business, but it'd be worth it. *She's* worth it."

"Oh, Dean." I place my hand on top of his. I want to argue, to tell him she's not, and explain what I know from her past. I want to rant and rave about how he deserves better than what this woman's offering, but is there any point? It's over now. And anyway, do we really have control over who we love? Do our hearts listen to reason? Unfortunately, I know they don't, so I whisper, "I'm so sorry."

I text Kace back, letting him know something came up and I have to cancel. Then I give Dean a hug, and my big, badass, tough-guy brother presses his face into my shoulder and cries. It's good that I'm here, that he can lean on me, but part of me knows why it was so easy for me to cancel on Kace.

It's Dean's turn for heartache today, but mine is coming.

❦

KACE

> Stella: Something came up and I won't be
> able to make it tonight. Rain check?

AFTER WALKING on clouds all day, Stella's text brings me crashing down. We've both been busy this week, but this is my only kid-free day until Saturday, when we're supposed to be moving Stella into the pool house.

The rational part of my mind tells me I should be patient, that there will be hundreds of opportunities to make love to her and just . . . be *near* her. Hell, she's literally moving into my backyard. I shouldn't be worried about this. I am, though. We've barely talked since the weekend, and I can't help but wonder if she's slipping away. This is supposed to be casual, and she's probably seeing other people—especially since I was the one who insisted we *not* be exclusive—but the idea of her with someone else makes me want to lose my mind. What if that's where she is now? What if one of the guys she's seeing showed up at her door, and she decided she'd rather spend time with *him*?

Maybe it's unevolved of me, but every primal instinct says she belongs to me, and I'm not willing to share. Which is bullshit, because that's not what we agreed on.

Dammit. I couldn't even blame her if she was with someone else right now. Why would she choose the divorced single dad who can't offer her more than sex and sneaking around?

I glare at the bags of groceries sitting on my counter waiting for tonight. I wasn't sure what she'd want, so I grabbed all the makings for two dinners: pasta carbonara, like my grandma made it, and filet mignon with gorgonzola potatoes. Doesn't look like I'll be preparing either.

I need to text her back and acknowledge her message without letting on how much it's fucking with me.

> Me: I understand. I guess I won't see you
> until Saturday, then, but I'm looking
> forward to it.

I read it three times. Short, not overly clingy, but still honest enough. It'll have to do.

STELLA

Friday night, I'm nothing but a ball of nerves about tomorrow's move. It's not the move itself that's making me miserable, but the idea that I'll be tied to Kace, geographically, at least, and when this ends, I'll have to see him all the time.

I'm sick of carrying around this fear—no, this *certainty* —that when Kace discovers the skeletons in my closet, he'll end things. Perhaps honesty would be less terrifying than omission. At least then I wouldn't have to wonder. But I'm so nervous he'll never look me in the eye again that my hands are shaking when I pull out my laptop, and they're shaking even harder when I start typing.

> ItsyBitsy123: Are you around?
> GoodHands69: Hey! Been a while. Yep. Just
>   put my daughter to bed. How are you?

I stare at the screen, hands shaking. I need to do this, but I don't know if I've ever been so scared.

> ItsyBitsy123: I want to tell you something,
>   and I want to say it now while I'm feeling
>   courageous.
> GoodHands69: Okay . . . I'm listening.

It takes me a long time to type out the message— deleting and rewriting details, adding more and then backing up to go with less. I wouldn't be surprised if Kace has fallen asleep or moved on with his night, but when I'm done typing, I still reread it three times and try to talk myself out of pressing send. I decide not to mention my college boyfriend by name, since Kace probably remembers him and I don't know that he wouldn't go after him.

I don't know why I want to share this story with Kace when I've been too chicken to share it with anyone else, but I do. For some reason, I need him to know this secret, need to remind him I'm still the mess who's never been good enough. So I send it.

> ItsyBitsy123: You know my last boyfriend took me on vacation. I thought we were good together for the most part, but the truth is, I struggle with getting guys to take me seriously, and I was trying extra hard with Bobby. Guys want sex and then get bored with me and move on, and maybe that's my fault, but . . . Anyway, I wanted it to be different this time, so I decided no sex until things were really serious. I thought our vacation would be the perfect time, but right after we got to the resort, his buddy sent him a link and Bobby decided he didn't want anything to do with me anymore.
>
> You see, when I was in college, I was dating this guy who was really into filming us in bed together. In retrospect, I never should've let him, but he said it turned him on, and I wanted him to like me . . . anyway, long story short, there were a lot of films, and I didn't find out until he'd broken up with me that he'd uploaded them to all kinds of amateur porn sites. I

don't even know how many. I'll probably never know.

Bobby's buddy knew my ex somehow and was told about the videos. So he tracked them down and felt it was his duty to let his friend know he was dating a—and I quote —"cheap porno slut."

Bobby was mortified. He was angry I hadn't told him. But you know what made him even angrier? I'd done these videos but hadn't once given it up to him in the months we'd been together. As if one had anything to do with the other. As if my mistake meant he should've been entitled to unlimited pussy from the beginning.

Anyway . . . it was ugly, with lots of tears and accusations, and Bobby called a cab to take me to the airport. Told me to have my stuff out of his apartment before he got home. Said he was looking for a life with a nice girl, and I was just a deceitful bitch. He told me he'd rather live alone the rest of his life than let a whore like me raise his children.

I think that's the part that hurt the most. Because Bobby was one of the few guys I've ever been with who actually talked about a future with kids with me. I want kids. I want to be a mom someday, but before Bobby, no one believed I was mother material. And once he got that link, he didn't either.

I probably should've told him sooner. The truth is, I may have consented to those videos, but I never would've agreed to share them with the world. And now they're floating out there, and there's nothing I can do to get rid of them.

Luckily for me, there's a lot of cheap homemade porn on the internet, and my stuff isn't particularly special. But it's there, and that's bad enough.

I know this thing between us is nowhere near the point where you're wondering if I'm "mother material," but every time I catch myself hoping this could go somewhere, I remember those damn videos and I imagine the look on your face if you ever accidentally stumbled upon them.

I wanted you to hear it from me.

My phone is quiet for too long after I press send. My stomach's in my throat, and my hands tremble. This is definitely not what he had in mind when he said he'd listen. He probably expected something along the lines of *I always wanted to be an artist*. Instead, he got my baggage. Why do I always have to dive in headfirst?

When my phone buzzes to alert me to his reply, I almost don't want to look. Of course, I do.

GoodHands69: I am so sorry. I can't wrap my brain around a guy treating a woman like that. Posting those videos was a violation, and Bobby treating you like that when he found out was unnecessarily cruel. You deserved better.

The screen blurs, and hot tears streak across my cheeks at those final three words: *You deserved better.* That's what I've been trying to tell myself, but after a series of mistakes and bad relationships, I started to wonder if maybe I *didn't* deserve better. Coming from Kace, I can almost believe it.

ItsyBitsy123: Thank you. It means a lot.

GoodHands69: What'd you do? After Bobby called you a cab, I mean. I assume you moved out, but . . .

ItsyBitsy123: I was so embarrassed. I thought this guy loved me, but obviously not enough. I didn't want to go home and have everyone ask why I left early. So I had the cab take me to this run-down little motel across the street from the beach. I stayed there for a few nights, then caught an early flight home so I could move out of his place.

GoodHands69: Good for you. I'm so sorry that happened.

ItsyBitsy123: Don't tell anyone, okay? It's just more evidence that I have shitty judgment in general, and I'd be so embarrassed if everyone knew those videos are out there.

GoodHands69: I can keep a secret.

My heart is in my throat. It's done. He knows. I don't

know if I would've had the courage to tell him any way but through this computer, but without seeing him in front of me, it's impossible to gauge his reaction. I'll have to see him in person before I can truly believe this doesn't change how he feels about me.

> GoodHands69: I don't know a single person
> who hasn't made a mistake. Don't beat
> yourself up for being human.

Gratitude and fondness and relief all tangle together in my chest.

> ItsyBitsy123: If you didn't have Hope tonight,
> I'd be over there right now climbing you
> like a tree.

CHAPTER NINETEEN

STELLA

*M*oving day comes, and Kace is the first to arrive. He pulls into Mom's driveway before seven. I meet him at the door, but he doesn't stop walking —just grabs my hand and heads straight to my bedroom, kicking the door shut behind him before pressing me against it and kissing me hard. His hands are all over me, as if he's trying to touch everywhere at once and can't get enough, and his mouth is relentless. He kisses me like he's dying and I'm the only thing that can save him.

When he finally breaks the kiss, we're both breathless. "You don't know how many times this week I had to make myself keep driving when I was passing here or your work. I wanted to stop the car, come in, and do that." He leans his forehead against mine and grins. "I want you so much."

"You do?" I ask. I can't keep the insecurities from my voice. "Even though I have . . . baggage?"

"More than ever," he says, and his voice is heavy with meaning.

My heart swells. Maybe it wasn't fair to think he'd push me away once he found out about the videos. Maybe I didn't give him enough credit. "I want you too."

He groans and grips my hips. "When can I finally have you alone again?"

I eye the boxes stacked all around us. "Not until we get this move done."

Straightening, he smacks my ass, leaving a pleasant sting behind. "Then get moving, woman."

ઠ

BETWEEN KACE'S truck and Dean's, my car, and the girls' vehicles, we managed to move my embarrassingly few possessions in one trip and less than four hours. By the time lunch rolled around, Dean was already back at Mom's, tearing up carpet and nagging Kace to help. Kace joined him—probably because the girls were here anyway, helping themselves to his pool, and he couldn't get me naked until they left. Once they were out the door, I barely got to say a word before Kace was on me, hand up my shirt, mouth on mine, fierce and possessive. *Hungry.* I lost my shirt and bra before we made it to the bathroom, and he didn't even finish undressing before he pulled me under the hot spray and kneeled before me, his hands on my hips and his mouth *everywhere.*

"I was beginning to think I was never going to get you back in this bed again," Kace says Saturday evening. We're in his bed, completely naked and satisfied after the most glorious shower in the history of mankind. He swallows, scanning my face again. He can't seem to stop looking at me, and I love that. "Listen, I know you don't want to hear about the other woman I'm talking to." I stiffen, and he chuckles softly. "Okay, that just proves my point. But I think we need to make something clear before this goes any further."

My heart stumbles into a whole different kind of racing than it was doing just a minute ago, and I sit up in bed. I'm naked and too vulnerable to have this conversation while he's holding me. "Okay."

"You're the only one I'm in a sexual relationship with, and that'll be true until this ends."

The cocktail of relief and disappointment has me feeling a little unsteady. I don't want him seeing anyone else while we're together. But knowing he still considers this temporary cuts a little too deep.

He takes a breath. "I'm not someone who can sleep with two people at the same time."

"Me neither," I admit.

His brows shoot up, as if this surprises him, and I try not to take offense. "You're not seeing anyone else?"

A lot of women have multiple partners at once, and as long as everyone's safe, there's nothing wrong with that. But why does he assume *I* would? I shake my head. "Only you, Kace."

"Thank God." He sighs and drags a hand over his face. "I can't share you, Stella. Even if this is a fling." He shakes his head. "For as long as this lasts, I need it to be just us. Are you okay with that?"

It's such an absurd question. I'd laugh if it didn't also prove he still doesn't quite understand me. Despite everything. "Believe it or not, I'm a fan of monogamy."

He grabs me around the waist and pulls me back down onto the bed with him before lowering his mouth to mine and kissing me hard. "Call me old-fashioned, but you've made my fucking week."

I laugh, though my emotions are too heavy and tangled for the sound to be light. "So you and this other girl . . ."

"We met on Random, and she's fun. I like talking to her, and I think she's been good for me, but . . ." He frowns as if he can't figure out how to say what he's thinking.

"But what?"

"I guess it's just I know enough about her now that I'm sure we'll never be more than friends." He shrugs. "Some things are just deal breakers."

And somehow my baggage isn't? "So it's just you and me?"

He nuzzles my neck, scratching me with his beard. "At least until your brother finds out and castrates me."

Meaning I'm still your dirty secret. But I don't say it. This is so much more than I ever could've imagined, and I need to take what he's giving me with both hands and make the most of it.

"Kace?" a woman calls from the hall. "Where are you?"

I freeze. "Is that Amy?"

He looks over his shoulder toward the opening bedroom door—just as Amy steps into view.

"Oh. I—"

"Out," he snaps.

Amy doesn't move. She stands in the doorway to Kace's bedroom and stares at me like I'm a roach she's found crawling across her food. "Hi, Stella."

I try to think of something to say but only manage a squeak.

"Out," Kace repeats, angling his body over mine to block me from her view.

"I thought you said you two weren't involved," Amy says.

Growling, he grabs the blanket and pulls it over me even as he rolls off the bed and walks bare-ass naked to shut the door in her face.

Once she's not staring at me anymore, I recapture control of my motor functions and jump out of bed, scrambling for my jeans. "I'm sorry. I'm so sorry, Kace. I know you didn't want anyone to find out about us, and—"

"Stella." He grabs the hand that's reaching for my jeans and pulls me toward him. "You do not owe me an apology. Not at all."

My shaking hands are only a mirror of what's happening inside me. I like that he tried to protect me from her angry gaze, but a little voice in the back of my mind is shouting that there's a red flag here. I was *surprised* he tried to protect me, surprised he didn't try to pretend nothing was happening, surprised he was harsh with her and kind to me. How screwed up is that?

I swallow. "I don't know where my shirt is." Probably somewhere in the hall where he stripped me. "Can I borrow one? I'll get out of here so you two can talk."

He pulls a Falcons T-shirt from his dresser and hands it to me. "I understand if you want to go, but don't run away because you think you have to. This is my house, and you're my guest. She's the one who showed up uninvited."

"I guess you two are even now," I whisper. I pull the shirt on over my head. "Tit for tat, right?"

"How do you . . . ?" He shakes his head, then mutters something about Smithy before sighing. "This was one score I never needed to settle." Grabbing me by the hips, he tugs me toward him and presses a kiss to my lips. "I don't want you to go."

"I don't think the conversation she wants to have will go any smoother if I'm here." I step back, away from his warmth. "Anyway, I'm supposed to meet the girls tonight, remember?" I paste on a smile. "I should go get pretty."

He sweeps his eyes over me. "You're already stunning."

A shiver of happiness trembles through me. I grab his cotton shorts from the floor and hand them to him.

He pulls them on. "Come over after you get home?"

I grin. "Why? What do you have in mind?"

His eyes go so hot that I'm surprised my clothes don't spontaneously combust. "I think what's in my mind is best when shown."

Those nervous tremors in my tummy morph into butterflies. "I'll be here."

I straighten my shoulders as I open the bedroom door, but luckily Amy isn't in the hall or anywhere in the path between Kace's bedroom and the back door.

KACE

Leave it to my ex-wife to be the biggest cockblocker in my life. I'm pissed. Not just because of the way she looks at and treats Stella, but because she walked right into my room like she had any right to do that.

I find her on the front porch swing, vaping. "What is *that*?" I ask.

"A vape pen."

I repress an eye roll. "I know that part. I mean, why would you start such a nasty habit?" I lean against the house, keeping my distance from her and her vapor. "Haven't you read the studies?"

"Sure, but I don't do it much, and never around Hope." She shrugs.

"Where *is* Hope?" I want to say, *Why the fuck are you here and walking into my house like you own the place?* But we'll start with the easy stuff.

"She's with my mom." Amy's expression is too serious. I haven't seen a look like that on her face since she told me she wanted a divorce.

"Why are you here?"

She takes another puff on her vape pen and shrugs. "I thought we could hang out. We haven't in a while."

Hang out? I know she wants us to be friends, but—

"So . . . Stella?" Her arched brow speaks volumes. It's Amy's signature *You're fucking kidding me, right?* face. "Is that really happening?"

I shove my hands in my pockets. I'm not going to give her the specifics about my love life. I don't owe those to her, and I wouldn't do that to Stella. "It's not really your business, Amy."

Her jaw drops. "Bullshit. Anyone you bring around my daughter is, in fact, my business."

"This from the woman who insisted I sign up for a hookup app and give sleeping with a stranger a try."

"That's different! You don't bring hookups home. You certainly don't *move them into your backyard*." She hops off the swing and paces in front of me. "She's so clever, finding her way in with you like that."

I sigh. "Didn't we already have this conversation?"

She stops pacing and glares at me. "She always hated me. Always wanted me out of the picture so she could have you for herself, and now she's going to be living with you—"

"Not with us. Living in the pool house."

"—and she's going to feed you all kinds of poison about me. Maybe she'll feed that poison to Hope too." She folds her arms and hugs herself tight.

"I never meant for this to happen, but—"

"You *accidentally* fucked her?" Her eyes are blazing with anger.

"Since when do you care who I fuck?" I've never raised my voice at Amy. Never. Until just now.

"Since you decided to pick the worst possible option."

"She's not what you think. Not at all. You were so wrong about what happened at Allegiance. There was nothing between her and Clint but Clint being a handsy douche."

Her gaze snaps up to mine, and I swear there's panic in those blue eyes. "Is that what she said? And you believed her? What else did she tell you about Allegiance?"

"Why do you care so much?"

She bites her bottom lip, leaving a mark. "I want to know what lies she's spreading about me."

"What the hell is your problem with Stella, and why are you so convinced she has it out for you?" I stare at her. There was a time in my life that I could read everything on that face. I could tell if she was hiding something or just stressed by body language alone. But it's been years since we had that kind of connection, and I can't for the life of me figure out what's behind this uncharacteristic tantrum.

"I don't trust her." She drops her arms and gives me a small smile. "Come on, Kace. This is Dean's little sister. You know how she is. You've always been so careful about what influences Hope. Just . . . think with your head and not your dick on this one. She's trouble."

"You're wrong about Stella. She's had some bumps along the way, but she's not the party girl I grew up with. She's . . ." I sigh. "She's one of the most caring, thoughtful people I know. I'm sorry you don't see what I see, but this isn't about you."

"There are hundreds of women who'd do anything for a chance with a guy like you, and you're giving everything to the first piece of ass who gives you a lick of attention."

I rock back on my heels. "I need you to leave. I already told you I won't let you talk about her like that. She doesn't deserve it."

Amy stares at me for a long time, eyes rimmed with tears, bottom lip trembling. Finally, she swallows and walks to her car.

I stand there and watch until she pulls away, turns the corner, and drives out of sight, and then I head inside to my computer.

I have an important message to send.

CHAPTER TWENTY

STELLA

Smithy's is packed. Even the outside patio is standing room only. Then again, it's a beautiful Saturday evening and this is the best bar in town—though I might be biased.

I spot the girls in a booth at the back and work my way through the crowd to get to them. Looks like everyone is here. Brinley's looking hot in a blue halter, and Savannah's showing off her perfectly sculpted shoulders in a strapless top. Abbi's the least flashy, as always, in a soft pink T-shirt that says, *I drink coffee and I know things*. I don't remember the last time we all made it to girls' night, but I'm glad to see their gorgeous faces.

"Stella!" Brinley shouts, spotting me before the others do. "We were starting to worry."

"Sorry I'm late." I slide into the booth beside Abbi. "I

was . . ." Shit. I can't finish *that* sentence honestly. Reluctantly, I settle on a lie. "I was studying."

"How's school?" Brinley asks.

I tense. "Not very well."

Savvy frowns. "But you're going to those study groups, right? Are those helping?"

I groan and sink into the seat. "Unfortunately, no. I know I was eighteen once, but I swear I understood how to stay on task even then."

Brinley snorts. "Knowing how and having the will to do it are completely different things."

"I just wish there were more people my age in the class. I need study help, but I don't have the patience for the chatter and endless detours off topic. For every hour of study group, there's maybe ten minutes of quality studying. This might've been a mistake."

Brinley reaches for my hand. "You always have a job with me. You know that, right?"

My eyes burn and I snap my mouth shut, afraid I'll cry if I say more, so I just nod.

"Ask Kace to help you," Abbi says. "You know he minored in chem, right?"

No, I didn't know that, but I'm not surprised. He's always been crazy smart. His degree is in some sort of biotechnical engineering—something I don't quite understand. I remember Dean spouting off about how Kace would be rolling in money once the government contractors picked him up. Yet somehow Kace ended up back in Orchid Valley building houses—and good for him. He found a career that pays well, and it's one he enjoys. If only we could all have that. "I'm sure he has better things to do than tutor me," I say, digging in my purse so I don't have to look her in the eye.

I don't know exactly how Abbi would react if she knew Kace and I were hooking up, but my instincts tell me she wouldn't love it. She's protective of him, and while I'd like to think she respects me enough to come around to the idea if we decided to take our relationship to the next level, I don't know that it'd be easy for her. Then again, maybe she wouldn't come around at all. Abbi and I are friends through Brinley and from working together at The Orchid, but our friendship is one of those that'd likely fall apart without external factors linking us together.

"He is really busy," Abbi says. "Actually, I think he might be seeing someone."

My head pops up. "What?"

"We were at Mom's for brunch last Sunday, and Mom was asking him if he'd started dating, and he got all weird."

I swallow. "Maybe he just didn't want to talk to her about it."

She shakes her head. "No. She asks him every week, and this was definitely different. He got all squirmy."

Savvy's staring at me, and I beg her with my eyes not to say anything.

Abbi chuckles, her brown eyes bright with amusement. "Anyway, he was tight-lipped about it, so I know nothing, but if any of you hear anything, you absolutely have to tell me."

"So you can give him shit about it?" Savvy asks with an arched brow.

Abbi shrugs. "It's my job as his little sister to give him shit."

"More like so she can do a background check on the

girl," Brinley says, narrowing her eyes at Abbi over her drink. "Don't give me that innocent, doe-eyed look. We all know you're mama-bear protective when it comes to Kace."

Another shrug. "Guilty, and I'm not even sorry." She frowns. "This divorce hasn't been easy on him."

"Let's talk about the wedding," Savvy says, because she's a goddess who knows when her buddy needs a subject change.

"Vow renewal," Brinley says, then shrugs. "Nothing to talk about. Everything's on track, thanks to my *fantastic* team at The Orchid." She grins. "It'll be nice to be able to *remember* saying my vows, though."

"For real," Abbi says. "Which reminds me, I still need to get my bridesmaid dress altered. Anyone have a good seamstress?"

"Let Mom do it," I offer. "She won't charge much, and she's great at that stuff."

Savvy nods. "It's true. She did mine for twenty bucks, and it looks perfect."

Brinley turns to me. "What about you, Stella? How's *your* love life going?"

I swallow hard. Brinley's the last person I want to lie to. Normally, she would've been the first to know about something as major as what I have going on with Kace, but she's been so busy with taking over The Orchid and getting settled in with Marston that I feel like we barely talk anymore. "It's fine." I force a smile.

"Did you finally take our advice and leave Random behind?"

"More or less," I say, which is true, if misleading.

Abbi chuckles. "Does that have anything to do with guys not swiping on you anymore?"

I frown. Because it's weird, but she's right. Aside from Kace, the only person who's reached out to me in the last week is that guy who suggested I was ugly. I've been so focused on Kace that I didn't think anything of it.

She extends a hand and turns up her palm. "Give me your phone. I need to show you something."

Something on *Random*? What if Kace has messaged me? He didn't freak out about Amy knowing about us, but how would he feel about Abbi knowing?

I swallow. "I deleted the app." I hate lying, but I want to talk to Kace about this before his sister finds out.

Savvy arches a brow. "You *did*?"

Abbi waves her hand in the air. "Smithy! Come over here!"

Smithy drops drinks off to customers at a nearby table and winks at them before heading our way. "How's it going, beautiful ladies?"

"Are you on Random?"

He gives her a long, slow smile and then drags his gaze over her in the lascivious way he usually saves for me and Savvy. Good. Abbi deserves a little male appreciation. "Why? You interested in getting you some *random*?"

Abbi rolls her eyes, unfazed by his flirting, and holds out her hand. "Give me your phone."

He digs it out of his back pocket and hands it over. Abbi grabs his hand and uses his fingerprint to unlock the screen before tapping and swiping like crazy.

"Do I want to know what she's doing right now?" Smithy asks.

"Probably not," Savvy says.

"There you are," Abbi declares, turning Smithy's phone toward me. On the screen is an image of . . .

"Is that Jessica Rabbit?" I ask.

"Jessica who?" Brinley cranes her neck as she tries to see what we're looking at.

An awful, yawning darkness opens in the pit of my stomach. I don't understand what's happening, but every instinct tells me this is very bad.

"The cartoon?" Savvy asks. "Man, I haven't seen that movie in forever."

"I don't think I've ever seen it," Brinley says. "Someone explain to me why you're looking at a cartoon rabbit on Smithy's phone?"

Abbi turns the phone so Brinley can see. "She's not a rabbit. She's a human."

Brinley's eyes go wide. "Oh. *She's* in a *children's* cartoon? She's so . . . booby."

"As is Stella," Abbi says, as if this explains anything.

"It's from a movie," Savvy says.

Smithy leans over the table to get a view of his phone, then nods. "Hottest piece of animated ass other than Ariel. I'd like to . . ." He holds one hand in front of him and waves the other, undeniably pantomiming "smacking that ass."

"You're gross," Abbi says.

"Nah, I'm just honest."

"Would someone please explain what's happening here?" I beg. What does a cartoon character have to do with my Random profile?

"This is your avatar." Abbi hands the phone back to Smithy. "Remember? You had that awful date and said you were going to take your picture down from Random, but I knew you wouldn't, and when I checked, I was right."

I can only stare at her, horrified.

I had dreams about Jessica Rabbit last night. I hope you're proud of yourself.

I swallow. "You got onto my profile and changed my picture without telling me? You got on my *phone* without my permission?"

"I was saving you from assholes who only want your body. And you've admitted yourself that it worked, which is pretty fucking ironic when you consider Jessica Rabbit is the caricature version of you, but no guy would guess that without seeing you for himself. The narrow-minded asses are too worried about meeting for a hookup and accidentally finding themselves face to face with a dude. Or worse —a fat chick like me."

Savvy and Brinley gasp at those words, but I'm too busy processing, and it takes me a minute to realize Abbi's just knocked herself.

"You are *not* fat," Brinley says at the same time as Savvy says, "You're gorgeous, and fuck anyone who doesn't see that."

I turn to Smithy, since that's his cue to say something about how she's "really rocking her curves" or how she's "fat in all the right places, if you know what I mean," but he's uncharacteristically mute and . . . staring at me like he's seen a ghost.

"You're Jessica Rabbit?" he asks softly.

I turn to Abbi. "When did you do this?"

"At Kace's pool party when you were in the bathroom. I snagged your phone before the screen went black and locked me out." Her smile falls away. "Shit, Stella, I thought you'd think it was funny."

At the pool party. Which means . . . before Kace swiped on me. Which means Kace didn't swipe on *me* at all. He swiped on some random chick with a Jessica Rabbit avatar. It means every time I thought it was weird that he talked about Amy and Hope like I didn't know them, he was really thinking *I* didn't know them. Every time it seemed like he was telling me something twice, he thought he was telling me for the first time. "I can't believe this," I whisper.

Smithy scratches his beard, his face screwed up in confusion. "So that means you're—"

"Thirsty." I jump out of the booth and grab his forearm. "Totally shocked by this information, and suddenly need a shot of something *very strong*." He meets my eyes, and I desperately try to communicate everything I'm feeling. *Please don't say anything. Please don't tell them whatever it is you know.*

"Come on, Stella," Abbi says, "it's not that big of a thing." But the delight that was on her face earlier is gone. In its place, worry has crept in.

Half of me wants to scream at her, but the other half is so fucking embarrassed by all of this that I just want to do whatever's necessary to keep my friends from asking questions. I give her a tight smile. "I'm sure I'll agree in a minute." I take a step toward the bar, dragging Smithy along behind me. I veer toward the bathrooms and freeze when I see there's a line.

"The kitchen," Smithy says, nodding toward the door labeled *Employees Only.* "Come on."

I follow him, but his staff is bustling around thanks to the packed bar, and I can't talk to him here, either. Hot tears press at the back of my eyes. I'm one wrong word or sideways glance away from totally losing it.

"This way." Smithy presses his palm between my shoulder blades and leads me into his office.

I push the door shut and fall against it. "Fuck." The silence of his office is worse than the cacophony of the bar, and I wish he'd explain this all away somehow. I'm hanging on by a string, and I need my friend to tell me it's all going to be okay. But when I look at him, he's worrying his bottom lip between his teeth. "Say something."

Smithy folds his arms across his chest and rocks back on his heels. "You're Jessica Rabbit?"

I flinch. "I thought we already established that."

"Kace told us about his little online piece—"

"Little online *piece*? What the fuck is that?"

He rolls his eyes. "He told me about his online *friend*," he says, emphasizing the word, like he's censoring for an overly sensitive elderly relative. "I don't think he has *any idea* you're the woman behind the avatar." He scrubs a hand over his face. "Unless maybe he was just saying that because Dean was there?" He taps his mouth with his index finger. "Could he have been pretending? Surely you talked about who you are at some point?"

I turn up my palms. "Maybe? I . . ." I shake my head. "I don't know."

"How do you not know, Stella? Isn't 'I'm Stella,' like, step one of connecting with someone online?"

"I didn't know he might think I was a stranger until a few minutes ago." And thanks to Random's disappearing-message thing, it's not like I can go back and look at our conversations to know for sure. "I wasn't trying to hide who I was. I thought he swiped on *me*." But I already know the truth. I was the other woman all along. The one I felt sorry for because he said it was only physical attraction with no substance. I remember thinking I knew what it was like to be the girl Kace thought was hot with no substance. *Still do, I guess.*

Then what did he say tonight? *Some things are just deal breakers.*

And that was after I'd told him about those videos. He said we all make mistakes, but he was probably trying to be nice, trying to make me feel better. The second I confessed my secret, he ruled me out as a possibility.

Part of me knew it was too good to be true from the start.

Smithy's face is long, his eyes wide. "But you're going to tell him, right? Just to be sure?"

"I think I have to." The words wrap around my stomach and squeeze too tightly. I press my hand to my belly and the gnawing ache there. "I need to."

Some things are just deal breakers.

"Yes, you have to. Fuck, Stell, he's *really* into you. Like, I wasn't sure he'd ever get over Amy, but he started talking about this Jessica Rabbit chick last week, and I . . ." His throat bobs as he swallows, eyes wide and worried. "He didn't talk about her like he would if he was hiding something from Dean. And he didn't seem as screwed up as he's always seemed about the fact that he wants to fuck you."

I blink at him. "Excuse me?"

He rolls his eyes. "I mean, who doesn't, right? You're a total snack cake."

I rub my temples. "Please don't call me or any other woman a snack cake ever again, Smithy."

He rolls his eyes. "My point is, Kace didn't know it was you."

"Maybe he knows," I whisper. "Maybe we're freaking out over nothing. Or maybe . . . maybe he'll be okay with it being me." I look up at Smithy, but it isn't until I see worry in the scrunch of his brow that I realize how much I needed his usual optimism.

I sink into the leather upholstered chair across from his desk, lean back, and close my eyes. I'm reprocessing everything Kace has said to me through the app and everything he's said in person. It's too much to puzzle out all at once, but every piece that clicks into place is further evidence all my fears were valid. Kace never wanted more than a physical relationship with me. I was his dirty little secret, and the only reason he connected to me on an emotional level was because he didn't know it was me at all. And now even that connection's ruined, because I opened my big mouth and told him about those fucking videos.

"Shit. Are you going to cry? Don't cry, Stell. Please?"

My phone buzzes, and it's complete faith in how fucked my life has become that lets me know it's Kace before I even look. He's texted. Probably about tonight. Probably something sexy, because . . . that's all I am.

I can't bring myself to open it.

"Smithy, promise me you won't say anything to Kace until I figure this out."

"You have to tell him," he says solemnly.

He's right. The girls all know about the avatar now, so obviously I can't keep this a secret forever. I just need a minute to deal with this ache in my chest.

I've always loved Kace, but I knew I couldn't have more. I *knew* I wasn't allowed to want more, so I was happy to settle for what he offered—the scraps of attention, the hot, lusty looks, and that one night in the pool house, the physical. But our conversations on Random changed everything. I got a taste of what it was like to have Kace see me—the real me, not just my bubbly surface personality, not just the sexpot party girl who liked to tease him. I got to know what it was like to have him crave my mind as much as my body, and now I don't know how I'm supposed to settle for less.

I've been talking to Kace. Falling for Kace. But he has no idea he's been talking to me. And when my online self told him her biggest secret, he didn't want anything to do with her anymore.

CHAPTER TWENTY-ONE

STELLA

I don't even remember the drive to Dean's. But I'm here, sitting in the middle of his living room floor in a puddle of my own tears.

I should've driven straight to Kace. I could've told him immediately. Ripped off the proverbial Band-Aid. Maybe he would've laughed about it. Maybe he would've gotten angry and walked away. But at least it wouldn't be this awful secret, and he'd know I never intended to trick him.

Instead, I drove to my brother's and word-vomited all my nonsense heartbreak the second he asked what was wrong. And Dean? He's wearing a path in the carpet with his pacing, and I'm pretty sure he wishes he didn't know any of this. Not that I'm "Jessica Rabbit," not that I'm in love with Kace, and definitely not that he has to keep this all a secret.

The doorbell rings, and his shoulders sag in relief. He

rushes to open it, and Savannah barges in. "Thank you," he says. "She said you were the only one I was allowed to call."

"What's wrong?" Savvy asks, coming straight toward me. "What happened? Why'd you leave the bar? Abbi feels so bad about the avatar."

"She's Itsy," Dean says.

Savvy scrunches up her face in confusion. "She's itchy?"

"No. She's ItsyBitsy, Jessica Rabbit, whatever—the girl Kace has been talking to on Random. The one he rejected after she told him some secret. Only, he just told Stella he was rejecting her and didn't tell online Stella, and now she doesn't want him to know who she is." He gasps and looks at me. "I don't understand it all, but the long and short of it is apparently my best friend is a fucking idiot, and I'm going to kill him."

Savvy looks my brother up and down, shakes her head, and points to his kitchen. "Go find yourself a drink. You need to chill." Then she crosses the living room and sinks to her haunches to look me in the eye. "Honey, don't panic. You can just tell him. You two have something now, right?"

That's not true, and it guts me. Even when I was curled into his side after we slept together for the first time, when he opened up to me about his marriage—it was about sex. Not about love or a future together. The only time he's connected with me on an emotional level was online. I was stupid enough to think he was opening up to *me*, but the awful truth is that those conversations never would've happened if he'd known he was talking to Stella. Either he wouldn't have hit me up at all or it would've been sexual banter—but at least if it'd been that, I wouldn't have ever hung so much hope on having more. "It's never been more than sex."

"The fuck?" Dean says. "You're *sleeping* with Matthews?"

I try to breathe, but my lungs are fucking trash and won't take the air I need. "I thought we had something because of our conversations on Random, but it was never more than physical. He doesn't even know I'm her, and now if I tell him, he won't want me because he knows too much about her and doesn't want her anymore."

Dean rubs his temples. "I'm so confused. Her who?"

Another sob rips through me. "He doesn't want *me* anymore."

"She is Itsy; Itsy is Stella. Kace rejected Itsy but doesn't want anything emotional with Stella." Savvy scowls at Dean. "Try to keep up."

I swipe at my tears with my palms. "She's the one he's been confiding in. Not me. I told myself what was happening between us meant something because of those online conversations, but all we've been doing is screwing around."

Dean's jaw is hard. "I trusted him. I thought he cared about you. He's supposed to protect you, and he's been taking *advantage* of you."

Savvy stands and takes Dean by the forearm. "Chill out, Bruce Banner. We don't like you when you're angry."

He scowls at her. "I'm not hulking out. She's my sister."

"She's also a grown woman who can sleep with who she wants." She tosses her purse on the counter, then lowers herself back onto the floor with me. She holds my gaze as she talks. "You've been talking to Kace on Random, but until today you assumed he knew it was you because you didn't know Abbi had changed your picture. And whatever you two have talked about on there has been part of the way you feel about him and part of your physical relationship—for you. But he . . . *definitely* doesn't know you're the girl he's talking to? Do I have this right?"

"He definitely doesn't know," Dean says. "At least, he didn't when he last talked to us about Itsy."

I sniffle, and Dean hands me a tissue. "Thanks," I whisper.

"You're welcome," he growls, and I almost laugh, because he does sound a little like the Hulk right now.

"Okay," Savvy says, all calm and collected. I'm jealous of her chill. No, I'm jealous of her choices. She told Alec they could only be friends, and now she's the one with a whole, healthy heart and I'm bleeding out. "I'm sorry I'm not understanding, baby girl, but why can't you just tell him?"

"Just tell him." Dean stops, blows out a breath, and nods. "Just tell him the truth. This doesn't have to be a thing."

Because I told him my secrets once, and if I tell him in person, it'll be like confessing the truth all over again. Because he changed how he felt about Itsy after she told him—after *I* told him—about the videos. Because I'm a coward and don't want him to know the truth now that I know how he'll feel about it. *Deal breaker.*

"Stella?" Savvy whispers. "Talk to me."

"I *should* tell him, but I'd do anything if it meant I didn't have to." I nod, and more tears spill down my cheeks. I swallow. "I thought he liked me, but he really liked her. Until he didn't like her because of her secrets, and then he only wanted me, but not for anything but sex."

"What are these big secrets, anyway?" Dean asks.

I shake my head. I just *can't* go there with my brother. Not tonight. Not ever.

"So if I'm following," Savvy says, "you're jealous of . . . yourself?"

Dean frowns down at me like I'm a perplexing puzzle. "That's fucked up, Stell."

"What if he thinks I did this on purpose? What if he doesn't believe that I thought he knew he was talking to me?"

"Oh my goodness, baby girl," Savvy says. "You're a wreck. He'll believe it was a mistake."

But what if he never looks at me the same because of what he knows about me now?

My phone buzzes beside me, and Savvy scoops it up, then hands it to me so I can unlock it. I numbly type in my passcode without taking it from her.

"It's a text from Kace," she says, cringing. "There are, like, four messages here. He says Amy's gone. He wants to know when you'll be there. Then he's asking if you're okay. He's worried." It buzzes again, and Savvy's eyes widen and she coughs. "Well, okay."

"What?" Dean asks. "What does it say?"

Savvy glares at him. "Stay in your lane."

"She's my sister," he whines.

Savvy hands the phone to me so I can see Kace's latest text. *Please tell me you're still coming over. An empty house means I finally get to hear you scream when I make you come.*

Dean stoops behind me and reads over my shoulder.

Savvy sighs.

"Ugh!" Dean stands and then paces. "Imma fucking kill that bastard."

"If you kill him, make it because he hurt Stell and not because he wants to pleasure her, 'kay?" She levels her calm eyes on me. "You also have a notification that BigHands69 has messaged you on Random. Should I open it?"

I shrug. Does it matter?

Savvy taps and swipes. Her face falls. "I'm sorry," she whispers.

I grab the phone to see the message.

> GoodHands69: Hey, this isn't an easy message to write, but it's past time. I've really enjoyed talking to you, but I can't split my attention between two special women anymore. I'm sure you'll find someone good, someone who isn't going to get hung up on your past. Don't give up, okay?

Meaning he's hung up on my past, or meaning he just wants me? And what a stupid question when I already know the answer. I shove the phone back at Savvy and hug my legs.

"What can I do?" Savvy asks.

"Buy me some time. Tell the girls . . ." I swallow back more tears and let numbness settle over me. "Tell them as much as you need to, but tell them they can't say anything to Kace about me being Jessica. I need to do that myself." *Somehow.* "And I need somewhere to live, because I can't look at him every day after I tell him the truth."

She nods then lifts up my phone. "And what do you want me to tell Kace?"

I squeeze my eyes shut. "Tell him I'm tired and going home."

KACE

I'm waiting on the patio when Stella finally gets home. I don't want to admit how long I've been sitting out here or how many times I had to stop myself from texting her and asking why she was canceling on me. I just had to come check on her.

"Hey, you," I call as she comes through the gate. She startles, then freezes as she meets my eyes. "I was worried."

She lowers her head and stares at her feet.

"Stell? What happened? Are you okay?" When I reach her, the streaks of her tears on her cheeks glow in the light from the streetlamps. I take her face in my hands and tilt her face up to study it. "Did someone hurt you?"

Her smile is shaky and no more believable than her excuse about being too tired to come over. "Nothing so dramatic," she whispers. "It's been a long day."

I smooth away her tears. "Let me come inside with you. I'll hold you and kiss it better."

"Kace . . ." She seems to search my face, and silence stretches between us, heavy with the words she's not saying.

"Talk to me. Who made you cry?"

"You did," she says, and I drop my hands like she burned me. "Not that I didn't see it coming, but still."

"What are you talking about?" I barely manage to give the rational part of my brain control of my mouth. "Did I hurt you? Did I say or do something?" I shake my head. "Tell me so I can fix it. Even if you never want to let me touch you again, please tell me what I did so I can make it right. I'm an idiot sometimes, but I can't handle thinking I hurt you."

"It's too late for that." She holds my gaze. "No girl wants the guy she's been crushing on for years to think she's just hot with no substance."

"I never—" I snap my mouth shut when the words really register. That was how I described my relationship with Stella when I was explaining it to Itsy. *No substance.*

"Stella—"

"Don't." She looks away. "I know we had an agreement. I'm just realizing maybe I'm not cut out for casual sex."

"What do you mean? You're the one teaching me how to do the whole casual thing," I say, and then I fucking hate myself, because that was the shittiest possible response. "I thought we were on the same page. I never led you on." But she's right. I'm treating her like a toy. And *I* sound like a child who's throwing a fucking fit because I'm not getting my way. But I hate this feeling—this feeling that I've hurt her, that maybe I don't deserve anything from her at all. This feeling that I've lost her completely.

"I can't do this." She swallows. "At least not with you."

STELLA

My phone buzzes as I walk into the pool house. After locking the door behind me, I pull it out.

> Savvy: The girls have been debriefed and all
> understand that they're not to say a thing

to Matthews or anyone else about Itsy's identity.

Me: Even Abbi?

Savvy: Even Abbi.

Me: Thank you, Savvy.

I wonder how much Abbi knows. What will she think when she finds out I've been sleeping with Kace? It shouldn't matter, but I hate feeling like maybe she was warning me off him at the bar that night. She knows her brother. She knows I'm not good enough for him.

I shove my phone back into my purse and drop it on the counter. I barely make it into the bathroom before I heave the contents of my stomach into the toilet. I heave again and again until there's nothing left. I rinse out my mouth then climb into the tub fully clothed, turn the shower on hot, and sit there for a long time, letting the water wash away my tears and wishing it could wash my mistakes away with it.

CHAPTER TWENTY-TWO

KACE

"It's my party day!" Hope announces Saturday morning, running in circles around the deflated rental bounce castle I'm spreading out on the back lawn.

"You excited?" I ask, grinning at her.

"Of course! My friends are gonna be here, and Aunt Abbi and Brinley and Stella!"

I swallow hard. "I don't know if Stella's gonna make it, Snickerdoodle. She's very busy with work and school." Never mind the fact that she's been living in our pool house for a week and hasn't said anything to me beyond a polite *hi* or *bye* since she ended our fling last Saturday night.

Every day's the same. I sit on the patio with my coffee in the mornings and inevitably catch sight of her, thanks to those floor-to-ceiling windows that overlook the pool. Then she leaves for classes and work and whatever she does after work. I watch for her car, and when it gets late, I think about texting to make sure she's okay, but then she's there, parking on the street and heading in to sleep and do it all again the next day.

I need to get a grip. I hurt her, and she doesn't want shit to do with me now. I need to accept that, but I'm pissed at Itsy, whoever the fuck she is, for telling Stella what I said. I can't help but think it was a reaction to my note ending our little online flirtation. Like I might not know her, but she knows me, and she told Stella because she wanted to get back at me.

When I catch sight of a swath of red hair from the corner of my eye, I can't help but turn my attention to the pool house. I shouldn't stare. I should definitely look away. But fuck. She's wearing headphones, a fitted tank top, and tiny light pink panties that show off her perfect ass, and she's . . . she's dancing.

The sight would make me smile if I weren't so horrified by my creepy landlord behavior. The truth is, I needed space this week too—to think about how I fucked up and to piece out how I feel about her changing the rules on me. She's the one who promised we could have a physical relationship without anyone getting hurt, but suddenly I'm an asshole for believing her?

My emotions are a fucking mess. I miss her. I miss how she made me feel. It's impossible not to feel happier when she's around. She's the type of person who'll take any reason to smile and run with it, because life's too short to be serious all the time. I might not understand it, but I respect it. In fact, I wish I were a little more like that. It'd make me a better dad.

She sways her hips side to side as she dances to music I can't hear, turning a slow circle until—*busted*. She meets my eyes and lifts her hand in a small wave before letting her gaze drift down over my shirtless chest.

A beat later, she looks down at her bare legs and then quickly back up to me—eyes wide, jaw unhinged—before she runs to the stairs and disappears.

Yep, I've officially become the creepy landlord.

"She's totally gonna come," Hope says, and I realize she was watching Stella too. "She's my buddy."

"We'll see," I say, and damn, do I hope my daughter's right.

My phone buzzes. I immediately think it might be a message from Stella and grab it so fast I almost drop it on the concrete.

> Amy: Fucking flight's delayed. If I'm LUCKY I'll be there sometime today, but there's no way I'm going to be back in time for the party, which means you're going to have to take care of the cake and decorations. I'm sorry, Kace.

And suddenly, I have bigger worries than my former fling's attendance at my daughter's birthday party.

STELLA

Kace has been running around his backyard like a chicken with his head cut off all morning. He's blown up a massive inflatable bounce castle, set up tables and chairs from the garage, and is now cleaning the pool. His bare chest is sweaty, and he has a scowl on his face that morphs into a polite smile when he spots me watching him. At least this time, I'm properly dressed.

Things haven't been comfortable between us this last week, and apparently that won't be changing now. My fault. I knew it'd end this way. But I can't see a guy work this hard for his daughter's birthday party and not offer to help.

I open the sliding doors and head out to the pool deck. "What's wrong?"

He screws up his face into that expression that tells me something's definitely not right, but he doesn't really want to say. "I hit some bumps with the party. It'll be okay. I just need to call my mom and see if she can come early to sit with Hope while I run out for some last-minute things."

"Don't be ridiculous. I can stay with her. Or I can run out and get stuff myself—whatever's easier for you."

"You don't have to work today?"

I took the day off to study for Monday's exam, but that can wait. "Nope. I'm at your service."

His shoulders sag. "Okay, well, Amy's stuck in New York. Her flight was delayed. She won't be home for the party. She'd insisted on getting all the decorations and the cake, but apparently she was just going to pick some up on the way home. Which means I have nothing. If you wouldn't mind running to the party supply store and maybe grabbing a cake at Costco, then I could stay here and get everything ready."

"That's no problem at all, but Kace . . ." I bite my lip, not wanting to sound like a snob.

"What?"

"What's Abbi going to say when she finds out you

wouldn't let her make Hope's cake but one from Costco is just fine?"

He scrubs a hand over his beard. "I don't know. When Amy wanted to take care of it, I assumed she had a plan."

I guess she did. If you can call swinging by Costco for a premade cake from their cooler a "plan." There's nothing wrong with Costco cake, but it's nothing like Abbi's—never mind that Abbi would decorate it to match the Elsa "ice princess" party theme. "I'll figure it out. Don't even worry about it."

His jaw twitches and he nods, but he's got that distant look about him, like he's focusing on an overwhelming mental to-do list.

I put a hand on his arm and squeeze, and he closes his eyes and exhales heavily. It's the first time we've touched since I ended things between us. Not that there was much to end. "It's just a party. She's turning five, and she's loved like crazy. It doesn't have to be perfect."

"It's not that." Finally, he meets my gaze. Is this what it feels like to snatch the bait and find yourself reeled in? I miss those eyes. I miss him looking at me like I'm the most beautiful thing in the world.

I miss believing there was something real between us.

I drop my hand. Kace studies it, opens his mouth like he's about to say something, then shakes his head. And turns away.

I clear my throat. "So . . . decorations and a cake. Anything else?"

He cringes. "Hope's very excited about the *games*, and Amy was also in charge of those." He shakes his head. "I know this is probably nothing a Google search couldn't solve, but I—"

"Say no more. I've got this."

❧

KACE

Hope's face is a perfect picture of five-year-old focus as she wobbles through the grass with a water balloon between her knees, trying to move as quickly as she can without popping it. On either side of her, two friends from her preschool do the same. Ten feet ahead, chalk spray paint marks the finish line. The adults cheer from the patio, and Brinley's ten-year-old daughter, Cami, stands at the end of the path to declare the winner.

The little girl with braids, Kara, picks up her pace and makes it a few strides ahead of the others, then shrieks when her balloon pops between her knees before she can cross the line.

"Slow and steady!" Cami shouts from the finish line. "Come on, Hopey! You got this."

Cami is Hope's honorary cousin, not to mention her idol, and at the sound of her voice, my daughter moves wrong and the balloon falls to the grass, busting between her bare feet. The last little girl standing giggles her way toward the finish line. All my focus is on Hope, though, and the big smile on her face.

I've had good birthdays, and I've had bad birthdays. I'm at the point in my life where it doesn't mean much either way. But birthdays are *everything* to my girl. She looks forward to them all year long. The only thing she's talked about this week is what her party's going to be like and who's going to be there.

Amy might be terrible about leaving everything to the last minute, but she's always pulled it together. After she texted this morning to let me know her flight was delayed, I worried this would be the year Hope's birthday was a disappointment on every level. Instead, she's so busy having fun that she's forgotten her mom's not here. At least temporarily.

"Who's ready for cake?" Abbi asks, sticking her head out the back door.

"Meeeeee!" the kids chorus, rushing toward the tables decorated with streamers and the rock candy "ice crystals" Stella sprinkled down the middle.

"Everyone sit down so we can sing to the birthday girl," my sister says before ducking back into the house. When she returns, she's holding a cake that looks like the castle from *Frozen*. Five candles blaze on top.

"Happy birthday to you," we all sing together as Abbi carefully sets the cake down in front of her niece. Hope sings along with us, with a spirited "Happy birthday to *meee*," and then takes one deep breath and blows out all the candles on her first try.

Everyone claps, and Abbi whisks the cake away to cut it. My mom helps, asking the girls if they want ice cream, and Stella and Brinley pass the plates out to the youngest guests, who dig in, making happy noises when the sugar hits their tongue.

My gaze lands on Stella, who's listening intently as Hope recaps the water balloon race and explains how the slippery balloon got away from her. Sometimes adults just humor kids, listening when they don't really care what they're saying. I've done it myself from time to time with other people's children. Do I really care about how you killed all those creepers on *Minecraft*? No. But I'll stand here and listen, because I know it matters to you. Hell, I've even done the half-assed listening thing to Hope when I've been particularly distracted by something else in my life, but that's not what happens when Stella listens to my kid telling a story. She laughs with Hope and adds her own observations. And it's not just today. She's always been that way. If she ever does have kids, she'll be an amazing mom. I hope that dream comes true for her.

The thought doesn't sit right, though, and I turn it around for a few seconds before I can figure out why. Stella's not the one who told me about wanting kids. That was Itsy.

Jesus, in retrospect, they're so similar. Itsy opened up more, but she had the same vibe Stella does. It's no wonder I was interested in her without ever seeing an actual picture. Now I wonder if I was just an idiot who was looking for an excuse not to fall in love again, and looking for a way I could be with Stella without risking my heart.

If I'd been honest with her—or even myself—I would've admitted that a physical relationship wasn't going to be enough for me, either. I like her too much for that. I have no idea if she feels the same about me or if she's interested in anything I have to offer, but it seems pretty narrow-minded of me to have assumed that just because she's single and carefree she wouldn't also enjoy a different kind of life.

"What's got you down?" Dean asks beside me. I was zoned out and didn't even realize he was standing there. "Baby girl's growing up too fast, isn't she?"

I nod. "Yeah, the years go quick, but I don't actually mind that she's growing up. I see all these parents saying they wish time would stop, but I don't feel that way. She gets cooler every year."

"She *is* cool. I like to think that's Uncle Dean rubbing off on her."

I grunt and shake my head. "Tell yourself whatever you want, but my kid is cool *despite* you."

He nudges me with his elbow and chuckles. "If that's not it, what's got you looking so morose?" He holds up a finger then tilts his head, studying my face. "Nope, I should've seen it the first time. That's the face of a man who's thinking about his woman. How are things with the, uh, online girlfriend?"

I swallow. "Over. We're not talking anymore." *And it's not the online girl I can't stop thinking about.* I hate keeping this whole thing with me and Stella from Dean, but what's the point in telling him now? "And before you ask, I'm fine."

"Right," Dean says. "So she wasn't a seventy-five-year-old granny playing you from her favorite recliner?"

"I thought she was supposed to be a sociopath living in his parents' basement."

Dean shrugs as if to say, *same thing.* "You know, no one's perfect. We've made mistakes and have secrets. Have you ever considered not being a scared little bitch about a new relationship?"

I narrow my eyes at him. "What do you know about it?"

He shrugs. "I just know you. You don't want to get hurt again, and that's understandable, but I'm wondering if maybe you're not giving this girl a real shot."

My attention is pulled off Dean when I spot Smithy sauntering across the yard, sucking on a Popsicle in the most lascivious way. I blink, and he winks at me. Because that's who Smithy is.

"What are you guys talking about?" he asks when he

joins us. He pops his Popsicle back into his mouth and slurps. Loudly.

"Kace was just telling me how much he misses his animated girlfriend."

Smithy's jaw drops, and he puts a pause on his little fellatio show. "Sorry, what?"

I jab my elbow into Dean's side. "Fuck off. That's *not* what I was saying."

"She's human and flawed and shit," Dean says. "So now he's going to move on and will probably end up with an AI in someone's lab."

I glare. "Since when do you care about my online dating life?"

"You're . . . not going to give her a chance?" Smithy asks. "Is it 'cause . . ." His not-at-all-subtle gaze drifts to Stella. I wonder if he knows about that. Luckily, Dean's fucking around on his phone and doesn't notice.

I give Smithy a hard look, and he shoves the Popsicle back in his mouth like it's a pacifier.

"Who are *you* talking to?" I ask Dean. He'd give me so much shit if I just started texting someone in the middle of a conversation.

He taps on the screen a couple more times, then slides the phone into his pocket. "Sorry." He glances around the party. "This turned out great."

I nod, grateful to move the subject away from Stella. "Yeah. I hope I got enough pictures for Amy. I think she's beating herself up for scheduling her flight this morning instead of taking the red-eye last night. This is the first time she's missed Hope's birthday."

"But at least she'll see her this evening," Dean says, and when I frown, he adds, "I mean, you know Amy. She'll find a way to get here so they can have their little mother-daughter birthday moment."

"Probably." I fucking hope so. While Hope is on cloud nine right now, she'll remember Mom's not here the moment everyone leaves.

Just like that, my phone buzzes with a text from Amy, as if Dean's some sort of psychic wonder. *Just landed in Atlanta. I'll be there soon!*

I turn the phone to Dean to show him. "Weirdo," I mutter.

"Whoa!" Smithy says, melted blue Popsicle juice dripping down his chin. "You've got the woo-woo, Dean."

Dean looks at the ground, then at the small group of parents gathering in a loose circle in the yard behind us, then back at Smithy. "It's just Amy." He shrugs. "Anyone could've guessed she wouldn't miss Hope's birthday."

Smithy cocks his head. "You're in a weird mood." He extends his Popsicle toward Dean's mouth. "Suck on this. It'll make you feel better."

Dean smacks his arm away. "Does that line work with your dates?"

Smithy waggles his brows. "I don't have to say it. One look, and they *know*."

I grimace. "Guys, there are small children within hearing distance. Could we dial the humor back to PG for a bit?"

Smithy chuckles and licks his blue lips.

Across the patio, Stella's clearing the plates off the table, and I rush in to help. "I can take those," I say at her side.

"I don't mind." She smiles up at me, and fuck. She looks so pretty today. She's wearing a pink sundress with big yellow happy-face flowers all over it, and her hair's brushed into a high ponytail. There's a new smattering of freckles on her shoulders, and I wonder if she's been studying outside on campus, wonder if those freckles would've come from an afternoon hanging out here if I hadn't screwed everything up.

For a beat, I feel like I can't breathe. The only thing I can focus on is the urge to bend and brush my lips over those spots, to taste this bit of her that I missed before.

I swallow back the urge and try to proceed like a fucking adult who's not ruled by his hormones. "Here." I take the plates from her hands. My fingers brush hers, and her gaze jumps to mine.

"Thanks."

"Did you get any cake?" I glance to the end of the table, where half of Abbi's creation sits untouched and half a dozen slices sit plated up around it. "Abbi's stuff is good."

She chews on her lip. "It's a weakness of mine." She leans closer and lowers her voice. "I was actually planning on waiting until everyone leaves so I could cut myself an inappropriately large serving and not have to filter out my foodgasm sounds."

I chuckle and pull my gaze off her mouth. I don't want to miss *that*, and the words to tell her as much are on the tip of my tongue, but I swallow them back. I want more than sex and teasing and innuendo with Stella, and it's about time she understands that. "Stick around later. Maybe we can talk."

Then I walk away, because I don't want to give her the chance to tell me she hates that idea.

CHAPTER TWENTY-THREE

STELLA

*S*hould I have spent today studying rather than planning a five-year-old's birthday party? *Yes.* How many regrets do I have about my choices? *None.*

The only thing better than seeing the stress lift from Kace's shoulders when I came home with the decorations and a plan for games was Hope's smile throughout her party. I know she's sad her mom wasn't there, and no amount of games or helium balloons can make up for that, but knowing I helped make her day fun is one of the best feelings I've had in months.

I expected our guest of honor to meltdown the minute her last guest left, but she didn't. She's sitting in the grass playing with her new presents while Kace and I clean up.

"Stella," Kace says, snatching the folding chairs from my hands. "Seriously, I've got this."

"I don't mind helping," I say, but I let him take them

because my arms are getting tired, and I should probably get out of the sun before I end up resembling an overripe tomato. "You can do the heavy lifting, and I'll go inside and load the dishwasher."

He smiles, his gaze dipping to my mouth. It's been doing that a lot today, and I like it. I also need him to *stop*, because I'm weak. "Okay, but don't forget we're having cake together once this is all cleaned up. I want—"

"Hopey, baby! Happy birthday, girl!" Amy shouts from the gate. Kace and I both turn to watch Amy stoop to her haunches and open her arms.

Hope drops her toys and runs across the lawn as fast as her little legs can carry her. "Mommy!"

I can't help that my attention shifts to Kace, can't help this masochistic need to see the longing in his eyes. Longing for his wife, for his family to be whole again.

He's smiling, but if he's feeling any sort of angst, he hides it well. Beyond happiness for his daughter, I can't tell what he's thinking. *Probably for the best.*

"I'll go work on those dishes," I say, stepping away before he can object.

Inside, the air is cool, and my sun-warmed skin prickles with goose bumps. I get to work loading the dishes and filling the sink with soapy water to wash the serving trays. When I'm still shivering a few minutes later, I grab one of Kace's hoodies from the back of a kitchen chair and pull it over my head. It's about three sizes too big, but it's soft and it smells like him. I bury my face into the neck and breathe in deeply.

"That looks good on you. It's especially cute with the dress."

I whip my head up as Kace closes the back door. He

strides toward me casually, but his eyes skim up and down, taking in my hoodie-and-sundress combo. "Yeah, I bet this ensemble will be all the rage this fall." I give him my best apologetic smile. "Sorry. After being in the heat all day, the AC felt super cold. I hope you don't mind."

"Not at all." He turns to the sink and shuts off the water. "You didn't need to do all this. You saved my ass today, and the least I can do is clean up myself."

"I wanted to help. Where's Hope?"

"She went to the arcade with her mom."

Which means we're alone. And I'm in his sweatshirt, the smell of him weakening my defenses faster than shots of tequila. And he's looking at me like . . .

"Cake," he says, and it jerks me from my hopelessly lovesick and desperate thoughts so fast that I actually feel a little dizzy.

"What?"

His smile is slow and lazy. The kind of smile inspired by a weekend wasted in bed. The kind given after a kiss stolen from a longtime lover. I love that smile so much. From the way his eyes crinkle in the corners to how it drags my attention to his soft lips. "I promised to feed you," he says. "Cake."

I grab the dishrag from the sink and swipe it across the counter. "I'll take a piece with me when I go. It's no big deal."

He's already cutting massive slices and sliding them onto dessert plates. "Every year since her first birthday, I've eaten a second piece of cake with my daughter after the guests left. Don't make me eat alone."

My heart sinks a little at this admission but is buoyed when he waves the plate in front of me. "Sure." I grab a fork from the drawer and lean back against the counter as I take a bite. As I anticipated, the sugary frosting melts on my tongue and pulls sex sounds from my throat before I can stifle them.

Kace pauses, his fork halfway to his mouth. "Can we talk about this foodgasm thing?"

I laugh. "Isn't it kind of self-explanatory?"

"We don't know what we don't know, right?" His eyes are glued to my mouth as I slide another bite of cake past my lips. I moan involuntarily—I would do a hundred extra chem labs for Abbi's buttercream—and he clears his throat. "I thought foodgasm was an exaggeration, but now I'm wondering if it's . . ."

I put my plate down to resist the urge to stuff my face while he's standing right there. "What?"

"Um . . . literal?"

I laugh—not a polite, small sound but a deep, full-belly laugh. God, that feels good. I'm sick of walking around sad and stressed all the time. "Like, could I ditch my vibrators and just stuff my bedside table with your sister's cake?"

He coughs. "That sounds really dirty. Can we not call it my *sister's* cake and just go back to the part where I got to watch you moan?"

Yes, please. I really, really want to go back to that part. My cheeks flame hot—not from embarrassment, but from the sheer struggle it takes to wield this much self-control. Kace wants me, and I don't want to say no. But even if he's interested in something more than a short-term fling, I can't bring myself to do what I'd have to do if I wanted to say yes.

"You have . . ." He cups my face in one big hand, and the feel of his rough callouses on my cheek sends a shiver of longing through me. He swipes his thumb across my bottom lip. "Frosting," he whispers, and tilts my face up to his, and I don't even know how we ended up close enough for this. At some point, he closed the distance between us. Or I maybe did. At some point, the air was filled with the magnetic vibration of attraction that turns everything over to physics. The two opposite forces must meet.

At some point, I fell in love.

He sweeps his thumb across the corner of my mouth. "Right here."

I swallow. "All better?"

"Not yet," he says, and slowly lowers his mouth to mine.

I spent a lot of years telling myself that my feelings for Kace were entirely rooted in the fact that they were unrequited. He was another example of my bad track record. Maybe he wasn't a bad guy, but a one-sided love isn't *healthy*.

But now, I can't even blame this blinding attraction on his resistance. There's no resistance in this kiss. There was the first time, when he wasn't sure about crossing lines with me. And even the second time, in my bedroom, when we handed the reins over to lust. But now, all the walls are down. Every sweep of his lips and flick of his tongue tells me he wants this. He wants me.

I pull away, breathless and needy but with my eyes burning with unshed tears. "We should stop." *Stop now before it's too hard. Stop now before you break my heart.*

"Stella?"

I place a palm flat against his chest and nudge him back. "I can't think when you're that close."

He retreats, but his slow, measured breaths fill my ears. He rocks back on his heels and shoves his hands into his pockets. "Can you explain what happened? What changed? Why are you pushing me away?"

"I just . . ." I shake my head. There's no way I can answer this very reasonable question without more of the truth than I can bear to give. And there's no way I can live outside his back door once I admit that truth to him. "I need to go study." I look around the kitchen, but I'm not seeing a damn thing. "Want me to help with anything else before I go?"

"No. I don't need you to clean up for me. I need you to *talk* to me." He presses his palm to his chest. "I want to make this better. How do you know Itsy? What else did she tell you?"

I don't know *Itsy. I am Itsy.* The words are right there—a bitter pill on my tongue that I desperately want to spit out. But I can't. "Nothing. And don't . . ." I trap the sob in my chest and struggle to breathe around it. How long will I feel heartbroken over this? "You told me all I needed to know with what you didn't say. I told you I couldn't do just casual with you, and you didn't say we could try more. You let it go."

"What was I supposed to say?"

Tears roll down my cheeks. "You were supposed to say you couldn't do just casual sex with me, either. You were supposed to give enough fucks about me that you wanted more than that too."

"Maybe I could, but I never expected—"

"Don't. It's better that you didn't. It's easier this way." I shake my head. I've said more than I want to. "I'll be out of your hair soon. I'll be living somewhere else, and you'll forget I was ever around to tempt you with easy sex."

"Stella, I want *you*. Not just your body, not just sex." He blows out a breath. "I screwed up because I wasn't ready. I wasn't looking for a relationship, and I panicked. But I'll figure it out. Give me a chance."

The universe must be laughing, because until him, until now, I've never wanted someone *good* who actually wanted me back.

Except he doesn't want me. Not all of me, mistakes included.

I turn to the back door. "We both knew this was a bad idea from the start." My voice cracks.

"Which part? Moving in, or being with me?"

"Both." I walk away, even though I know I haven't fixed anything, and even though it hurts so much to leave another chunk of my heart behind.

KACE

"Dean!" I run outside, fresh out of the shower, in nothing but a pair of cotton shorts. It's barely daylight, and Dean and Smithy are loading Stella's bed into Dean's truck. Her couch is already in there. "What's happening?"

"Just moving Stella," Dean says, avoiding my gaze.

Smithy's eyes go big, like I'm gonna take him out or something.

I spin around, looking for Stella, feeling frantic. Last night she said she was moving *soon*, but I didn't think *soon* meant in less than twelve hours. "Where is she?"

Smithy ducks his head and jogs back to the pool house.

"She's gone. She didn't want you trying to convince her to stay," Dean says, and there's something hard in his eyes, like he knows more than he's letting on. He looks at me for a long time, then shakes his head and sighs. "I'm just trying to be a good brother. I don't want to get in the middle of it."

I step closer to him and keep my voice low. "Where's she going to live?"

"She doesn't want me to say." Dean cringes and casts a glance over his shoulder toward the pool house. "Listen, I haven't been a very good friend lately, and I want to do better, but right now, I need to be a good brother first."

I wouldn't respect him so damn much if it were any other way, so I back off, even though part of me wants to argue this is the best place for her right now. "Make sure she's safe, wherever she goes. I couldn't live with myself if some asshole . . ." I cringe just thinking about her old landlord.

He nods. "I know, man. I will."

I retreat another step. "I'll get out of the way, then."

SHE'S GONE. I watched my own motherfucking best friend pack up Stella's shit and drive off.

I can't blame her. It's a special kind of torture being this close when we're doing nothing but hurting each other. But watching the guys' trucks drive off with her stuff felt so damn *final*, and I don't want to believe it's over. It wasn't supposed to be this way.

CHAPTER TWENTY-FOUR

STELLA

I've been sad all week, but today is a happy day. Today I got to watch my lifelong best friend renew her vows with her first love. I watched Brinley and Marston make their promises, and instead of feeling sad or jealous, I felt hopeful. I'm still hurting. My feelings for Kace run too deep, and I won't get over this anytime soon, but if those two found their way back to each other after all the heartache and obstacles life threw at them, maybe there's hope for a cheap porno slut like me.

Brinley's staff turned the patio from a ceremony site into a reception venue seamlessly, and then there was food and cake and toasts, and then I got to watch the best couple I know look into each other's eyes as they danced.

All my sadness will be there tomorrow, but today's a good day.

"Hey, beautiful," Abbi says, wrapping her arm around my waist. "Are you hanging in there?"

I lean my head on hers and sigh. "Yeah. Thanks to about three and a half glasses of champagne."

She giggle-snorts. "Right? I'm going to regret the bubbly tomorrow, but it is so good." She turns her head and studies me. "You're really okay?"

"Not completely. I'm getting there, though. Thanks to you guys." Because my friends have come together for me in a big way over the last two weeks. Not only have they all kept their mouths shut about who Itsy really is, they listened when I cried and second-guessed. They plotted new living arrangements for me and even helped me study, though my chemistry grade is looking like a lost cause. Nursing school might not be in the cards for me. I'm sadder about not having a prospective solid income than I am about not getting to be a nurse. That was my mom's dream, anyway. The part that appealed to me was the paycheck and maybe the respect. Not many people are impressed when they find out you're a receptionist, even if you're the best receptionist a business could want.

"I don't want to rush you," Abbi says, "but if you wanted to tell him, there's no one in the office across from Brinley's, and I left it unlocked."

I close my eyes. "I kind of don't want to ruin the day, but there's another part of me that knows I should tell him while I'm feeling at peace about everything."

She takes my hand and squeezes. "For what it's worth, I think he's being an idiot and he should throw himself at your feet and offer you the world."

I scoff and shake my head. "You wouldn't feel that way if you knew the whole story."

She gives my hand another squeeze. "I knew Reggie back in the day, and he liked to run his mouth," she says, referring to my college boyfriend.

"God." I squeeze my eyes shut. "Does everyone know?"

"Personally, I never believed his stories. I thought he was just full of it and trying to look like a badass," she says. When I open my eyes, she's frowning at me. "What he did wasn't just wrong, it was illegal. None of this is your fault."

I swallow hard. "Thank you. That means a lot."

"I emailed you some links to sites that explain your rights and the contact info to a lawyer friend. That is, if you want to do something about it. I'll support you, whatever you decide."

"I appreciate that, Abbi, but I can't afford—"

"She'll do it pro bono. She has experience with this, so helping women like you is a passion project for her."

I don't know what to say. I'm so grateful and overwhelmed, and after years of feeling like my best option was to hide, it's hard to wrap my head around an alternative. "Thank you," I whisper.

"Of course. This is what friends are for." She cocks her head to the side. "If those videos really are a deal breaker for Kace, he doesn't deserve you."

I bite my bottom lip and nudge her shoulder with mine. "You're going to make me cry." I'd expect those words from Savvy or Brinley, but Abbi and I aren't as close, and considering how protective she is of her brother . . . "That means a lot."

"Then again," she says, smirking, "in order to find out, you'll still have to tell him the truth."

So true. "Maybe another glass of champagne first."

KACE

Stella is stunning. I know I'm supposed to be giving all my attention to the bride and groom, but how can I when the woman who has my heart is in the room dressed in a slinky bridesmaid's dress and laughing with all our friends? I've wanted to ask her to dance about a dozen times, but stopped myself.

She catches my eye and smiles at me, which is unexpected, but not as unexpected as her nodding to the door then walking inside The Orchid, casting a glance over her shoulder like she expects me to follow.

I wait a minute to make sure no one's watching. If she's finally going to talk to me, I don't want our friends interrupting.

Once in the building, I'm not sure where to go. There are dozens of rooms and offices in here. Voices are coming from the kitchen, and I follow them to find my sister and Dean standing nose to nose, faces red like they're arguing. I open my mouth to ask them if they've seen Stella when Abbi smacks both hands against Dean's chest.

"How could you?" She's crying, so I take a step forward. "You're risking the best friend you've ever had, and why?"

I stop, dread curdling my stomach.

"I know," Dean growls. "I fucking know, okay, but I love her. It's not just sex. We have a *connection,* and I think she could love me too if she'd take me back."

"Amy will chew you up and spit you out, and all you'll have to show for it is a ruined friendship. Is she worth that?"

What. The. *Fuck?*

"This isn't your business," he growls. "I'll tell Kace eventually, but—"

"No need." My voice is a croak.

Dean spins around. "Kace." He pales and his jaw works, but he can't seem to find any words. "Just let me explain."

I try to swallow. It feels like there's something lodged in my throat. "You want to *explain* why you're talking about *loving* my ex-wife?" I shake my head, backing up. "Nah. I'll pass." Then I realize Stella's walked in the kitchen at some point, and she's looking back and forth between me and Dean. "Did you know about this too?" I ask her.

She nods. "I'm sorry." She runs from the room.

"Kace," Abbi says, suddenly at my side and gripping my arm. "You're okay, right? You've moved on. I know you have. You have better things ahead of you."

I shrug her off, turn on my heel, and get the fuck out of that kitchen. I stop dead in the middle of the hall. I don't want to head back to the party—back to the friends who'll see the shock on my face and want me to explain. I turn to head to the front of the building and step into the darkened reception area. A single light glows down the hall, and I follow it like a beacon.

Stella's standing in an empty office, staring out the windows. "I'm sorry I couldn't tell you about Dean and Amy," she says without turning around.

I close the door before crossing the room. She'll send me away any second, but I can't stand this distance between us. My chest aches with how much I miss her.

"I know you want your wife back, and—"

I usually overthink, but not this time. This time, I pull her into my arms and kiss her hard. She gasps against my mouth, and I half expect her to push me away, but she pulls me close instead—hands fisted into my shirt, mouth opening under mine. She tastes like champagne and smells so sweet, and I'd stay in this room all night, all week, all fucking month if it meant she wouldn't leave my arms.

"I don't," I say when she pulls back. "I don't want Amy back, and I don't care who she sleeps with." I blow out a breath, the adrenaline tapering off. "I care that Dean kept it from me."

"Oh," she says. "Well, you should talk to him, because he's a mess."

I slide my hands down her back. "I'm talking to *you* right now."

"Kace . . ."

I take a deep breath. "Why don't I get a chance? Because of what Itsy told you? I was never saying *you* had no substance. She misunderstood me. I was saying I thought our relationship was superficial, and I was an idiot for ever thinking that, but you need to give me a break here. Our plan at the beginning was for this to just be a physical fling."

"I know," she whispers, bowing her head. "I can't blame you for the way you feel."

"But I don't feel that way anymore." I tip her chin up with two fingers so she can look me in the eye when I explain. "There's *nothing* superficial about how I feel about you, and I'm sorry I didn't say so sooner. I'm a coward, okay? I was scared to try for more. But now I just want a fucking chance to prove we can be good together—to prove how much substance we have. *Please.*"

Her lips part and she stares at me, and I can't help it. I swoop in and steal another kiss. Then more. On her mouth, her jaw, her neck.

"You look so beautiful today. I couldn't take my eyes off you the whole ceremony."

"I know." Her hands roam across my back, over my shoulders and chest. She nips at my lips and gasps into my mouth. "I like it when you look at me. I'm so weak for it."

"Nothing about you is weak." I yank up her skirt and stroke her thigh, working my way around to the thin band of her panties at the top of her hip. I follow that silky scrap of fabric down between her legs and stroke her there. She bites back a cry. "I'm the one who's weak for you, and I'm sick of trying so hard to resist it. Let me touch you. Let me feel this." I slip two fingers into her panties, and she gasps at my first pass over her clit. "Shh. Later, you can scream as loud as you need to, and I'll fucking relish every sound you make, but right now I need you to be quiet."

"Kace." Her hands are shaking as she unbuckles my belt, unzips my pants. "Just tonight, okay? I need you."

Just tonight? Fuck that. I want more than tonight, and I'm going to make her see she does too. I tease her again and again until she's trembling in my arms and I feel her orgasm building. "You're so slick. I can't stop thinking about how this would feel on my cock." I drive two fingers into her as I press my mouth to hers, muffling her needy whimper. Slowly, I drag in and out and watch her face—her heavy-lidded eyes, her teeth sinking into her bottom lip. "I want to spin you around and fuck you against this window." I withdraw, softening my touch as I circle her clit—once, twice, three times—before plunging my fingers inside her again.

"Please."

I don't know if she's asking me to fuck her or let her come, but then my dick's in her hand and she's stroking me, and I can't think about anything but getting closer. Closer to her slick heat, closer to her soft whimpers, closer to the woman who stole my heart and then ran away. "You have no idea how much I want you. How much I've missed you," I say, jacking up into her hand as I continue to tease her slick sex.

I spin her around and yank her hips back to tilt her toward me. She writhes and rubs her sex against my dick until the tip notches inside her.

She jerks away, her dress falling back down, then stumbles backward. "I'm sorry," she says. She closes her eyes, and tears roll down her cheeks. "We can't."

Shit, shit, shit. "Stella, please."

"You don't want me, Kace. You'll realize that soon enough." Then she opens the door and runs away.

CHAPTER TWENTY-FIVE

KACE

I'm working on my laptop at the kitchen table when the front door opens with a crash, and Hope announces, "We're home!"

I close my laptop and stand just in time for my daughter to run at me and wrap me in a hug. I stoop down to press a kiss to the top of her head.

"She was up at four a.m. asking to watch Elsa and Anna," Amy says, appearing from the hall. "So be warned—she might be cranky tonight."

"I can handle it." I turn my attention to Hope. "Hey, Snickerdoodle. Did you have a good night with your mom?"

"The best. I got new 'Merican Girl dolls." Her eyes go wide. "*Two* of them."

I arch a brow at this and look to Amy, but she shrugs. "They're her birthday presents from me, Kace. Relax. They just took longer to get here than I expected."

"Can I go play with my dolls?" Hope asks, bouncing.

I nod. "Only for a few minutes while I talk to Mommy, then I want you to help me clean your room."

She runs off before I can even finish talking, and I laugh. I'm sure she didn't hear what I said about her room and probably doesn't want to.

"She loves those dolls," Amy says, but when I turn to her, her mouth is pulled tight in a grimace as she stares out at the backyard.

"Are you okay?" I cock my head to the side, studying the anguish contorting her features. "Ames?"

"I heard Stella moved out."

I swallow hard. "Yeah. She found another place."

When Amy looks up at me, tears spill down her cheeks. "I'm afraid I made a mistake."

"About what? Dean? Because you did." My jaw is tense, and it's almost funny. I'm angrier with her for leading Dean on than I am with Dean for sleeping with my ex-wife. "That was a ridiculously bad move on your part."

"I know, but that's not the mistake I'm talking about."

"Then what?"

"Us." She swallows, and the next thing I know, her arms wrap around me and she's pressing her lips to mine. Call it hope or habit, but I kiss her back, and when her tongue touches my lips, I meet it with my own. *This is my wife. I'm kissing my wife.* But no matter how many times I say the words to myself, they still feel wrong.

She's not my wife. She's my ex. Finally, my brain's caught up.

I push her back, gently but firmly.

"Sorry," she says, bowing her head.

"That's not who we are anymore." That hasn't been who

we are for a long-ass time. And Christ, why did it take me so long to figure that out?

She looks up. "It could be. Maybe it should be." When she steps close again, I back away, and she wraps her arms around her middle. "I know I have no right to ask, Kace. I *know*. I thought I wanted more freedom, but I miss the routine of our lives. I miss knowing that if things fall apart, I won't have to fix them alone. I miss having someone there to remind me to lock the front door and someone who'll fix the shower when it leaks. I miss knowing that if I'm at a loss for how to respond to Hope's obstinance, someone's there to lead the way."

I blink at her. "What are you saying?"

"I'm saying I miss our life." She reaches for me, then drops her hands to her sides. "I miss our marriage."

For months and months after she moved out, I waited for her to come home and say those words. For more than a year, I let myself believe that what we had, what our marriage had been, was good enough for me. But I know better now. I see what she saw all along. "Amy . . ." I hang my head. "You were right to leave."

She draws in a shaky breath. "I was stupid."

When I lift my head and meet her eyes, I know I have to say the words I promised myself so long ago I wouldn't. "If our relationship were truly all you needed, you wouldn't have had an affair."

Her eyes go wide and she stumbles backward. "What?"

"I know you had an affair with Clint. It was never Stella. It was you. And she knew about it, didn't she? That's why you started telling me all those things about her. You were afraid she'd tell me, and you didn't want me to believe her."

Amy's eyes fill with tears. "I didn't want her to destroy our *family*."

I scoff. "No. You didn't want me to find out *you* had already destroyed it." I look away, because it's too hard to reconcile what I understand now with the woman I thought she was. God, it's all so obvious. The way Amy suddenly didn't want me to touch her anymore. I thought it was motherhood, that she was too tired and run-down from working all day and then coming home and trying to make up for all those lost hours with Hope.

When I turn back to her, she's staring at me, her expression desperate. "I did it for us." She swallows. "Clint was always flirting with me. I told you that."

"Yeah, but somehow you left out the part where you were fucking him."

"You and Dean were on the verge of losing your business. Without that promotion, I wouldn't have been able to give the company a loan. I did it for *us*."

I shake my head. There's a gaping hole in my chest—not because I want my wife back but because I'm realizing I spent years married to a woman I don't even know. Because I spent years lying to myself about what we had. "You did it for yourself." I swallow back the hurt and betrayal. "And I don't know whether it was for pleasure or because you wanted to be the hero, but if you knew me at all, you'd have known I'd rather lose the company and work some mind-numbing desk job for the rest of my life before sleeping next to a woman who'd betray me like that." I squeeze my eyes shut, but there's a storm happening in my mind, casting every happy family memory under the pall of her choices. "Did I somehow make you think my business was more important to me than our marriage?"

"No." She shakes her head, blond curls bouncing.

"Did Clint force you?" I remember Stella's description of how he put his hand up her skirt, tried to touch her without her consent. "Was he—"

"No." Tears roll down her cheeks, and she blows out a breath. "I liked the attention, okay? He made me feel sexy and wanted for the first time since Hope was born."

I flinch. I did everything in my power to make her feel those things. I failed.

"I don't think I would've done anything if it weren't for the job. We *needed* the money, Kace."

"The job gave you an excuse to do what you wanted to do, and then when Stella found out, you decided to run a smear campaign to make sure I'd never trust her."

She swallows. "You don't understand. I was *terrified* I'd lose you and Hope. I knew what I was doing was wrong, but in my mind it was a temporary transgression, and you and I would have a better life because of it."

I drop into a chair and cradle my head in my hands. "I've spent years blaming myself. I couldn't figure out where I went wrong. Why you wouldn't let me touch you anymore, why you withdrew . . ."

"I made a mistake. A terrible mistake." Her gentle features twist into ugly rage. "I can't believe she told you. But you know what? She's made mistakes too. She's in online *porn*, Kace. Why do you think I'm so against her being around my daughter? That stuff never goes away. It'll haunt her for the rest of her life."

My head snaps up, and I hear screeching tires in my mind as I replay Amy's words. "Online porn?"

"Yes! Oh my God, she tries to act like it's not there, but it is. The internet is forever, as they say."

I didn't find out until he'd broken up with me that he'd uploaded them to all kinds of amateur porn sites.

The room tilts off balance. Itsy was so scared to tell me that secret, but she forced herself to do it because she thought it could ruin us, and she needed to know how I felt about it before we got any closer. And I made things exclusive with Stella, only to have her pull away that same night . . .

Fuck. I feel like someone just pulled back a curtain, and what I should've known all along is plain as day before me. Itsy . . . Stella is Itsy. Itsy is Stella. It's so obvious that I'd laugh if it weren't also a disaster. Why didn't she tell me?

I close my eyes and drag a hand over my face. I told her the other woman I was seeing had shared more about herself with me and that it was a deal breaker. I didn't specify what, but Stella knew I was talking about those videos. She knew, because she'd just confided it the night before.

I have so many questions, and I don't understand how this happened, but it's obvious now why she's pushed me away. Why she knew things I'd told Itsy.

"You understand," Amy says softly. "You deserve better than someone like that."

"You don't know her at all. There isn't anyone better than Stella—not for me." I swallow the lump of emotion in my throat. It was one thing to not understand why she was pushing me away, but it's another entirely to know why she did. I don't blame her a bit. "As for those videos of her? I'm disappointed you'd use something like that as ammunition." My lips twist in disgust. "I thought you were better than that."

Her mouth works for a minute, making her look like a

fish out of water before she finally finds her words. "That was our deal. If she told you about Clint, I'd tell the world what I'd learned about her."

"She didn't tell me about Clint. I figured it out myself."

She pales. "How?"

I huff out a laugh, but there's no humor in it. "I suspected there was someone long before you moved out." I swallow. How fucked up am I that I ignored those instincts? That I would've rather lived a lie than lose something that was already broken? "I was never sure, but I didn't want to be, so I told myself I was wrong. That my suspicions were totally off-base. I didn't want to lose you."

"It was a mistake, and I'd never let it happen again. I just—"

"You want someone to take care of you."

She shrugs. "Is that a crime?"

"But you don't want *me*, Amy. Don't you see the difference?"

She opens her mouth to speak then snaps it shut again.

"Be honest with me—with yourself—did you feel anything when you kissed me just now?"

"I wanted to." Her bottom lip trembles. "I really did."

"What do you want from me?"

Her entire face crumples as she sobs. "I want to keep my family. I want us to be *okay*. Please don't hate me. Don't keep my daughter from me."

"Hey." I stand and pull her into my arms. Shit. She curls into my chest, shaking. "I don't hate you, Amy, and I'm not going to keep Hope from her mother."

When she pulls back, her face is red and streaked with tears. "I'd *hate you* if you did this to me."

I grunt. There's some honesty, at least. "I didn't say I'm

not angry. I don't *like* you very much at the moment. That doesn't mean I'd keep you from Hope. You weren't a very good wife, but you're a great mom."

"Maybe we could try again," she says, her words squeaking a little. She pulls out of my arms and studies me. "Maybe we could make it work now that the truth is out there."

"I don't want to." If this whole thing weren't so fucked, I'd laugh to hear myself say those words. I've wasted a year of my life waiting for Amy. Our marriage was over the minute she decided sleeping with her boss was a good idea. "I don't hate you, but I don't want to be with you, either."

She flinches. "I understand. I betrayed you, and you can't be expected to forgive—"

"I'm in love with Stella."

Her eyes go wide. "Oh." She nods. "Right, well, who didn't see that coming?"

"Ames . . ."

"No. It's fine, Kace. I'm happy for you. I just . . ." More tears spill down her cheeks, and she backs away. "I know what it feels like to be loved by you, and I know what it feels like to throw that away because life's left you . . . discontent. I just hope she's not an idiot like I was."

I shake my head. "Nah. I'm the idiot here. I fucked up."

"Then apologize." She shakes her head. "The path that made me lose you—lose our *marriage*—it started with one kiss. One kiss in the boardroom at the end of a long day. He just touched his lips to mine and told me I was beautiful, told me he'd like to spend more time with me. I went home and convinced myself I couldn't tell you about it, convinced myself I could turn something bad into something good, justified a whole affair. After that, nothing was ever the same between you and me." She touches my cheek. "Don't be like me. Don't let the small mistake turn into something you two can never recover from."

"It's not that small," I whisper. And it's not my first mistake, either. What I said about her to Itsy in the beginning—that was my first mistake. Or maybe my first mistake was thinking my attraction to Stella was ever just physical.

"Did you cheat on her? Did you break your vows?"

I blow out a breath. "Obviously not."

"Then fix it, Kace."

"What about Dean? Are you going to apologize to him? Are you going to fix that?"

She turns her head and studies the wall. "I don't want that. He's the one who wants more. He knew I wasn't looking for anything but no-strings fun."

"You can't have no-strings fun with someone you already have feelings for," I say. And it's another truth that's so obvious now it's been laid out there. "When there are already strings, pretending there aren't just makes a tangled mess."

"But I never had—"

"*He* did. And fuck, Amy, you and I used to talk about the way he looked at you, how badly my best friend was crushing on my wife. So don't pretend you didn't know."

"I liked the way he looked at me," she whispers. "And I know that makes me selfish, but I've been lonely."

"Give it to him straight, and then get out of his life." I see her so clearly now, and I'm disappointed that she's not a better woman. "Don't drag it out like you did with me."

Grimacing, she nods. "Good luck with Stella." She walks away, and . . . it doesn't hurt. She's not tearing out my heart as she goes. She's leaving room for something new.

❧

"DADDY, UNCLE DEAN IS HERE!" Hope says from the front window. She knows she's not allowed to answer the door without me, but that doesn't stop her from wanting to be the first to know who's here.

"Thanks, kiddo." Fucking finally. I texted him hours ago telling him I needed him to come over so we could talk. I pull open the front door and immediately burst into laughter.

Dean Jacob is standing on my front porch with a bouquet of flowers and three Mylar balloons with the words *I'm sorry* printed on them. "These are for you," he says, a lopsided smile twisting his lips.

"What the hell?"

"Not 'posed to say *hell*, Daddy," Hope says, scooting in front of me to get to her favorite honorary uncle. "Pretty flowers!"

"Just call it a *bromantic* gesture, and don't give me any more shit about it, okay? You wanted me to come over. I thought I should be prepared to grovel." He stoops to his haunches and whispers to Hope, "Tell your dad to take them and ask me in. I feel pretty silly out here."

I grab the flowers from his hands and turn into the house. "Come on in, you weirdo."

His steps echo behind mine as I lead the way to the kitchen. I set the flowers on the island before returning my attention to my friend.

Dean hands the balloons to Hope, who accepts them with jaw-gaping awe. "Thank you!"

"I am sorry," Dean says softly when we're finally eye to eye. "I handled everything terribly, and I wouldn't blame you for hating me forever, but I hope you'll forgive me instead." His jaw tightens as he tilts his face up to the ceiling. "If she'd been mine, I'd certainly take issue with you sleeping with her after we broke up."

I shake my head and try to figure out where to start. "Three things. First, you did handle it terribly. You should've been upfront with me." I sigh. "But second, I feel pretty bad for your brokenhearted ass, so I'm not going to make you grovel too much."

"Thanks," he mutters. "I don't deserve that."

"How are you holding up?"

He shrugs. "I don't feel like I should complain to you about how your ex broke my heart, so maybe we should just skip that part?"

"I'm sorry. She . . ." I shake my head. "She's not as perfect as I always thought she was."

"I could've told you that a long time ago," he says, looking at his shoes, "but I never wanted her because I thought she was perfect." He rolls his shoulders back and lifts his head. "And the third thing?" he asks, looking like he's bracing himself for the swing of my fist.

"Third, I'm in love with your sister, and I want you to help me get her back."

His eyes go wide. "You're not gonna hurt her again?"

I swallow. "I never meant to hurt her the first time, but I was an idiot and didn't realize she was the one I was talking to online, and . . ." The rest of his words sink in. "You already knew? How? Did Stella say something?" *Did she tell you how I can fix this? Do you think I have a chance?*

"Yeah, I knew. A couple of weeks ago, she found out your sister had swapped her picture on Random with that pic of Jessica Rabbit, realized you hadn't known who you were talking to all that time, and completely flipped out. She cried so much she about flooded my living room." He punches me in the shoulder. *Hard.* "Bastard."

I rub the throbbing ache, open my mouth to defend myself, then snap it shut again. "You . . . knew all this time? And you haven't kicked my ass yet?"

His mouth hitches into a crooked grin. "I wanted to, but Stella swore me to secrecy." He opens the fridge and pulls out a beer, pops off the cap, and takes a long pull. "And anyway, it's not like I had a leg to stand on, considering what I had going on with Amy."

Shit. I blow out a breath. "How much do you know?"

"Just that she told you some secret online, and you didn't want anything to do with the online version of her after you found out."

It's not exactly that simple. I loved so many things about Itsy, but since I didn't know she was Stella when she told me that secret, since I thought I needed to choose between her and Stella, it was easy to walk away. It wouldn't be honest to pretend that secret wouldn't scare me off a stranger. But Stella's not a stranger. She's the woman I love, and her secrets aren't deal breakers. They're part of who she is.

"And, listen, I don't really understand how you two got yourself in such a mess to begin with, but I can't stand seeing my baby sister this sad. Now that you know she's Itsy, can you please just . . . fix it?"

I swallow. "I want to."

"When she talks about this secret—whatever it is—do you know what she's referring to?"

"Yeah," I say, my voice rough.

"You said it was a deal breaker. Is it? Because I can't help you if you're going to put her through that again."

"It's *not*. Maybe it would be with someone else, but it gave me an excuse to choose Stella." I shake my head. "I still don't understand what happened. Abbi changed Stella's profile pic?"

"Yeah, so when you swiped on Jessica Rabbit, Stella thought you'd swiped on her normal profile picture and assumed you knew who you were talking to. It wasn't until Abbi fessed up that she realized she was the 'other woman' you'd mentioned. And at that point, she knew how you felt about her secret. She didn't want to tell you the truth until she could move out, and then she didn't want to tell you because she was so embarrassed."

"And now she's gone and wants nothing to do with me," I finish.

Dean grimaces. "I don't think that's true. She doesn't want to own up to whatever it is she told you. How she feels about you hasn't changed." He drains his beer and tosses it in the trash. "Do I wanna know what this secret is?"

I shake my head. "Not all secrets need to be shared with the world. You're better off not knowing this one."

"What are you gonna do?"

I grab a beer for myself and think of Stella as I take a long drink. "I think I have an idea."

CHAPTER TWENTY-SIX

STELLA

> GoodHands69: I know we don't talk
> anymore, but I could use a friend
> right now.

I blow out a slow breath and read it again, hearing the words in Kace's voice and feeling a little more heartsick. I keep telling myself I'm going to delete my account. But I never do. And this is exactly why. I hoped he might eventually message me again.

"What is it?" Savvy asks softly.

I'm sitting at her kitchen table and gathering information Abbi's lawyer friend needs while Savvy futzes around in the kitchen. When I moved out of the pool house, we took all my furniture to a storage unit, and I moved into Savvy's with two suitcases, a pillow, and a broken heart. Her couch isn't the worst I've slept on, but I sure hope I can find a long-term solution soon.

I turn my phone so she can see the screen. "He wants to talk."

Savvy frowns. "You have to tell him anyway, right? Eventually? So talk to him. Be there for him. He might not know this is you and you're her, but *you* are the one he wants to talk to." She screws up her face and shudders. "What a mess. Go be the one to listen."

I know I need to tell him. Putting it off has only made me dread doing it that much more. But then when I tried last night, he ended up finding out about Dean and Amy first, and then I almost let him fuck me against a window. Clearly, I have no self-control.

> ItsyBitsy123: Are you okay?
> GoodHands69: Not really. Remember how I told you I was seeing someone else? She dumped me, and while I didn't really understand it at the time, some things have come to light that helped me understand. I'd do anything for another chance with her.

My heart stutters, revving for a race I'm not sure I'm ready for. Does he know?

> ItsyBitsy123: Maybe she's not who you think. Maybe it's better that it's ended now.
> GoodHands69: Actually, I know her pretty well. I've known her since we were kids,

and I've always cared about her. But I
fucked up. My divorce left me pretty
insecure about relationships, and I thought
all I wanted from her was sex, but it was
always more than that. From the very first
touch, it was more. In fact, I think that's
why I liked talking to you so much. Every
message you sent me reminded me of her.
I always heard your words in her voice and
imagined her talking to me.

And then I fell in love with her.

He *loves* me? But he wouldn't if he knew the truth.

I drop my phone and put my face in my hands. "I can't do this."

Savvy scoops up my phone, draws in a ragged breath, then strokes my hair. "Girly, I think you need to keep reading."

I take the phone back and reluctantly look at the screen. There's a new message.

GoodHands69: We all have secrets, and I
used yours as an excuse to choose Stella.
Which, as I'm sure you're aware, is pretty
damn ironic. Just so we're clear: I don't
give a shit about the videos—though I'd
like to get a crack at the guy who
uploaded them. All I care about is the
sexy, freckle-faced woman I love giving
me another chance.

GoodHands69: Come to the door so I can
tell you to your face how I feel.

I look up at Savvy. "I don't understand. Does he know?"

There's a knock at the door, and I gasp and press the back of my hand to my mouth. Maybe he doesn't mean that he knows. Maybe that's not him. I'm too scared to hope.

Savvy folds her arms, and the knock comes again. "Get the door, you fool."

I'm shaking. I'm surprised my legs carry me, and when I pull the door open, I'm so happy to see Kace on the other side that I nearly fall to the ground.

He's carrying a giant bouquet of yellow roses and a *Who Framed Roger Rabbit* DVD. "ItsyBitsy," he says softly. "Always climbing, always getting knocked back down."

"I'm sorry." My voice cracks. "I should've told you. I thought you knew, and then . . ."

"I know," he says. He presses the hand holding the DVD to his chest. "I know you have every right to send me away and shut me out of your life, but I'm asking you to listen to what I have to say. If you still want me to leave after that, I promise I won't bother you again."

As if I've ever been able to resist giving Kace Matthews exactly what he wants. "I'm listening."

He pulls in a deep breath. "When you were seventeen and crawled into my bed, I wanted to touch you. You were so beautiful. And I wasn't oblivious. I knew you were special. You always made me laugh. I never took myself quite so seriously when you were around, and if anyone needed that, it was me. But I wasn't ready for what part of me already understood you deserved. I couldn't give you one night because I already knew that when we got together, we'd need more than that."

He lifts a hand, arm extended, and I think he's going to touch me. Then he drops it. "If you crawled into my bed now, I'd recognize it as the beginning of something. I'd kiss you because I'm dying to taste you again, but also because I'd see that kiss as something we could build on."

How can a hollow chest ache? I didn't think there was anything left in there anymore, but his words are washing away the numbness.

He takes a breath and lets it out. "When you visited after you started college and you teased and flirted with me?" He laughs. "Actually, some of your suggestions were more propositioning than flirting, and I wanted to take you up on your offers. So badly. But I wasn't ready. I couldn't understand that the way you made me feel lighter could be part of something real between us. And then there was Amy, and I'll always be grateful for my marriage and my daughter. Amy taught me what I do and don't want in a partner. And my daughter taught me the most beautiful things in our lives can indeed get better with time."

"Kace," I whisper.

"And then you were there again. And I should've been ready. You were more beautiful than ever, and despite being an idiot who believed all the lies he'd been told about what you'd done at Allegiance, I still knew you were special. But I wasn't ready. I believed the only explanation for my divorce was a failure on my part, and I didn't want to fail again. Watching Amy walk away was the hardest thing I've ever done, but I think I already knew it wouldn't compare to the pain of losing you."

My internal organs feel like they're rearranging themselves. My stomach is where my lungs should be, and my lungs are all twisted up with the shattered bits of my heart that have been festering low in my stomach. "Then why . . .?"

"I've never been able to separate the physical from the emotional, and that was no different with you." He shakes his head. His eyes are bloodshot, his cheeks pale. "I still wasn't ready when I fell in love with you."

Actually hearing those words makes the floor fly out from under me, and I have to brace myself on the wall and bite back a sob.

"I knew I wanted you and I thought about you all the time. I knew I'd make up excuses to be in the same room as you, but I wasn't prepared for anything bigger than I've ever felt before. If Amy held a knife to my heart, what I feel for you is a grenade. It's too big. You could destroy me. But I don't even care if you pull the pin, because the alternative? Letting you walk away just because I'm scared?" He steps into the apartment, puts the flowers and DVD down on the table in the foyer, and stands before me, palms up. "It's not even an option. And I'm sorry it's taken me this long to get here, but Stella, I am ready for whatever you can offer me, whenever you can offer it. It doesn't have to be today or next week, because I know I fucked up, but if you'll give me another chance, I promise you I'll do everything in my power to remind you how much I love you every single day. I'm ready whenever you are."

"Kace, those videos . . ."

He brushes a stray curl from my face and tucks it behind my ear. "Someday, when she's older, you're going to be the perfect person to explain to my daughter why she shouldn't let idiot boys have intimate pictures or videos of her." He takes my hand and brings it to his mouth, kissing it hard. "I'm sorry I ever made you believe a mistake like that meant you weren't worthy of me. I love you, Stella Elaine Jacob. Give me a chance."

"I love you too, but . . ."

"But what?" he whispers, not angry, just . . . hopeful.

Hot tears roll down my cheeks, and I want to throw myself into his arms, but I'm afraid he still doesn't understand just how imperfect I am. "I'm a mess."

"Lucky for you, I'm pretty steady."

"I'm failing chemistry," I blurt. "I'm probably not even going to get into nursing school."

He pulls me into his arms, and his mouth hovers over mine. "If I need a nurse, I'll go to the hospital." He smiles against my lips. "I want *all of you*. A relationship, not a fling. I want your promises and your smiles and your vulnerable moments—not perfection."

"I want to give you all that," I whisper.

"No takebacks," he says.

I slide my hands into his hair and finally let myself kiss him.

EPILOGUE

KACE

Two months later

"*K*ace," Abbi says, leaning into my arm, "I'm so glad you bought this place. I swear I want to *live* at your pool. I love it, and I love *you*, brother."

I blink down at my sister, taking in her expression in the moonlight. "Are you *drunk?*"

"Totally drunk," she says, nodding. "But you said I can crash in your guest room anytime, so it's *fine*."

I look to Dean with my best *Can you fucking believe this?* face—because I don't think I've ever seen my sister drunk—but he's so busy grinning at said drunk girl that he doesn't even notice me.

Then my gaze snags on Stella, and I'm struck dumb by

297

the sight of her in a black dress and heels that could qualify as deadly weapons. Her hair's down around her shoulders and her lips are painted bright red, and my brain jumps to the memory of them wrapped around my cock last night and the sounds she made when she took me deep. Yeah, that's never gonna get old.

I swallow and take my time looking her over again. She sips a White Claw and watches me with that sexy little smirk on her face. The one that says, *I think about you when I touch myself.* Okay, maybe a smirk can't say that, but that's sure as fuck what I'd like to think is going through her head.

"Would you two get a room?" Smithy says, his gaze bouncing back and forth between me and my beautiful girlfriend. "The eye-fucking is *out of control.*"

"Jealous, Smithy?" Stella calls.

"Damn straight I am. It's not fair that you get that fine ass in bed with you every night, Stella."

Stella laughs, all lightness and smiles tonight.

Smithy points at Dean and then Abbi. "Those two are just as bad."

"What?" Abbi squeaks.

Jesus. Is that why Dean's been acting so weird? It's been like when he was seeing Amy all over again. Is he messing around with Abbi? And what a fucking hypocrite am I that if he is, my first instinct would be to tell him to back the fuck off?

Taking a deep breath, I dig deep for a rational reaction. But I know Dean. He's not about the long-term stuff. Well, with the exception of Amy, who wasn't interested in giving it to him. He's not a dick, but he's not exactly *boyfriend material*, either. "Are you two . . . ?" I wave a finger back and forth between them. "Seriously?"

Abbi's eyes go wide. "No! Why would you—"

Dean steps close to her and wraps his arm around her waist before dipping his head to whisper something in her ear. When he pulls back, he searches her face with a gaze more serious than I've seen on him in a long time.

Abbi swallows, but she doesn't take her gaze off Dean when she says, "There's nothing happening here."

"The lady doth protest too much," Smithy says. He offers his knuckles to Dean, who arches a brow and leaves him hanging.

"Weirdos," I mutter, letting my gaze slide back to the woman of the evening. Stella just got home from her first day back as lead receptionist at The Orchid, so naturally we had to gather and celebrate. Brinley practically kissed Stella's feet when Stell asked for her job back. Then offered her a raise and begged her to never leave her post again. Apparently, my girl is fucking fabulous at her job. This doesn't surprise me at all.

Stella watches me with that boozy, relaxed half-smile on her face, and it suddenly occurs to me that if my drunk sister needs a place to sleep, we won't get the house to ourselves tonight. At least Stella will still be in my bed—unlike the five other nights a week, when she insists on sleeping in her new apartment—but sometimes a guy needs to hear his woman moan.

As Abbi and Dean turn the tables on Smithy, asking him about his love life, and Marston and Brinley snuggle together in a chaise, I walk across the patio and slide my hand through Stella's. "Proud of you."

"Thanks." Her teeth sink into her plump bottom lip. "You want me to grab you a drink?"

"Not really. But we should go inside."

She arches a brow. "Why?"

Grinning, I step forward until there's little more than a wisp of air between us. I feel the shiver that runs through her as I lower my mouth to her ear. "You look good enough to eat, and I can't do that here."

She barks out a laugh and shakes her head. "Let's go, then."

So I lead her into the house, through the kitchen, and around the corner into the dark hallway, where I press her against the wall and show the woman I love just how good it can feel to give an idiot like me a second chance.

THE END

Thank you so much for joining me in Orchid Valley for Stella and Kace's story. I hope you'll return for Abbi's story in my next release, *Every Time I Fall*. If you'd like to receive an email when I release their book, please sign up for my newsletter: lexiryan.com/signup

I hope you enjoyed this book and will consider leaving a review. Thank you for reading. It's an honor!

AUTHOR'S NOTE

Dear Reader:

Non-consensual pornography or "revenge porn" is illegal in forty-six states and the District of Columbia. Many victims feel helpless or too embarrassed to do anything about their private pictures or videos being shared. However, if you've been a victim, please know you have rights, even in places that don't have explicit laws against this horrible violation. For more information on your rights and the steps for getting the images or videos removed, please visit the Federal Trade Commission's website.

OTHER BOOKS BY LEXI RYAN

Orchid Valley

Every Little Promise (Brinley and Marston's prequel)

Every Little Piece of Me (Brinley and Marston's story)

Every Sweet Regret (Stella and Kace's story, coming late 2020)

Every Time I Fall (Abbi's book, coming spring 2021!)

More to be announced soon!

The Boys of Jackson Harbor

The Wrong Kind of Love (Ethan's story)

Straight Up Love (Jake's story)

Dirty, Reckless Love (Levi's story)

Wrapped in Love (Brayden's story)

Crazy for Your Love (Carter's story)

If It's Only Love (Shay's story)

The Blackhawk Boys

Spinning Out (Arrow's story)

Rushing In (Chris's story)

Going Under (Sebastian's story)

Falling Hard (Keegan's story)

In Too Deep (Mason's story)

LOVE UNBOUND: Four series, one small town, lots of

happy endings

Splintered Hearts (A Love Unbound Series)

Unbreak Me (Maggie's story)

Stolen Wishes: A Wish I May Prequel Novella (Will and Cally's prequel)

Wish I May (Will and Cally's novel)

Or read them together in the omnibus edition, *Splintered Hearts: The New Hope Trilogy*

Here and Now (A Love Unbound Series)

Lost in Me (Hanna's story begins)

Fall to You (Hanna's story continues)

All for This (Hanna's story concludes)

Or read them together in the omnibus edition, *Here and Now: The Complete Series*

Reckless and Real (A Love Unbound Series)

Something Reckless (Liz and Sam's story begins)

Something Real (Liz and Sam's story concludes)

Or read them together in the omnibus edition, *Reckless and Real: The Complete Series*

Mended Hearts (A Love Unbound Series)

Playing with Fire (Nix's story)

Holding Her Close (Janelle and Cade's story)

OTHER TITLES
Hot Contemporary Romance

Text Appeal

Accidental Sex Goddess

Decadence Creek (Short and Sexy Romance)

Just One Night

Just the Way You Are

ACKNOWLEDGMENTS

I'm always so grateful to the village it takes to help me get from an idea to a finished book, but perhaps this time more than ever. I started writing Stella's story the same week the COVID-19 lockdown began. The world was uncertain, everything was changing, and since my kids were out of school, I was never, ever alone. *insert maniacal laughter* Despite all the challenges, we made it to the finish line and I love this couple and their story so much.

As always, to my family first. Brian, Jack, and Mary—thank you for believing in me and inspiring me to be my very best. To my mom and siblings—thank you for all of your support and for making me want to write big casts of characters forever.

Thanks to all my writing friends who sprint with me and talk me off the ledge when the book looks like a disaster. To my hand-holding, hair-stroking, and pep-talking best bitches, Mira Lyn Kelly and Lisa Kuhne, my eternal gratitude to you and to unlimited texting plans. To the Goldbrickers and the ladies in my Slack group, thank you for helping me remember the power of consistency.

To everyone who provided me feedback on this story along the way—Heather Carver, Samantha Leighton, Lisa Kuhne, Nancy Miller, and Janice Owen—you're all awesome. I appreciate you all so much! Tina Allen, this book is for you because I think you're awesome. Thanks for being a beta reader and a friend.

I am so grateful for the best editorial team. Lauren Clarke and Rhonda Merwarth, thank you for the insightful line and content edits. You push me to be a better writer and make my stories the best they can be. Thanks to Arran McNicol at Editing720 for proofreading. I've worked hard to put together this team, and I'm proud of it!

Thank you to the people who helped me package this book and promote it. Sara Eirew took the gorgeous cover photo and Hang Le did the design and branding for the whole series. To all of the bloggers, bookstagrammers, readers, and reviewers who help spread the word about my books, I am humbled by the time you take out of your busy lives for my stories. My gratitude will never be enough, but it is sincere. You're the best.

To my agent, Dan Mandel, for believing in me and always believing the best is yet to come. Thanks to you and your team for getting my books into the hands of readers all over the world.

Finally, the biggest, loudest, most necessary thank you to my fans. Because of you, I'm living my dream. I couldn't do it without you. You're the coolest, smartest, best readers in the world. I appreciate each and every one of you!

XOXO,

Lexi

ABOUT THE AUTHOR

Lexi Ryan is the *New York Times* and *USA Today* bestselling author of emotional romance that sizzles. A former academic and English professor, Lexi considers herself the luckiest girl around to make a living through storytelling. She loves spending time with her crazy kids, weightlifting, ice cream, swoony heroes, and vodka martinis.

Lexi lives in Indiana with her husband, two children, and a spoiled dog. You can find her on her website.

Printed in Great Britain
by Amazon

20037629R00185